WINTER WONDERS

WINTER WONDERS

TWELVE MAGICAL HOLIDAY STORIES

ROBERT J. MCCARTER

LITTLE HUMMINGBIRD PUBLISHING

CONTENTS

PART 1
THE MAGICAL CARTERVILLE CHRISTMAS LIGHTS

ONE

MONDAY, DECEMBER 17

We do Christmas right here in Carterville, Arizona.

If you picture a snow globe of an old mining town built out in the late 1800s draped on a steep hill that is perched on a tall mountain, a quaint, cheerful little town of about three hundred with a Main Street lined with festively decorated old red brick buildings, you wouldn't be far off.

The center of town is Carterville Circle, a roundabout that connects Main Street and Cedar and dominates a brief flattening of Carter Hill. In the center of that roundabout is a fir tree planted when the town was founded that is over sixty feet tall.

The businesses are, of course, all decked out for the holidays with Christmas lights and cheerful scenes painted on their windows. Early snow has come, and by mid-December the scene is beautifully flocked in white. The stately old streetlamps that line Main Street have colorful lights wound around them, and the mighty fir tree in the middle of Carter Circle is festively decorated with oversized ornaments and giant faux presents underneath.

It looks perfect, so perfect that it is the kind of scene that would work beautifully in a snow globe. These days, you can buy that snow globe in a number of shops here, but the story I want to tell happened a few years ago, not long after the meteor hit and the residents of Carterville got their powers.

Right. I didn't include that in the snow globe description, did I? I've written a lot about Carterville powers, how they only work within five miles of the center of town, how they can often be minor or quirky, how they occasionally can be called "super," and how there are no masks or capes, just small-town folks dealing with small-town problems with a bunch of powers added on top.

And I've written about the murder, fire, scheming, and power struggles that were a result of that meteor and those powers, but just because it is the season that it is, I want to tell a different kind of Carterville story.

You see, that snow globe image of Carterville was nearly perfect, except for that majestic fir tree in the center of town. It was decorated, but it didn't have any Christmas lights.

At first, it was just a matter of budget. Before the meteor hit, Carterville was trying to become a tourist destination but sitting on the north side of the San Francisco Peaks about thirty miles from Flagstaff, it was just a little too far off the beaten path.

But when the word about the powers spread, the tourists started coming and the town council thought it was high time that the fir tree be properly decorated, that Carterville live up to its potential as a one-of-a-kind Christmas destination.

This is the story of how the tree was first lit in a way that could only happen in Carterville.

MY NAME IS HENRY CARTER, AND I AM THE DUTIFULLY elected chief of police of Carterville and an ancestor of Samuel Carter, the founder of this town.

I knew all about the attempts to light up the tree, but the meteor had struck only a few months ago and my job had turned into nothing short of sheer madness as we came to grips with what had happened to us.

There were the outbreaks of narcolepsy until we figured out that Annie Smith, the owner of the Carterville Inn and my girl-friend, could put people to sleep. I was currently tracking strange bursts of unexplained violence and dealing with the most bizarre calls you could imagine.

It was Monday night, and I was in my closet of an office in the Carterville Police Department desperately trying to catch up on the mountain of paperwork that dominated my desk. Annabelle Unger came rushing in, bringing in a waft of cold air with her, the red blossoming on her cheeks almost matching her hair.

"The tree, Henry," she said, her lovely southern drawl thicker than usual in her excitement. "The tree. It's lit."

Annabelle was encased in a red down jacket and, in an acknowledgement to the slick conditions, had actual boots on instead of her favored heals. Back then she was in her early fifties, she had just quit the habit but still had the fine lines of a multi-decade smoker decorating her face. She was my office manager and was as buried as I was in this madness.

I sat back, my ancient office chair creaking loudly.

"They finally figure out how to get power to it?" I asked.

That was the problem. They had gotten all excited about it when Arnold Hughes, who was the local insurance guy and could now levitate, had offered to help. It had suddenly seemed easy until they all realized that you couldn't just run an exten-sion cord across the street. A generator had been considered, but the rattling racket of it would have destroyed the whole vibe. Batteries and an inverter were considered next, but there were security and safety issues, and the frequent switching of heavy batteries was problematic logistically. A power line from a nearby building also had safety issues.

Everyone was still arguing about it, such was politics in a small town.

Annabelle shook her head, the smile on her face so wide that I got a view of what she had been like as a child. That red hair of hers, especially the purple streaks, was chemically aided now, but I could suddenly see the kid she was coming down the stairs and looking at a tree packed with presents.

"No," she said, breathlessly. "It just lit up. All by itself. It's a..." She was going to call it a Christmas miracle, but her face darkened and she cut herself off. We had both seen a lot on this job, the kind of things that can make you cynical. She extended one gloved hand towards the door and said, "Come on. You have got to see it!"

The town had gathered, cars had stopped, as everyone stared at the fir tree in the middle of Carter Circle, everyone's exhales turning into small blooms of condensate in the cold.

It was certainly a stare-worthy sight: the tall fir tree flocked in fresh snow the texture of powdered sugar with the red, green, and white lights pulsing gently underneath; the faux presents below wrapped in shiny paper with big bows, a sprinkling of snow on them; the two- and three-story turn-of-the-century red brick buildings behind the tree; and finally the sharp outline of the San Francisco Peaks rising up into the starry sky behind it all.

If the cold didn't take your breath away, this certainly would.

Karen Winslow, the mayor, was always babbling about marketability and drawing tourists in, how it would make our town more economically viable. My eyes always glazed over when she talked like that, but this? This was a sight to see, and knowing that it was somehow the Carterville powers that was making it happen...? Well, even a middle-aged cynic like me could see it.

Annabelle was standing next to me, her mouth ajar in childish awe. She was holding the CPD Digital SLR in her hands, which is what she had run back to the station for, but in her state of wonder had forgotten to take pictures.

Annie Smith walked over, her dark hair hidden under a faux-fur-lined hood, her high cheekbones rouged by the cold. She had a sharp beauty that went well with the winter, but her face was still tanned by her love of the sun. She slipped her arm under mine and said, "This is..."

She didn't finish the sentence—she didn't need to. I had always loved this town, felt that this town was part of me and I was part of it, but that night, for the first time in a long time, looking at the sparkling lights, it felt like things were going to turn out okay.

The tree sat in the center of the roundabout, a low rock wall around it and a sidewalk circling the wall. There were parents holding their kids on that little wall so they could touch the magical lights.

"Are these special lights?" I asked Annie. The Carterville Inn being right across the circle, she had kept me up to date on the tree.

"No," she said. "Just normal Christmas lights. LED, I think. Why?"

"They are not acting like normal Christmas lights," I said.

And they weren't. The colors twinkled and pulsed like

someone was altering the flow of electricity. At first it was just minor variations, a delicate twinkle here and there, but then they began to pulse brighter and brighter. There was a star on the tip-top of the tree that pulsed so brilliantly it almost looked like an actual star.

Maybe somewhere there are fancy Christmas lights with circuitry that can do this, but not the cheap lights the town could afford and not without power hooked up. I could see the dangling cord draped over one of the presents. I knew they had dragged an extension cord over and tested the lights, but that was yesterday.

As the pulsing of the light intensified, waves of sparkling color starting at the bottom and flowing to the top, the murmuring voices stopped and it was all oohs and aahs. The lights were dancing under the clear starry night, joyfully dancing —there is no other way to describe it.

And then with a crescendo of color, the star burning brightly, the tree went dark.

***

Officer Martin Lester is tall and lanky with dull blue eyes and a prodigious and nearly grey mustache. He's about five years older than me, having beaten me crossing that dreaded Rubicon into his fifties.

He was a police officer, the only other one in town, and we were both poking around under the great fir tree, our cell phones out as flashlights.

Being smarter than me, he had a grey beanie on against the cold while I stubbornly had my cowboy hat on, my ears rapidly going numb.

"Ain't no power hooked up," Lester said, holding up the cord I had seen earlier. "Clear as can be, you know."

I nodded and sniffed. The freezing air prickled my nose, but I thought I smelled ozone.

"Chief," a woman said from behind me. "I'd like a word."

I almost groaned. I knew that voice. I knew that tone. It was the mayor, and she was currently talking to my ass, which felt beyond awkward. I duck-walked out from under the tree, stood up, and said, "Good evening, Karen."

Karen Winslow was a few years older than me, her hazel eyes intense and her greying blond hair in its usual elegant French braid, her head capped with a pompom-topped beanie that probably cost more than I made in a week.

"This is important," she said nodding up at the tree, her eyes getting this dreamy look. "Imagine how they'll flock here to see our tree, our lights with no power source, our little Carterville Christmas Miracle."

I nodded but didn't say anything. She loved tourists, I did not. I had to deal with the messes they created but I could also see how more tourists could make this a good Christmas season for the town.

"Find out what happened. How we can keep the lights on. This is your highest priority," she said and then promptly turned and walked away.

I didn't bother telling her that even though she was mayor, she was not my boss. It never seemed to do any good.

When Karen was gone, there was some mirthful chuckling coming out from under the tree. Lester, being smarter than me, again, hadn't come out.

"You look tired," Annie said after she crossed the street, her blue eyes glittering and a playful smile on her lips. She grabbed my hand and started pulling me back across the street. "Stay at the inn tonight. I'll make sure you sleep well... eventually." Her words were punctuated by a throaty laugh.

Annie had been my high school sweetheart and we had

gotten together earlier in the year once I was well clear of my divorce. I happily followed her, all thoughts of powers and Christmas trees forgotten.

ANNIE WAS BEHIND THE PRODIGIOUS COUNTER OF THE Carterville Inn dealing with a guest issue. "Prodigious" is the right word, because this used to be a saloon and that counter used to be the bar.

When you think "historic" building in the West, you just might picture the Carterville Inn. It dates back to 1890 and has the original stamped tin ceiling and arched windows in the red brick walls. The lobby is long and narrow with a creaky wooden floor, the walls hung with large black-and-white prints of Carterville when it was first settled. There was an elegantly decorated Christmas tree in front of the window and baskets of shiny Christmas tree bulbs decorating the coffee tables that antique chairs crowded around.

"Why are they here?" Wendy, my big sister, asked, nodding towards the guest Annie was talking to. "Aren't they locals?"

We were sitting in a couple of those high-backed antique chairs. Annie had been sidetracked by work, so we had been chatting while I waited.

Wendy looked a bit too much like me, like a Carter, to be considered pretty, her chin a tad pointy, her shoulder-length brown hair mousey, her eyes a little deep set. But those eyes held intelligence and kindness both, making her beautiful. She was a nurse, the kind that made hospital stays bearable, and that made her gorgeous.

"Ken and Amelia Reed," I said of the young, dark-haired couple who were holding hands as they talked to Annie. "Just got married a week ago. Heater fried and pipes froze, so they are staying here for a few days until it gets sorted."

Amelia was taller than Ken, slim to his stocky with thick-rimmed glasses, and she clearly loved Christmas. On the counter was a hat that looked like a Christmas tree complete with little lights, though they were dark. To match it, she had on a long green jacket with patches that looked like blue and red ornaments.

The two of them were attached like just-married people in love usually are. Annie and I had achieved that, briefly, in high school, but we were too old and jaded for that at this point.

Wendy nodded and leaned forward and looked at me, her brown eyes intense. I knew that look, it was her often used big sister look, and I suddenly wanted a drink.

"How are you, Henry?" she asked.

Wendy's daughter, Lilly, was going to Northern Arizona University in Flagstaff and Wendy had driven down from Colorado where she lived to collect her for the holiday and was staying for a few days. The last few years had brought a lot of change and I think Wendy wanted to get a look at Carterville post powers and check up on me.

I sighed and said, "I'm tired. It's all a bit much. We still get regular calls, noise complaints, some domestic violence, but most of them now are... they are so bizarre."

She just stared at me, a question in her eyes.

"Take Arnold Hughes," I said. "Loves to show off that he can levitate. I mean, *loves* to show off. They rigged him with some canisters of compressed air when he was decorating the tree, because levitation ain't quite flying. Karen had reporters in for the publicity."

Wendy rolled her eyes.

"Anyway, he does it in his backyard, for the hell of it, all the time. His neighbor constantly calls in peeping tom complaints and I have to keep talking to him."

She laughed, which was the point, and then got serious. "I'm sure it's not all silly like that," she said.

I shook my head. "Random fights keep breaking out," I said. "There are a lot more thefts, no idea if a power is involved, and the influx of tourists has complicated everything."

She nodded out towards the circle. "And now you have to find out how a Christmas tree puts on a world-class show it shouldn't be able to with no electricity."

I nodded. "I guess I do, although I don't have one clue how."

TWO

TUESDAY, DECEMBER 18

Word spread about the Carterville Christmas lights at the speed of gossip and in a small place like Carterville, that's just short of the speed of light. A good two hundred people showed up—at least half of the town plus a good portion of people from out of town—to stand around and wait for the magical Carterville Christmas lights.

Karen had reporters there and scientist from NAU. Ken and Amelia Reed, the newlyweds staying at the Inn were there, gloves clasped, and hopeful looks on their young faces. My best friend Frank Paulson and his wife Lisa were there, which meant that the Carterville Diner was shut down for this, which rarely happened. Mary and William Reilly had found a place close to the tree, looking like the quintessential grandparents that they were.

This made Lester, Annabelle, and me very busy. Lester was directing traffic around the circle, telling people to go park at the lot at the bottom of the hill. Annabelle and I were on crowd control trying to keep people out of the street and out from under the tree. We were understaffed and I got a nerve-racking vision of Carterville's future if Karen had her way. We were overrun, but all the businesses were busy as people ducked in to try to escape the cold.

Carter Hill sits between 6,400 and 7,100 feet in elevation on the north side of the tallest mountain in Arizona, so it gets cold here.

"Out!" I yelled at a teenage boy named Bo Larson skulking under the tree. He had a mop of curly blonde hair that was always flopping into his eyes. This was the third time I had rousted him. "One more time and I'll call your mother, Bo," I said.

He gave me an angry look like I was the worst person in the world, a look that reminded me of my own teenage son who was with his mother in Phoenix, and it just made me miss him.

"He's a good kid," Mary Reilly said, her hazel eyes bright and her white hair peeking out of the beanie I knew she had knitted herself. "LA to Carterville is quite the difficult transition for a young man like that."

"Must be," I said with a nod. "Too many hormones and not enough for him to do here."

Mary was all of four-feet-four and looked like the kindliest of grandmothers, but her power was one of the super ones. If she told you do something, said it in the right way, you did it. Period.

Mary and William had discovered her power pretty early on. They had been having a fight when Mary told him to go to "hades" and William almost had a mental breakdown trying to figure out how to execute that command.

I heard voices raise not far away and then a shout in what sounded like a fight breaking out. I looked back under the tree and a tourist was poking around now.

"Do you mind?" I asked Mary, nodding under the tree. "Just be gentle, okay. Tell them very kindly to leave and stay out."

Mary stood up straight, got this very un-grandmotherly twinkle in her eye, and said, "You got it, Chief."

As I ran off to deal with the fight, I resolved to keep Mary close. She was useful, but her power was one of the ones that needed watching.

———

THE CROWD WAS MOSTLY DISPERSED BY 10 P.M. THERE HAD been three fist fights but no magical Christmas lights. Mayor Karen Winslow summoned me up to her apartment on the second floor of one of historic buildings on the circle.

Karen didn't have a power. She and her husband had horse property close by and had been outside of town when the meteor hit. I had to wonder what that felt like for her. She owned half the town and was lacking something very fundamental to the new Carterville.

I appeared to be lacking the same thing as I hadn't experienced a power yet. I really didn't care. Sure, the little boy in me wanted a power, any power, but the middle-aged man knew better.

The living room of her apartment was elegant, filled with uncomfortable antiques, dark wood, and somewhat cliched Western paintings. She loved horses, more than people I was pretty sure, so the horses were the stars of the artwork.

"It's disappointing," she said. She sat with her back perfectly straight dressed in a long wool skirt, a turquoise sweater, and an authentic Navajo squash blossom necklace made of turquoise and silver. Her flowery perfume was expensive and too strong for my taste.

I nodded gravely. "These fights," I said, well aware she was refereeing to the tree. "Very disturbing. Not like us."

She gave me a sharp little smile and said, "The tree."

"Oh," I said in faux surprise.

"What are you going to do about it?" she asked.

"Unlike the fights," I said, "this is not a law enforcement matter, Karen."

While my position was an elected one, my budget was controlled by the town council and I knew what lever she was going to pull. It was the same one she always did, but I was going to make her pull it.

She took a deep breath and sighed. "Very well. I wonder where in the city budget I can find the funds to get the investigation this city needs?"

I sighed right back and said, "We've been working on it. We don't know anyone with this kind of power, but there are so many powers we still know nothing about."

She rose and it was clear I had been dismissed. "Figure it out," she said. "I expect lights tomorrow night."

THREE

WEDNESDAY, DECEMBER 19

We were conducting what Officer Martin Lester called a "Sword in the Stone" test. Annabelle had run all over town, gotten donations from most of the merchants, and put together a very nice Christmas gift basket for the person that could light the tree.

It was a good idea. We were also asking each person what their power was. Everyone that participated had their name put in a raffle for the gift basket in case no one managed to light up the tree.

We started in the late afternoon and went until well after dark. About sixty people tried and some of it was pretty funny.

Mary Reilly, everyone's grandmother, shouted at the tree, demanding that it light up. We all held our breaths, the power in her voice obvious, but apparently inanimate objects were immune. Everyone laughed nervously when she was done.

Bo Larson, a stocky bundle of teenage angst and anger, held the end of the cord tightly, scrunched his face up until sweat beaded on his forehead, but to no avail.

Ken and Amelia stopped holding hands long enough for

each of them to try. I had hope there for a moment when Ken told me his power was "static electricity," demonstrating by, weirdly, rubbing his shoes on the snowy sidewalk until his black hair rose up like he was a mad professor and a spark jumped from his index finger to thumb.

He tried, and he might have gotten the first bulb in the long chain to light, but it was so brief that it was hard to tell.

Amelia, the walking Christmas tree, had no idea if she had a power but it was clear she had the Christmas spirit, scrunching up her young, pretty face to no effect.

Trent Bashir, a small man of Indian descent, whom everyone knew talked to his many dogs and cats, constantly, registered his power as "animal whisperer." He told me he not only talked to them but could now "with near certainty know what their reply would be if they but had a voice."

This was the new Carterville, so I believed him. He tried giving the tree gentle encouragement like it was a puppy reluctant to go out in the snow to take care of business, listened for an answer, but none was given and no lights.

After some raucous encouragement from the crowd, I tried halfheartedly. Annabelle, who could levitate small objects tried. Arnold Hughes, the super levitating showoff tried with great drama—that involved him levitating, of course. Dozens more tried and not one was able to do it.

Karen watched from her window above us most of the time, her arms crossed.

The tree did not light up, but it was a good night. I think it was the first time the town as a whole had acknowledged what had happened to us in a positive way.

FOUR

THURSDAY, DECEMBER 20

As darkness descended on Carterville, the crowd around the great fir tree in the middle of Carter Circle was small, maybe twenty people.

We hadn't made any progress and I was starting to think that the mystery of the Carterville Christmas lights was going to go in the same category as the mystery of the Carterville powers. Something we would never truly understand.

As Annie and I stood in front of the Carterville Inn, cups of spiked hot chocolate in our hands, that was fine by me. I mean, it wasn't exactly a mystery, was it? The Christmas tree lit up the same way Arnold levitated, or Mary could command people to do things. It was the meteor and the power that lay underneath our town. And while some scientists had entered the mine looking for answers, the old tunnels were not safe, and they didn't get very far.

"It's still beautiful," Annie said. "Really beautiful."

"It still feels like Christmas," I said. "I don't want us to get too dependent on these powers. We have no idea if they'll even last."

Annie gave me a look of surprise, her blue eyes intense. "Really?" she asked.

I nodded. "I kind of miss the old Carterville when it was a little more Mayberry and a little less Twilight Zone."

She nodded, grabbed my arm, and leaned her head against me.

And then it happened. The lights on the tree flickered to life. Not all at once, just a gentle spark of light here and there, so at first it wasn't clear, like maybe it was just a reflection. But then ripples of light went up and down the tree, gentle waves of red, green, and white and Annie gasped in delight, a sound echoed by others in the crowd, phones coming out to record it.

"Henry..." Annie said, awe in her voice and she looked a lot more like she did when we were both kids running around our small town.

"It's happening," I said, but I felt myself dampening the delight, looking around the circle, trying to figure out who was doing this—and if there was even a "who" involved.

I saw Karen Winslow standing nearby along with a couple other of the town council members. They had been talking but had stopped to watch. Mary and William Reilly were hugging each other in excitement as they looked up at the tree in awe. Annabelle had the department camera and was taking pictures this time. Officer Lester stared gape-jawed at it. There were about a dozen other locals and a handful of people I didn't recognize.

The gentle waves of color flowing up the tree got more intense, the waves coming faster and faster until every light was on and shone brightly.

I stopped doing my job and stared agog like everyone else. There was nothing else I could do.

And then the lights did things they shouldn't be able to do. First, they went all red and then bled into blue and then green, some lights more intense, sparkling among the brief mono-chrome, the lights pulsing as they gently slid through the color spectrum.

And then the lights started doing both tricks. Waves of light moved from the bottom to the top, gently flowing through the color spectrum. The waves started gently and got more and more intense until they flared white, so bright they left an after image, the star on top briefly shining like a real star, and then it was over.

I stood there feeling weak and strong at the same time, like I had just run a race—as if I would do such a thing. I felt more awake than I had in ages, and I was happy and content.

"What was that...?" Annie whispered like we were in a church.

"A gift," I said with a satisfied sigh. But "satisfied" was not the right word. I felt good. I felt alive. But I felt something else, something very powerful. "I feel..."

"Horny?" she asked with a girlish giggle and a squeeze of my hand.

"Yeah," I said. "Like it's Sunday morning, there's nothing much to do, and everything is right in the world."

"I'm just so sorry Amelia missed it," Annie said. I looked around and she was right, the newlyweds weren't here.

"Too bad," I said.

"They were going stay in their room tonight," she said. "The won the raffle for the basket which had plenty of food and wine. They are out of funds and have to leave in the morning."

"Really?" I asked, something tickling at the back of my brain.

"Yeah," she said. "The repairs at their house are dragging on, so they are off to Tucson in the morning to stay with some rela-tives. This is their first winter here and Amelia is desperate for a white Christmas."

I was still staring at the tree when the pieces fell into place, and it was suddenly clear.

"You are brilliant," I said, kissing Annie soundly.

FIVE

FRIDAY, DECEMBER 21

My job forces me to have many awkward conversations. Carterville powers doubled down on that, but this was... well, it was beyond the pale.

"Are you sure?" Annie asked. It was 8:30 a.m. and Annie had a tray of breakfast expertly balanced on one hand, dressed in her elegant Carterville Inn uniform which was black slacks, a white shirt, and a black tie and vest with her long dark hair pulled into a ponytail.

I nodded and she knocked. "Room service," she said politely.

Ken Reed answered the door, his short black hair a nimbus around his head once again in "mad professor" mode wearing a white robe monogramed with the Carterville Inn logo. He smiled and then saw me and shut his mouth.

"Everything's fine," I said, holding my palms up. I was working so I was in my police blues and that always makes people nervous. "I have a plan to keep you two here in the Carterville Inn until your house is repaired if we can just have a quick word."

He nodded and Annie swept in and placed the tray on the

small table near the window, the room filling with the smell of coffee and bacon. Their room didn't overlook the circle, but Carter Hill and the houses farther up.

The space had high ceilings with the same stamped tin as the lobby, a small, antique dresser, and a high four-poster bed.

"Thank you," I said, taking my cowboy hat off and stepping into the room. Amelia was wrapped snuggly in a robe that looked exactly like an extra-long Santa jacket.

Everyone was staring at me. "The tree... It lit last night... and... well..." I just couldn't find the words as my cheeks flushed hot.

"Shall I?" Annie asked.

I nodded, gratefully.

"We believe that it isn't a single Carterville power lighting up the tree," she said, her tone neutral.

"No?" Ken asked.

Annie shook her head. "Ken, clearly your power involves electricity, and Amelia, you are Christmas's biggest fan. And when you two..." She paused, her cheeks flushing enough for me to notice it underneath the tan she maintained even in the winter. She took a breath. "We have reason to believe that it is your act of... of *love* that lights the tree."

Amelia's mouth formed an "O", and she got up grabbed her Christmas tree hat from the dresser. She pushed up her glasses and her cheeks flushed red as she said, "The lights busted. A long time ago. But I... you know..." She ended looking pointedly at her husband.

"She likes to wear it... you know... sometimes," he said with a bashful shrug. "It lit up the last two times when we... you know..."

It was 7:58 p.m. and I was as nervous as a cat in a room full of rocking chairs. Karen Winslow was there along with half the town, a news crew, and a whole lot of reporters.

I had promised her that the tree would start lighting at precisely 8 p.m. when the Reeds were scheduled to express their love to each other while Amelia wore her Christmas tree hat. Not that Karen knew about that—we had promised to keep it a secret.

Everything lined up. Everything fit together, but I just wasn't sure. How could I be? This was the first time we suspected that it took two Carterville powers to make something happen. Ken's part made sense, but what was Amelia's power? Did she transmute and amplify other people's power? Was her love of Christmas taking Ken's power, lighting the hat, and that somehow transferred to the nearby tree? There was one thing that was undeniable, the feeling of being in the presence of the magical Christmas lights was decidedly passionate.

"It's going to work," Annie said, taking my hand.

I swallowed and nodded but didn't say a word.

At 8 p.m., the tree was still dark, and the mayor was giving me the stink eye. At 8:03 p.m. people started mumbling and I decided it was time for me to find another job. At 8:06, when the tree finally started its show, my knees went weak with relief and then the swirling, sensual lights was all I could see, and I felt young again.

Once I thought about it, it was amazing that the tree lit up only six minutes late. If it had been me and I had been asked to "perform" on a schedule knowing that the whole town would experience it...? Let's just say that youth is a gift.

Later that night, I was summoned back up to Karen Winslow's apartment and found myself sitting on her expensive but uncomfortable furniture.

"So, who is it?" she asked as she sat down across from me.

"I haven't tracked the source of the violence down yet," I said with a mischievous smile. "We'll get it, though."

She shook her head and crossed her arms, looking at me like I was a recalcitrant child. "The tree, Henry. The tree."

"I'm afraid that information is confidential," I said. "But if you want it to continue, it will take some funding."

She cocked her head and stared at me. "How much?" she asked.

"Two hundred dollars a day," I said. "Cash." That gave Annie a decent rate for the room and gave the Reeds enough money for food and a little fun.

She looked shocked, like I had just said a dirty word or something. "That is ridiculous. The city can't afford it."

"But you can," I said with a smile. "You'll make it back easily in increased tourist traffic at your businesses."

Her mouth opened in protest but then closed, and I could see the wheels turning behind her hazel eyes which looked green tonight.

"This sounds like extortion," she said tartly. "How do I know you aren't just going to pocket it?"

"You don't," I said with a smile. "But you know me. I am a man of my word. I promise these funds will be used to light the tree up every night and none will stay with me."

I got up and headed for the door. I could still feel the heady effects of those very special Christmas lights and Annie was waiting.

"Can tell me who it is?" she asked.

I turned and said, "No."

"Henry, I am afraid I must insist."

"Sorry, Karen. I work for the people," I said. "Anonymity has been requested and will be honored. I gave my word." I smiled and added, "Merry Christmas!"

I chuckled as I left. Of course, Karen would come up with the money, it was a good investment. And for the rest of us, it looked like it was going to be one hell of a Christmas.

BACKSTORY—THE MAGICAL CARTERVILLE CHRISTMAS LIGHTS

Holiday: Christmas

This story stands alone, quite nicely, actually, but if you have been reading my Carterville books, there's a lot more in here, with appearances from most of the main characters in the five Carterville mystery books and a few hints as to what is to come.

All the Carterville stories are mysteries, as is this one, but I wanted to go with something a little lighter than the other stories.

As of this writing, this is, chronologically, the first Carterville story, taking place months after the meteor hit and five years before the events of the first novel, *Out of a Christmas Sky*.

It's worth noting that *Out of a Christmas Sky* takes place on Christmas Eve and Christmas Day because of my writing for the *Holiday Spectacular*. This story, in turn, was inspired by *Out of a Christmas Sky*. Everything, at some point, tends to end up in my writing.

For this story, It was fun to go back and envision things before they got so crazy, to see Henry and Annie getting along, to view some of the small town conflicts before they all came to a head.

PART 2
EMILY LOVES CHRISTMAS, EMILY LOVES MURDER

EMILY LOVES CHRISTMAS, EMILY LOVES MURDER

"But, Walter..." Emily whined, her four-year-old voice climbing up an octave, her fists on her hips and a frown on her chubby face. She stood in front of a Christmas tree at two a.m. on Christmas Day in the living room of an upscale Tucson, Arizona, neighborhood. The house had the green swath of a golf course behind it, and beyond that, the cactus-covered Santa Catalina Mountains rose up into the moonlit night.

Emily is a ghost, as am I, but she's been dead for eighty years and can at times be like a wicked old lady and at other times like the four-year-old she was when she died.

She had just "popped" us from our graveyard where I was happily being miserable about my afterlife and how I was stalled on solving my own murder. Popping is when a skilled ghost, like Emily, goes instantly from place to place. There is a bit of a sound to it, thus the name. If I could "pop," I would have probably left already.

For once she wasn't wearing her ever-present shorts and lollipop-print T-shirt, but had "changed" into a sweater with alternating red and white stripes with a Christmas-tree pattern in the opposite color of the stripe. The sweater just gave me a headache. She even had a red ribbon corralling her blond Shirley Temple curls. Being a skilled ghost, she was only slightly transparent, the details of her appearance perfect, and believe me, this takes skill and concentration.

Emily loves Christmas. Just like you would expect a four-year-old would.

The Christmas tree she stood in front of was decked out in tinsel, shiny red and blue ornaments, and white Christmas lights. A pile of perfectly wrapped presents, green and red and blue, underneath.

"Honey," I said, adjusting my fedora and shoving my hands into my trench coat, trying to steel myself against the intensity of her four-year-old will. And yes, I'm dressed like a 1940s' movie detective, as I have been since we solved our first murder. Emily's idea, as you might imagine. "I'm just burned out. We've been doing case after case all year. I just want to—"

"But, Walter! Look." She pointed to the corpse that was under the tree along with the shiny presents. The woman appeared to have fallen, crushing some gifts and ripping off some of the lights, ruining the postcard-perfect tableau. I hadn't taken a close look yet, but judging from the blond hair, pajama-covered legs, and slippered feet, this appeared to be the woman of the household. The rest of the house was asleep and wouldn't discover the body for a few hours. Not the kind of thing one wants to see under the tree on Christmas morning.

You might think that she'd had a heart attack or a stroke but for the blood seeping out from under her and staining the polished wood floor, creeping steadily towards the white area rug.

Emily loves murder. Like only a being who has been a ghost for eighty years can. And in general, the dead do love death. What can I say?

Every day of the year Emily loves murder. I know ghosts that can do some curious things, but she somehow has a sense for murder. Strange, odd murders.

"Walter! This... it's all I want for Christmas. Walter, pleeeeaaasseee."

She smiled at me with a wattage that could have given me sunburn had I still been alive.

"And then we can take a break?" I asked, slowly.

She nodded, her smile intensifying. She knew she had me and I was smart enough to know that her promise would be forgotten as soon she sensed the next murder.

But what was I going to do for Christmas? Haunt my old casino and watch the sad sacks gambling instead of being with their families? Go to LA and watch my ex-wife live her glamorous Hollywood life? Go to my ex-dental practice, my second-choice career after acting didn't pan out, and look again for clues to my own murder, a case that had long ago gone cold?

"How long ago did she die?" I asked.

Emily looked up and to the left, her mouth twisting in concentration and her tongue sticking slightly out. "Thirty-four minutes."

"Long enough for the spirit to start separating."

She nodded, her blond curls bouncing.

"So she moved on and won't be able to help us," I said.

"Nope. But she's got Walter Anchor, Ghost Detective, on the case."

I really hated the term "Ghost Detective," but I am a ghost and my third career is solving murders, so it fits.

I sighed. "Well, let's get to it then."

Emily squealed her delight, a sound so high-pitched and piercing, I'm surprised it didn't wake the living.

WE DIDN'T CALL OUT ANCHOR'S IRREGULARS, THOSE ghosts that helped us on cases sometimes, especially when we need eyes on suspects. Neither of us even mentioned it, and for me it was because if this was Emily's Christmas present, it was only right we do it together, like our first few cases.

Since there was no ghost, there were no witness we could interview, and since we have no sense of smell and not much of a sense of touch, but we can see and hear extremely well, we went about seeing and hearing.

Emily hovered right above the body, her garish red and white sweater only slightly lighter than the pooling blood, it contrasted harshly with the green of the tree.

"Not a bullet hole," she said. "It penetrated right between the ribs and looks like it went straight through to the heart. Poor dear didn't suffer long."

"A knife?" I asked as I slowly walked the living room. There was a baby grand piano with not one fingerprint on the black finish or on a series of photographs.

"No," Emily replied. "It looks kind of round."

The pictures on the piano showed the story of a perfect family. Mom and Dad went to high school together, when he was a muscular, dark-haired football player and she a shapely blond cheerleader. They had married young and had two children, one boy and one girl, both of which appeared to be teenagers now.

Mom and Dad had aged with dignity and grace, still handsome in their middle years. Dad letting the distinguished gray invade at the temples, and Mom still retaining her blond hair and the general shape of her youth.

There were more pictures on the oak entertainment center and on the wall of the hallway leading back to the bedrooms, and these all reinforced the "perfect family" story they were trying to tell.

There are no perfect families.

The murderer was likely in the house right now.

"Ummm… Walter," Emily called from under the tree. "You better come look at this."

I walked over and squatted down. Emily was out from under the tree and sitting on the floor right on top of the darkening pool of blood looking at the victim.

"I don't think that's the mom," she said, pointing to the face of the victim.

And it wasn't. She was too young. This was the daughter.

I sighed, not really wanting to dig further into this "perfect family."

We switched gears and did what we should have done in the first place. I took Emily's little hand in mine and we did away with the niceties of "walking" and flew through the house, finding Mom and Dad sleeping in their large master bedroom suite, their blond-haired daughter asleep in her fastidiously clean room, fencing foil hanging on the wall above her bed, and lastly we found the son, their eldest, asleep in his sports-trophy-festooned room.

I cursed. This was no longer a simple case. I liked simple cases when I would interview the ghost, go tap out my report in the SECI chamber—that typewriter for ghosts we all have been using—and get on with my day being grumpy about my own murder.

"Language, Walter!" she hissed. "There are children present."

Try waking up dead in your dental practice with a needle in your arm, someone having faked your suicide via propofol. That'll make you grumpy.

I cursed some more. The girl was asleep and wouldn't be able to hear me anyway, and Emily was not quite a child.

We kept moving and soon found that one of the guest bedrooms had been occupied, the satin sheets and royal-blue comforter having been thrown back.

The murdered girl was a guest.

We checked the rest of the house and found nothing but what a lot of what money can buy. We went back and observed each family member as they slept. And they all slept quietly, peacefully, not like a normal person sleeps after committing a murder.

"This is just practice, you know," Emily said as we watched the son, his eyes twitching under their lids in REM sleep.

I nodded. Emily says this to me a lot.

"We're going to find your murderer," she added.

"It's all I want for Christmas."

Emily sniffed and tears leaked out of her big ghostly eyes. Big, fat, four-year-old tears. She swallowed hard. "And after you solve your murder, you'll..." She devolved into a hard cry.

I squatted down in front of her. "I'll move on."

She nodded, snuffing and rubbing at her nose. Emily has no body, no biology, but the girl can sure cry.

"Move on" is one of the euphemisms around here for the next stage after being a ghost. You move on when your unfinished business is finished. And my murder is presumably that unfinished business, not that I have a clue as to where I might "move on" to.

I took her and held her and let her cry. I didn't tell her what she wanted to hear, that I would stay with her always. That's just not the way life is. "We have no leads on my murder, honey," I said gently. "I'm sure we have lots of cases left together. This is your Christmas case. Let's go solve it. And let's do it before anyone wakes up and finds out what's waiting for them under the tree."

"Before?" she asked, pulling away, her green eyes wide.

"Yeah. Before. Just to prove we can. After all, Emily and Walter, Ghost Detectives, are on the case."

Her face changed and took on what was a comical level of determination on her young, round face. "Before dawn!" She made a fist and nodded her head, her curls bouncing, and marched back into the living room.

WE RECONSTRUCTED, AS BEST WE COULD, WHAT HAPPENED in that plush living room in front of that perfect Christmas tree. Mary snuck out of the guest room at around 1:30 a.m. to...

Okay, so we don't know that Mary is her name, but it seems like we shouldn't just call her "guest girl," so Emily came up with Mary. It was her mother's name, which is sweet and twisted and oh, so Emily.

"Mary was carrying this gift," Emily said, referring to a gift that had skittered out of the living room into the marble and stainless-steel kitchen. And it was instantly clear. The wrapping paper was different, just your regular old cheesy print Christmas paper with Santa and reindeer, not the slick, satiny stuff that the other gifts had. And it wasn't wrapped perfectly either.

On it was a tag written in sloppy print: *for kyle from your secret admirer.*

A quick trip to the son's bedroom and a glance at his trophies revealed that his name was Kyle. Mary, who looked to be fourteen where he looked to be seventeen, had a big ol' crush on him.

"Awww..." Emily began. "Sweet Mary snuck out in the middle of the night to do the nicest thing for the object of her affection..." She paused and her face scrunched up. "And we're going to get the bastard. We're going to get him good!"

Emily doesn't curse. "Bastard" for her is big deal and gone was the sweet four-year-old and front and center was the pissed-off eighty-year-old ghost. She walked over to Mary, her fists balled up, and started looking around.

"Murder weapon?" I asked.

She nodded. "We find that. We nail the bastard."

And suddenly all little Emily wanted for Christmas was justice... well, I hoped that's all she really wanted.

That "hell hath no fury like a woman scorned" saying. Yeah, it may be rather sexist and overgeneralized, but I can attest from personal experience that there is something to it. And I gotta tell you, hell hath no fury like a little girl/ancient ghost scorned on behalf of a recently dead teenager in the middle of a desperate crush.

And Emily, being dead eighty years, is a very skilled ghost. She hides it under cuteness and curls, but she's got abilities to put my recently dead ghost skills to shame.

I sometimes think that when we hit a case, Emily already knows who did it, can just sense it, but she slows it all down and gets me involved so I can have something to do.

Like her goal with all this is keeping me busy, helping me navigate this afterlife, and not letting me drown in my own regret.

But now? It was like I was seeing her for the first time.

Her voice took on an aged growl and that stupid Christmas sweater morphed into her normal T-shirt with the colorful lollipop print. Keeping up an appearance that isn't your default takes some effort, so this was a sign that she was redirecting her formidable energies somewhere else.

"You look for the weapon," she growled at me, her finger jabbing out vaguely around the house. "I'm going to search for signs of blood. There wasn't enough time for a good cleanup and we are likely looking at a crime of passion, so this should be a snap."

She marched off towards the bedroom, her fists balled and her little arms pumping, and I started searching for something round and sharp.

I considered following her. I was wondering if she was mad enough to hurt someone—not that it is easy for a ghost to do that. But given her tone and demeanor, I did what I was told.

As a ghost, I can see well, even in minimal light, but I can't see in the dark. I also can't open drawers or dig through the garbage. I took a moment and thought. A crime of passion means it wasn't planned. The weapon would be something at hand.

I went over to the "so useless in Tucson" fireplace—no stocking, maybe that was a classy upscale thing to skip—and sure enough there was a poker there, but the end wasn't right. I searched every nook and cranny of the posh living room, stuck my head under every piece of furniture, behind the entertainment center, into the cabinets which had enough light leakage for me to see. I gotta say being incorporeal can come in handy sometimes.

I moved to the kitchen next, which was as big as some apartments I'd lived in, and did the same. I kept my ears open, but Emily was quiet, and no one had woken up. I found an ice pick in one of the drawers, but no signs of blood, and it was buried under a lot of other stuff. I stuck my head in the disposal and didn't see any signs of blood, and nothing I could discern in the trash can.

Round hole. Sharp object. What could it be?

And then I had it. It was so obvious and so terrible. I just hate crimes of passion.

"HE DID IT," EMILY HISSED WHEN I GOT TO THE SON's bedroom. Red flickered on the edges of her form, her rage becoming manifest. I had never seen her like this before.

"Honey," I said, putting my hand on her shoulder, the normally numb ghostly sense of touch a bit prickly. "Did you find something?"

She looked at me, tears in her eyes. "No. No weapon, no blood, and he's sleeping so... so... peacefully!" She spit the last word out. "But I know he did it. He didn't like her. He didn't want her. He killed her!"

I squatted down. "What happened to you, Emily? What is this all about?"

She chewed on her lip and looked away, her normally bright green eyes clouded, but didn't answer.

"You've just seen too much," I said gently. "Too many times when men used their strength against women. Against girls." I suspected there was something personal in her past but didn't go there.

She nodded, her nostrils flaring as she sucked in a deep "breath." "And this one's going to pay." She turned back, the red flickering along her form taking on the deep red of fresh blood. She floated above the bed, her fingers gripped into a claw, reaching for the boy's head. I didn't know what she could do. And I didn't want her to do it, because if she did, if she lashed out in anger, it would change everything. Forever.

"No, Emily!" I shouted. "He didn't do it!"

She stopped and looked at me, her fierce eyes sending a shiver down my nonexistent spine. "What?" she spat out.

I held my hand out. "Come with me. I'll show you."

She swallowed hard, her smooth brow furrowing, and turned back to the boy who was now tossing and turning as if in the grip of some horrible dream.

"He didn't do it, Emily. I know what the murder weapon was." I sounded sure, but I hadn't checked yet and there was a sliver of doubt.

She blinked, the flickering red getting softer and then subsiding as she floated to the ground next to me and took my hand.

"He didn't?" she asked, her voice sounding like a little girl who had just woken up from a dream.

I walked her to the daughter's bedroom and pointed at the foil hanging above her bed. "It's square, but the wound would look round enough. If you pull off the plastic orange tip, I bet it's sharp enough."

"Hold me up," Emily said, walking to the wall, and this was a very good sign. Sure, she could fly, but her wanting to act like the living meant she was back to normal.

I picked her up and she eyed the thin blade. "There." She pointed near the tip. "A spot of blood. Tiny. The living would never even notice it."

I put her down and took her hand, walking back into the living room where we looked at the corpse of the girl under the Christmas tree.

"A crime of passion?" she asked quietly. I sighed. Sure, I'm a ghost and don't breathe, but there is a ghostly analog of the action with a similar effect. "Jealousy, I think."

She looked up at me, her face puzzled.

I shrugged. "Old-fashioned love triangle. Mary loved him and she loved Mary. Imagine Mary waking up and confessing to the daughter how she felt. The daughter listened, but her blood boiled. She had invited her crush over for a Christmas Eve sleepover only to find out she wasn't wanted. She encouraged Mary to go place the present and in a fit of hormone-amplified jealousy, grabbed her foil, ripped off the protective tip and..."

Emily's shoulders slumped. "I don't like crimes of passion, Walter."

I chuckled. "Me neither, honey. Let's go write this one up for the police at the SECI chamber and then go try to find a good old-fashioned crime of greed."

Her green eyes lit up and suddenly she was wearing that awful red and white Christmas tree sweater again. "Are you sure? I promised you a break."

"What else would Emily and Walter, Ghost Detectives, do for Christmas anyway?"

She nodded and smiled and we were off to our next case.

BACKSTORY—EMILY LOVES CHRISTMAS, EMILY LOVES MURDER

Holiday: Christmas

Walter and Emily have appeared in a lot of stories of mine. A lot. They made their first appearance in my third novel, *To Be a Fool: A Ghost Memoir, Book 2*. It was just a cameo, but my brain was already working on telling other ghosts' stories and the idea of a pair of ghosts that go around solving murders was irresistible. And with one of them being a ghost that has been dead for over eighty years but looks like, and sometimes acts like, the four-year-old she was when she died? Yeah, I had to write that, didn't I?

This story is my most successful attempt at writing an actual short story with Walter and Emily. They are so much fun to play with, the stories tend to get a little long. Their collection, *Unfinished Business: The Cases of Walter Anchor Ghost Detective* is about 475 pages long, most of the stories telling the larger tale of how Walter solves his own murder.

In the Walter and Emily time line, this story takes place sometime after *Detecting Haley* and before *The Red Arrow Murders*.

I have some other stories floating around with these characters and writing this has made me remember how much fun they are. Hmmm... maybe it will be time for ghosts solving murders again soon.

This story was originally published in *Pulphouse Fiction Magazine: Issue #15*, a Christmas issue.

You can find out more at *RobertJMcCarter.com/WalterAnchor*.

PART 3
MEET CUTE: THE MUSICAL

ONE

I think I've wandered into a Christmas Movie.

You know what I mean. It's three days before Christmas and suddenly the historic downtown of the mountain town I call home is glistening with fresh snow, bits of it sticking to the historic red brick buildings. There's an off-brand version of a Christmas song I can't quite place floating through the air, but not scratchy like usual—it's clear and perfect. People are smiling. Children are laughing. Every single store has Christmas lights up and they glisten and twinkle as the last warm light of the day shines on the snow-covered peak that frames the festive scene.

Snowflakes are dancing in the air, and while it's cold enough for it to snow, it doesn't feel that cold. There's snow on the road and on the sidewalk, but as I walk along I don't feel in danger of slipping.

I stop in my tracks not far from our local coffee shop, the scent of it elevated above the normal glorious scent of coffee, and look around. Something isn't right.

Or, rather, something is *too* right.

"Merry Christmas!" a short lady with rosy cheeks says. She's bustling along the sidewalk with an armload of packages.

"Merry Christmas," I mumble back.

I look around and it's like the saturation levels of the town have been turned up a couple of notches, the colors just a tad too bright for reality. Life just isn't this perfect and this colorful except in the movies.

I mean, Christmas is a beautiful time of year around here, but not *this* beautiful.

It's one of those moments when you can just feel the change in the air. Something is going on, something is different, I just can't figure out what it is. It's almost like I'm having a senior moment even though I'm only twenty-eight.

I hear the bell ringing on a shop door opening and a woman's voice, one that's like music to me, says, "Thanks, Gus!"

I look across the two lane, one-way street and see a young woman with a long brown ponytail dressed in a red down jacket and a purple scarf step out of a local giftshop. You know, the one that sells trinkets and tchotchkes and really leans into the season. Her arms are overloaded with bags and packages that are presumably full of gifts.

I don't know her name, but I've seen her a hundred times. She has a splash of freckles on her cheeks and her blue eyes glitter like gems. She's a die-hard runner, her long, lanky frame serving her well in that regard. She loves coffee and is a student at the local university and she's just about perfect for me if I could only get up the courage to introduce myself to her.

Suddenly, the scene darkens a touch and the happily generic Christmas song stops playing. I hear the rev of an engine and the scent of oily fumes mixes with that of the coffee.

The young woman steps out onto the street and sees someone she knows to her right and calls to her while I see a black pickup truck with a snowplow blade mounted on the front barreling down on her from the other direction. The packages are stacked up to her head and she can't see the truck.

Time slows down and I can't hear anything but the beating of my heart.

I see the driver of the truck. I don't know his name, but I've seen him around. There's a snow blower in the back and I know he makes a living clearing snow this time of year.

Even though he's a ways away, I can see him clearly as he spots the young lady and a surprised look takes over his ruggedly handsome face, and then fear. He moves an oddly convulsive way, like he is trying to stamp on the breaks but it isn't working.

I don't think, I run into the street right in front of a blue sedan which honks and stops just in time.

My steps are true and I surge towards the young woman with the ponytail who still hasn't noticed the truck.

"Watch out!" I shout, but the words come out slowly, like time has slowed down. Each step takes an agonizingly long time as I run towards the young woman, as the black pickup barrels closer.

My heart is beating hard, thump-thump-thump, and all thoughts of this strange evening are gone. This is a one-way street, there are two lanes, but traffic is backed up behind the blue sedan that stopped for me and the truck has nowhere to go.

I plow into the young woman right before the truck gets to us and we and all her packages go rolling onto the snowy sidewalk just as time speeds back up and the roaring truck surges by, its horn blaring, and then there is the sickening crunch of metal as the truck runs into a streetlamp just past us.

The young woman is lying on top of me, her breath coming fast. My head really hurts, I must have bumped in on the sidewalk, but I still get lost in those sapphire blue eyes of hers.

I try to speak, but it comes out as in inarticulate grunt.

"You..." she begins, blinking repeatedly, and I notice how

long her lashes are. "You saved my life," she says, her breath is warm and it smells like coffee.

"I... I guess I did," I manage to say.

The moment deepens and I can feel it. This is it. This is the moment. She is the one. I feel warm all over and a smile lights up her face and I have no choice but to smile back.

"Is everyone all right?" another voice asks. It's a deep, manly voice, and without even looking you can tell it belongs to a muscular man.

I don't look, but the young woman does, her eyes widening and suddenly music is playing, crystal clear and floating on the air. It's not a Christmas song, at least not one I know.

"I don't know what happened," the manly voice continues. "My brakes wouldn't work. I... I ran into that streetlamp to make sure I didn't hurt anyone."

"Oh, but you're hurt," the young woman says, and quicker than I thought possible she is off of me and I feel cold and alone.

The music builds and I look and that deep voice belongs to the ruggedly handsome driver of the truck. He's dressed in jeans and a flannel shirt that can barely contain his barrel of a chest. His face is covered in an ultra-short beard and his brown eyes are annoyingly soulful.

"I'm Amanda," the young woman says. She's blinking. A lot. More than she just was with me.

"Clint," he says with a nod.

"You're hurt," she says. "Let me." She takes a handkerchief from her pocket and starts dabbing at the blood on Clint's forehead. Even his damn forehead looks strong and imposing.

The music changes, the tune growing, and then...

Okay, bear with me here. This is about to get weird, but I swear to you this is what happened.

A shiver passes through Clint and Amanda says, "You're cold."

He shrugs it off, the music gets stronger, and he opens his mouth and—I swear to God—starts singing:

It's winter in our little city
It's cold but the snow sure is pretty
But my heart warms when I see you

And he can sing, his voice a rich, deep baritone that would do just fine on a Broadway stage.

And if that wasn't weird enough, Amanda back sings to him:

It's winter in our mountain city
It's cold but the Christmas lights sure are pretty
You're hurt, let me take care of you

And yup, Amanda belongs right on that stage with Clint. What in the world...?

Suddenly there is no traffic and people with arms full of colorful packages are out in the street and they all start singing, taking the song in a more up-tempo direction:

It's winter in our city
It's cold but Christmastime is so pretty
It's time for a little romance between these two

And then Clint and Amanda are dancing, the flash mob twirling around them as they all sing the chorus, their voices beautiful, their dancing energetic, and I'm on the ground feeling cold and alone my head hurting. Wasn't I the one that just saved her life? Didn't Clint almost kill her... and me?

The dancing flash mob forms a circle around Amanda and Clint and they are illumined perfectly like the nearly full moon just turned into a spotlight and his voice rises as he sings to her again:

> *It's winter in the city*
> *It's cold but the snow sure is pretty*
> *And I don't care about my smashed truck*
> *Even though I won't be able to make a buck*
> *Because now I've met you*

Amanda then sings to him:

> *It's winter in the city*
> *It's cold but the decorations are pretty*
> *My heart was as smashed as your poor truck*
> *But now I think I've had some good luck*
> *Because now I've met you*

The flash mob starts spinning with the precision of a marching band as they toss red and green packages to each other like a troupe of crazed jugglers and they all start singing the chorus again:

> *It's winter in city*
> *It's cold but Christmas time's so pretty*
> *It's time for a little romance between me and you*

OMG! It's not just a Christmas Movie I've somehow found myself in. It's a musical, and it's not even about me.

TWO

I flee the scene of the ongoing Christmas rom-com musical. It's just too much. Part of me knows something isn't right, something weird is going on, but that is just a soap-bubble of a thought that just keeps getting popped by the technicolor brightness of this night and the two other flash mobs I pass singing romantic songs.

It seems meet cutes are happening all over this town and everyone just feels the need to sing and dance about it.

Maybe it's the bump I took to my head. Maybe I've completely lost it. Whatever it is, I've never experienced anything like this.

And now I realize that I haven't introduced myself. My name is Jeff George. Yeah, I know. I didn't name me. I was born in this lovely mountain town and returned after college because with my English Lit degree, no one was pounding on my door to offer me a good job.

I live in the mother-in-law quarters behind my parents' house, so it's not as bad as living with them, but almost.

As you must have determined by now, I am single and not

one of those happily single people. My mother and father are still in love, in a way that is quite embarrassing at times, and I want that. I want to be so in love it's ridiculous and embarrassing.

What else do you need to know about me? I read a lot, obviously, and I love to run. At 5'5", I'm rather short, so I'm not all that fast, more on the slow and steady side of things.

So I literally run away from all the musicals through my snowy mountain town which is decorated to the nines for Christmas and end up at my home away from home which is a former food truck sitting in a parking lot next to the city park. The white panel truck has "Words on the Run" emblazoned on it in dark blue, with the outline of a mountain behind it and the outlines of a bunch of runners holding books while they run.

This is my baby. I sell sports drinks, coffee, tea, and power bars for the runners and books and non-Paleo treats for the readers, and both to the narrow crowd of folks like me who love to read and love to run.

When I get there, my best friend in the entire world, Isabella Morales, is there.

She's just a touch taller than me with long black hair and dark brown eyes, her skin the color of coffee with lots of cream.

Our eyes meet and we both start talking. I tell her about saving Amanda's life and how Clint and her made eyes at each other while singing and dancing. She tells me about witnessing the often used meet cute where a poorly secured tree slides off the woman's car almost causing the handsome man to crash before their eyes met and they all broke out in song.

This rushed exchange provides me with some comfort. At least I'm not the only one experiencing this madness.

"It's sexist," she says, ending her story her hands on her hips. "It's clichéd. It makes the woman out to be useless and dumb, like women can't tie knots."

That's Izzy. She full of opinions and unafraid of voicing them.

"That's what's freaking you out?" I ask.

She shrugs. "Well, that and all the musical numbers going on around here."

We met in college where she was wisely studying law while I had my nose in books.

I shake my head. "That should have been my meet cute with Amanda, but Clint with his cleft chin stole it."

"Poor baby," Izzy says, her voice going saccharine as she pats me on the shoulder. "I've had more meet cutes than I can count and not a one of them—"

She stops talking because music is playing, different than before but crystal clear, like we are right next to the band playing the tune.

I feel this energy tingling through my body and my feet feel like moving and then Izzy's eyes get wide and she starts to sing, this pained look on her face as if the words are forcing themselves out:

Every rom-com has a meet cute
But how many meet cutes have I had?
There's the runaway luggage and the mistaken identity
The stuck elevator and the loose Christmas Tree
A meet cute doesn't mean a romance and that's so sad
How many meet cutes do I have to have?

Izzy dances across the parking lot with a startling amount of grace. She's strong and solid, lifts weights all the time, and I've never seen her dance. She ends in a flourish, her hand pointing at me and her eyes wide.

I must get the same look on my face, because words start

forcing their way out and I start dancing around the parking lot singing:

Every rom-com has a meet cute
But how many meet cutes have I had?
There's the messy spilled food and the fender bender
There's the babbling like an idiot and getting stuck in
snowy weather
A meet cute doesn't mean a romance and that's so sad
How many meet cutes do I have to have?

And then the parking lot is filled with another flash mob, the tempo on the music kicks up a couple of notches and we form a circle and all start singing and dancing. For each one of the meet cutes we sing about, a couple goes into the center of the circle and quickly acts it out:

Meet cute!
Spilled orange juice
Meet cute!
Mistaken identity
Meet cute!
Babbling like an idiot
Meet cute!
Poorly secured Christmas tree
Meet cute!
Saved you from the slimeball
Meet cute!

The flash mob scurries away, the tempo slows back down, and it's just Izzy and me and she sings:

Every rom-com has a meet cute

But how many meet cutes do I have to have?
Until I meet my partner and I'm not so sad

And then I'm singing:

Every rom-com has a meet cute
But how many meet cutes do I have to have?
Until I meet my partner and I'm so very glad

We end up in the middle of the parking lot hands joined, both of us breathing hard.

"What the fizz!" Izzy says, and even that's weird, too. It's not like Izzy ever had any trouble lobbing an f-bomb or two.

THREE

In the morning I wake up groggy, my tongue thick and my stomach sour like I drank way too much. I stare up at the white ceiling until it hits me.

Christmas. Rom-com. Musical.

Oh my God!

I grab my phone and a text is waiting from Izzy, *Did that shirt happen?*

I stare at it. Did she really type "shirt" when she should have typed something spicier?

I sit on my bed in my messy one-room mother-in-law quarters thinking about it. I love musicals, I really do. I think the skilled weaving of song and story can lead to a potent experience stronger than either one by itself. But I never wanted to be in one.

I take the childish route and text back, *Did WHAT happen?*

Izzy's response is quick. *Don't mess with me or I will destroy you. That whole life is a freaking musical rom-com thing last night.*

I stare at my shelf of books, my eyes being drawn to my classics shelf where I have a copy of *The Wizard of Oz* right next to *Alice in Wonderland*.

I type back to her, *Guess it wasn't a dream.*

What are we gonna do? she texts back.

No clue. Meet me at the truck when you can.

THE MOTHER-IN-LAW COTTAGE I LIVE IN IS NOT FAR FROM where the "Words on the Run" truck is usually parked. It runs okay, but I don't drive it unless I have to. As I walk down the snowy streets, as the sun is just rising, I look around expecting people to start breaking out in song.

Things are bright, the sun is shining and the world has that beautiful "just snowed" look, but nothing strange happens. So I go to work supplying caffeine and calories for the body and stories for the soul.

It's about 9 a.m. and things have slowed down. The morning runs on the trails around here are over and those that can breakfast with what I provide are gone. I'm sitting on a stool in front of the window scanning *The Wizard of Oz* on my ereader looking for some clues.

"I thought that was you," a woman says. The voice is musical and my heart speeds up.

I look up and Amanda is there. Her freckled cheeks are flushed from the cold and she's got her shiny red down coat on, her lovely brown hair pulled back into a ponytail.

"I... Ummm... Yeah..." I say, clearly having lost the ability to speak. Partially from her presence, partially because I didn't think she knew who I was.

She laughs, and it's so lovely and I feel like a teenager facing his first crush, my cheeks burning hot.

"You kinda disappeared last night," she says, those gemstone blue eyes dancing. "After I took care of Clint, you were gone."

She leaves it hanging there, obviously I'm supposed to say something, but can I?

"Well... Sorry...?" I manage, sounding like an idiot, but at least that's an upgrade.

"All good," she says. "I just wanted to thank you for saving my life. I see you're busy though."

She turns to go, but it's slow and hesitant and clearly not what she wants.

"Coffee," I say. "Want some?" Oh good, I've upgraded to caveman level speech patterns.

She turns and the smile on her face makes my knees weak and I'm glad I'm sitting. "Please."

I take a deep breath and force my brain to start working properly. "It's warmer in here," I say, pointing towards the back of the van.

"Umm..." she begins.

Yeah, I did save her life but she has no idea if I'm a creep.

"I'll come out," I say as I pour a couple of cups of coffee into paper cups and put them on the stainless-steel pass-through which has cream and sugar set up on it.

I walk to the back of the van, squeeze my eyes shut, and say to myself, "No expectations. She's just thanking you. No expectations."

But my hands are a little shaky as I climb out. And as I do, I have this fear that I'm going to start shaking and tell her how nervous I am, how much of a pedestal I put on her on even before we had said one word to each other.

She's sipping her coffee when I walk around and I grab mine.

She suddenly seems shy and I am hoping my ability to speak has returned. "Strange evening, huh?" I ask

She nods, her eyebrows raising. "I'll say."

"All that singing," I say, because that's what's on my mind.

"Singing?" she asks.

I panic. My heart starts racing. Doesn't she know that she was singing and dancing last night? "Umm... you know... there were some carolers in the square."

She gives me a "you crazy" look and tries to cover it with a smile.

It's pretty weird from there. We talk about running and the races at a lower elevation we are planning to do for the winter. She thanks me again, but it's all flat and disappointing.

How can she not know about the musical she was a part of last night? Did I hit my head that hard? And if I did, how come Izzy is experiencing it too?

What is going on?

FOUR

Izzy shows up after the lunch rush during the afternoon lull, the van bouncing a little as she opens up the door in the back and climbs in.

It's winter, so the lunch rush isn't much, but people still run here year-round and read too.

Izzy wears a perfume that has hints of lavender so I know it's her. I don't look up from my ereader, where I'm scanning *Alice in Wonderland* again, and ask, "Any singing or dancing for you today?"

"Thankfully, no," she says. "My day has been the big fun-time circus of getting ready to prosecute a rapist."

Izzy is an atheist and as such is very conscious about never thanking God for anything even in a colloquial way.

I look up and the sour look on her face reinforces what she just said. "So you'd rather be singing and dancing?"

The space in the "Words on the Run" van is tight. The serving window where I'm perched on a small stool is up front with lots of shelves stuffed with food. I pulled the stove out when I bought the van, so behind me is a station for making tea and coffee above a small propane fridge. The rest of the van is shelf after shelf of books, mostly used. It means the default scent of the truck is coffee and old books with a touch of sweat.

"I think I would," she says. "I hate cases like this."

Izzy pushes past me, her hands briefly on my shoulders, grabs a muffin, and pours herself some green tea, the earthy scent of it filling the van.

The passenger's seat swivels and she swings it around and plops herself down with a long sigh. "Any musicals for you?" she asks.

"No," I say, putting my ereader down, a goofy grin taking over my face.

"What?" she asks.

"Amanda came by to..." I begin feeling my cheeks flush. "To thank me."

"With her body?" Izzy asks, her brown eyes glittering.

"Izzy!"

"Well, then with what?" she asks.

"Her mouth," I say, realize what I said and my cheeks flush really red.

"Way to go J-man," she says before I can correct myself.

"No, no," I say. "With words, you know, the usual way humans thank each other."

"Sounds boooor-ring, but dish," she says.

And I do. In detail. Izzy is my best friend, she knows exactly who I am.

She munches on the muffin, which I know she won't bother to pay me for, and sips on her tea, her face a squished up mask of empathy as I recount the very awkward encounter.

"What am I going to do?" I ask.

She opens her mouth to speak but then looks up and cocks her head a bit. I hear it too, there is that music playing, that perfectly clean music that presages a musical number.

"No..." I begin.

"Shirt!" she says, her eyes getting wide when the right word clearly doesn't come out.

It hits me first and I stand up without really thinking about it and walk out the back of the van. Izzy follows me and I look at her and her eyes are as wide as mine.

I have no choice. I take a dramatic step forward into the parking lot, spread my arms, and start singing:

The love of my life
Didn't want to be my wife
It turns out she didn't want a mister
She ran away with my sister
Whaddya gonna do?
Whaddya gonna do?

I executed some slow-motion dance steps during that verse that felt decidedly old-school Fred Astaire.

When I stop, Izzy twirls in front of me, her moves reminiscent of Grace Kelly. Her jacket is off and her long dark skirt swirls around her strong legs and she starts to sing:

The girl of your dreams
Wasn't what she seemed
Turns out she didn't want a female
Now she's married with kids in Glendale
Whaddya gonna do?
Whaddya gonna do?

Her dance steps wind her back to me and our eyes met. They are still wide, there is still some freakout there, but there is also a smile on her face like she is enjoying it.

So I let go, I let the music take me and I dance and sing:

My books never let me down
But sometimes I play the clown
Because I really just want a lover
That's also a really great partner
But whaddya gonna do?
Whaddya gonna do?

Izzy twirls in front of me and sings:

The man that I thought I loved
When he got drunk he pushed he shoved
I just want someone gentle
Someone that loves the movie Yentl
But whaddya gonna do?
Whaddya gonna do?

Our dancing brings us together and we join hands and dance and sing like Fred and Ginger, our voices harmonizing beautifully:

We are a pair that aren't part of a pair
But whaddya gonna do?
Whaddya gonna do?
We two lonely hearts never make a good start
Whaddya gonna do?
What the heck you gonna do?

When it is over we're in the middle of the parking lot, holding hands and breathing hard. Our eyes meet for just a second and it's... weird. Things are never weird with Izzy.

"Umm..." I begin. "I think this is your fault. You said you'd prefer a musical."

She blinks, takes her hands back and rubs them on her skirt.

"Yeah..." And then a smile lights up her face and burns away the weird. "I think I'm starting to like it. Weird as heck, but not the same-old, that's for sure."

"Sorry about what you went through with Mr. Asshole Lawyer," I say, her bit about "he pushed he shoved" brought it all back and I knew it was worse than that. Much worse.

"Thanks," she says with a bleak little smile. "I guess it turned out okay. He made me into the woman I am today." She gets a distant look in her eyes and that bleak smile remains.

What she meant by that is she started studying Judo and lifting weights after Mr. Asshole Lawyer so the next guy or girl that tried that kind of crap would be sorry. Her eyes focus back on me and she says, "And sorry about the alleged love of your life marrying your sister. I know holidays are heck for you now."

I reflect her bleak smile back to her and nod. It is always a bit torturous when my sister comes home with the woman I used to love and their kid and I have no one. I shrug and say, "I just focus on my niece and studiously ignore the PDAs."

The mood has fallen and I search my brain for something to lift it up. "Hey, want to watch *Yentl* tonight? And maybe *Chicago*? We haven't had a musical marathon in a while."

Her face gets weird again and I feel weird because I don't know what's going on with her and that's so unusual.

She looks down and kicks at the pavement, and when she looks up, she her face has a wide-eyed "eureka!" look.

"Better idea," she says. "Now that you know perfect runner girl's name, I have a much better idea."

She rushes back to the van, grabs her coat, and starts walking away. "I need to do a little research first. I'll text you where to meet me later."

I just stand there for a while and watch her walk purposefully away. What in the world is going on?

FIVE

Sam Darling is an Afro-Cuban, cross-dressing drag queen and my one part-time employee at "Words on the Run." He's also a bartender, a dance instructor, a personal trainer, and one of the most emotionally intelligent people I know.

He spells me at the truck for a few hours on weekdays so I can go buy supplies and take care of other business things.

I am still standing in the parking lot near the park trying to figure out what was going on with Izzy when he walks up.

His face is chiseled with a strong nose, cheekbones you could slice cheese on, and a perfect complexion. Today he has on red lipstick, false eyelashes, mauve eye shadow, and a wig of short black hair with a pageboy cut. He has a long wool peacoat which reveals pantyhosed legs and nice Ugg boots.

"Drag show tonight?" I ask, even though I know the answer.

"Never mind that, boy," he says with a pursing of those red lips. "That girl is in to you."

"Izzy? No," I say.

He folds his arms, shakes his head, and snorts. "Need I remind you how you all met as newbies in college?"

"What do you mean?" I ask, but I'm distracted because I hear music playing again. Oh God, not another musical number.

"Meet cute," Sam says. "Classic."

I shake my head and am distracted by the growing music which has a heavy beat. "She had a girlfriend at the time," I say.

"As if..." he says with a dismissive roll of his eyes. "Let me lay it out for you, boy."

He takes off his jacket and tosses it away to reveal a strappy, lacy, short black dress covering his athletic form. That and the hair and it clicks. He's going to be Velma Kelly from *Chicago* at the drag show tonight.

He opens his mouth and starts rapping, his bass voice a rumble, the pattern of the rap feeling rather old-school:

It was about ten years ago when you were still a teen
You both were so young not used to that college scene
Pretty Isabella clawed her way up from the streets
Her dream to become a lawyer and help give poverty a
defeat

It is strange to have Sam dressed as Velma Kelly and rapping. But he is also doing a Chicago-esque dance with staccato movements like from "The Cell Block Tango" but thankfully not the murderous message.

Shy bookworm Jeff with his head in the clouds
Was much more used to his fantasies than the college
crowds
Izzy so serious, so studious, so always in such a hurry
She was late for class so she had to scurry
Shy bookworm Jeff was reading while waiting in line
His stomach was grumbling and it was dining time
Izzy had her smoothie and it was a dash and go thing

*Bookworm Jeff with a tray of food thinking about Lord of
the Rings
They collided with a crash, their heads knocking together
His pants were ruined and so was her very best sweater
But shy eyes met and there was an undeniable connection
Best friends from that moment on, always love and
affection*

It ends and Sam has his jacket back on. "Honey," he says, his bright red lips pursed. "She followed you here."

"She's an orphan, no family," I say, my voice sounding a lot more pleading than I like. "We were close, it makes sense."

He points up a finger with a long red nail perched on the end. "One, top of her class, she could go anywhere, no reason to come to this little town."

I open my mouth up to speak, but he gives me that cocked-head look and I stop short.

"Two. Let's face it—you don't turn down twice the money to move up to the cold unless there's a really good reason. Not a girl that smart. That driven."

"But..." I began.

"Three. Sam sees how that girl looks at you when you are not looking at her. It Love with a capital 'L.'"

Is this why Izzy was just so weird?

"Look deep in your heart," Sam says, his voice gentle. "I know she ain't a tall skinny girl like the kind you are always chasin', but how did you feel after your collision way back when?"

I shrug. "Embarrassed. After that, I was glad I had a friend."

One of Sam's eyebrows raised. "And you didn't wonder?"

"Well... she told me she had a girlfriend early on," I say.

"So the straight boy that you are you assumed she was gay," he says.

I nod.

He stares at me, a disappointed look on his face.

"And then after my fiancé left me for my sister she was with that asshole," I say. "After that she really needed me to be her friend."

"And that means you weren't being a complete idiot then," he says with a wag of his finger. "But you are now."

We stand there and the silence is thick and awkward. "Hey," I say. "Weird question. But has there been any dancing around here in the last few minutes?"

His brow furrows and he gives me a disapproving look that would put my mother to shame. "You wanna see dancin', then come to the show tonight. You'll see dancin'. Now scoot, boy. Let Sam go do his job. I know you got stuff to do too."

There is a couple walking up to the truck and Sam waves at them and shouts, "I got you all." He trots to the truck, leaving me alone to think about the past.

SIX

The rest of the day is a blur. A trip to the bank. Shopping for supplies. Tweaking the website to show the latest specials. But throughout all of it I keep thinking about Izzy and how we met.

It wasn't just a meet cute, it was a double meet cute, with the food collision and the bonking of heads.

She had followed me back here after college when she could have gotten a big job in a big city.

I did love her, she was like family to me, but romantic love had never been on the table.

First she had a girlfriend, and then when I learned she was bi, I was with the woman who is now my sister-in-law. And since then... Well, it was never a thought.

The sun is down and I am alone in the van restocking when the text comes in from Izzy.

I fumble with the phone and feel suddenly nervous. The text says, *Time for your Christmas present. Wear something nice and meet me out front of 2Sweet at 8.*

"2Sweet" is our local sweet shop with truffles, caramel apples, homemade ice cream, that kind of stuff.

I'm a mess as I finish up at the truck and go home and shower and get changed. Something fundamental about my world has changed and all the musical numbers are the least of it. It's like I can't think anymore.

2Sweet is on the same street that I had saved Amanda's life last night, just up a block. It is nestled in between a fancy Italian restaurant and a pita sandwich place in a hundred-year-old red brick building. The window is painted with a Christmas scene and that's framed with colorful Christmas lights.

The town feels like it did last night, all glittery and bright with Christmas music floating in the air like this is a scene from some cheesy Christmas movie.

Izzy is waiting in her long puffy jacket and looking nervous.

"It happened again," she says when I get there, puffs of condensate lingering in the cold air.

"What happened?" I ask, still feeling like my world is so changed. This is my best friend Izzy, but could she be more?

She shakes her head just a little. "One of those crazy meet cutes. This time it was the guy that couldn't attach his stupid tree to his car and the girl it almost took out was me."

I just stand there blinking.

"And it included a damn musical number about how Christmas trees brings people together. He's a little young, but I really need some fun."

"Okay..." I say. Izzy had a meet cute. Izzy is obviously so preoccupied by it so she doesn't even see how weird I am acting.

"So, we gotta do this quick," she says. "I've got a date in a bit."

"Do what?" I ask.

"First, let me see," she says, unzipping my jacket and examining the blue cable knit sweater and tan chinos I'm wearing. It feels like a weirdly intimate act although it's normal for us. She sighs. "Good enough. A button-down under the sweater would have been better."

I think she finally notices my confusion and pulls me in front of the window of 2Sweet and nods.

Inside Amanda is womaning the ice cream station, a bright smile on her face.

"This is your Christmas present," she says. "Put your earbuds in, call me, and I'll get you over your inability to talk to the girl."

"We're going to Cyrano her?" I ask, still confused.

"Just to break the ice and get you a date," she says, a playful smile on her lips. I notice they are nice, full lips. Why hadn't I noticed that before?

I must still look confused. "Look," she says, "you've been pining after her before you even spoke to her. You just saved her life. She came to see you. There is clearly an opening here."

Izzy has a date. Izzy is setting me up. Izzy is just my friend.

The weirdness of the world corrects itself. Sam doesn't know what the heck he's talking about. Besides, I'd never do anything to threaten our friendship.

"Okay," I say with a smile. Izzy thinks I'm just saying that about the Cyrano thing with Amanda, but I'm saying it about all of this. Why couldn't that have been my meet cute last night? After all, in every rom-com the relationship has to have a few bump along the way.

As I walk in, 2Sweet smells like a cavity waiting to happen, the smell of caramelized sugar and fat thick. It's, frankly, a little too much for me.

You got this, Izzy says in my ear.

"Hey," Amanda says as I approach ice-cream freezer she is behind. There's not thirty-one flavors there but a good dozen. I can see the colorful, open, five-gallon tubs through the glass. "If it isn't Jeff George, the savior of silly girls like me."

The store itself is all bright colors and glass display cases with shelf after shelf of treats.

Amanda has a bright red apron on over a brown sweater and jeans, her long brown hair back in its perpetual ponytail, her sapphire eyes brighter than any of the treats in here.

I smile and listen to Izzy and repeat what she says only rephrasing it slightly. "Hey," I say, hiding my sweaty hands in my pockets. "Sorry I was so weird earlier. I think I owe you an explanation."

She gets a bemused look on her face, one delicate eyebrow raising and nods. "I'm listening."

"I... I just think you're an amazing runner," I say after listening to Izzy. "And I hear you're getting a doctorate in anthropology, so you must be smart. And anyone can see that you are beautiful.

"You're the whole package and just my type. Is it any wonder I turned into a blathering idiot earlier?"

As I say it, it sounds way too cheesy but she looks down and her cheeks flash briefly red. I didn't know that anthropology bit, Izzy had done her research.

"Thank you," she says, and I swear her eyes are even brighter.

You got this now, Izzy says in my ear. *Just ask her out. Be curious. Be interested. Over and out.*

I shove thoughts of the muscular, square-jawed Clint out of my mind and really look into those blue eyes and will my knees not to get weak.

What is it about her? This isn't my normal reaction to the opposite sex.

"Maybe we can get a drink some time," I say, proud that I am able to get a coherent sentence out without prompting.

"Sure," she says with a smile. "I'm off in 90 minutes. How about tonight?"

SEVEN

Our postcard perfect Christmas town has a "speakeasy." The fun way to enter is through a bookshelf at the back of a homemade soap and lotion shop.

This is where I take Amanda.

This is where the drag show is going on.

It's a fun evening as we have a few drinks and get to know each other.

She tells me that her parents are divorced and I tell her about my parents, still in love after all these years. She tells me about working her way through college and I tell her about my strange little business. We talk about her three older brothers and my sister. She's spent a lot of time overseas in her studies of anthropology and hopes to do more. We talk about our mutual love of running and how it helps you get out of your head.

If Amanda were a drink, she'd be champagne, expensive champagne. She's bright and effervescent and being around her can make a guy like me dizzy.

The speakeasy is crowded, a long narrow room with the bar on one side and lots of small tables on the other. The far end has a small stage and the walls are red brick and the high ceiling is covered in period stamped tin panels.

We don't get a lot of time to talk before the drag show, which is amazing. It ends with Sam and five other queens doing "The Cell Block Tango" on the small stage.

It's one of my favorite numbers in any musical, despite its murderous theme. It's so fierce, so innovative, so electrifying.

After the show, I've had enough alcohol and we've talked enough that I'm starting to get comfortable, maybe too comfortable.

"Can I ask something?" I say over the din of the bar. "Feel free to not answer."

She cocks her head to the side, those sapphire blue eyes searching mine, and says, "Sure."

"It... umm..." I begin, sounding like an idiot again. "It seemed like you and Clint really hit if of last night, so..."

The question peters out and I'm unable to continue.

"So why am I out with you tonight?" she asks.

I nod, not trusting my words anymore.

She nods slowly and there's a real sadness to it. Music starts playing, that kind of ultra-clear, just in the air music and a spotlight clicks on and Amanda stands up.

Another musical number?

She suddenly has a microphone in her hand and Sam and a similarly dressed drag queen show up on either side of her and yank at her brown sweater which tears away, and underneath it is a black slinky dress like the queens are wearing.

The bar is suddenly quiet and Amanda starts singing, the song is slow and sad:

I don't want to be tied down, can't you see
I just want to live my life while I'm young and free
Exploring this crazy world and my sexuality

Sam and the other queen also have microphones and they sing together, their tempo much faster than hers:

Let her be free
Have some fun
Just you and her on life's run

The two queens lift Amanda up so she's reclined back and twirl her around in the air while the spotlight follows her and she sings another verse:

Every man it seems wants to tie me down
It makes me feel like I'm going to drown
Every man wants to be served like he wears a crown

And the queens put her down and sing:

Let her be free
Have some fun
Just you and her on life's run

Amanda sings another verse as she struts around the bar gently touching and flirting with man after man:

There'll be time for kids and finding a place to belong
I want to find my way and sing my own song
I just want to be happy while my days are long

She ends up back in front of me flanked by the queens and they all sing:

Can't you see, she's got to be free
Have some fun

Just you and her on life's run

And then the spotlight clicks off and the sounds of the bar crash around us and Amanda is sitting across from me back in her sweater and asks, "Does that make sense?"

I lick my lips and nod. I get the whole swipe left, swipe right thing and have done my share of that and Amanda is a total swipe right.

Before I know it, Amanda is leaning over and kissing me and it's... Well, her lips are soft and warm and she still smells a little like coffee and tastes like the champagne she's been drinking. It's a kiss full of promise and my body responds to it, but my mind, seemingly of its own accord, goes to Izzy.

I'm kissing Amanda and all I can think about is Izzy and I'm wondering how she kisses.

Amanda pulls back and asks, "What's wrong?"

I shake my head slowly, I can't believe I'm doing this. "I... I totally get where you're coming from. Maybe it's because thirty is right around the corner, but I want to have what my parents do. I want to be ridiculously in love in thirty years."

"That's a tall order," Amanda says.

I nod. "It is. But I've been close with an amazing woman for ten years and I... I never thought of her as more than a friend, but..."

Amanda smiles and it's a genuine smile that lights up her lovely face. "Then go get her, Jeff."

"But... we're on a date," I say.

She snorts. "I'm a big girl and I take care of myself. Go! Go get her!"

EIGHT

I've never been so nervous in my life. Just around the corner with Izzy and me is an amazing future or disaster.

When I get out of the bar and the cold hits me, I remember that she's on a date tonight too. Shirt!

But I'm committed, so I fumble out my phone and text her, *I need to see you ASAP.*

It's late, past midnight, and I realize I may not get an answer. I pace the sidewalk, my stomach pretending it's a skilled contortionist doing a make-or-break show and pulling out all the stops.

When my phone bleeps, I jump. The text back from Izzy says, *I'm home.*

No asking how my date that she arranged went. No inviting me over. I know Izzy, and this isn't good.

I have a moment there outside the speakeasy when I think I'm insane. I should go back in and be with Amanda. I shouldn't tempt fate with Izzy.

But my world changed when Izzy and I sang that "Whaddya gonna do" song and there is no going back.

I run to the "Word on the Run" truck, fire her up, and drive

"

to Izzy's place which is a house in a nice neighborhood on the other side of town.

I'm sweating like I'm in the middle of a marathon when I knock on the door. When Izzy opens it, she's wrapped in a ragged grey robe with her bunny slippers on, a frown on her face. Her long black hair is rumpled and falling over her shoulders in a way that is more than a little distracting.

"Date didn't go well," I say.

She shakes her head. "Too young. My head just wasn't there."

I walk in and she closes the door. "Wait a minute, what about Amanda? You didn't blow it, did you?"

I shake my head. "No. We went out. I took her to the drag show. She's a little too much for me," I say. "And my head just wasn't there."

We're in her living room, which is sparse Zen elegance, a flatscreen TV mounted on the wall, hardwood floors, a simple couch, chair, and coffee table, a couple of sparsely populated bookshelves.

Because of what's been happening the last two days with this musical madness, I can see our history with a clarity I never had before.

We had a meet cute but circumstances weren't right then so we became the best of friends. After that it was timing with one or the other of us in a relationship or needing to heal for so long that I never thought of her as more than my best friend.

"You're staring at me, Jeff," Izzy says, her arms folded in front of her. "Why are you looking at me like that?"

My heart is pounding in my head and I just stand there. I look up and cock my head. I'm waiting for the music to start. I'm waiting for a song to pour out of me so Izzy knows how I feel and I don't have to come up with the words myself.

Why else would this musical madness have been happening?

"Are you having a stroke or something?" she asks, the concern clear in her voice.

I shake my head. "No. I was hoping for a musical number."

She cocks her head, one eyebrow raised. "Why?"

"To make this easier?" I say.

"To make *what* easier?" she asks, a small smile playing on those full lips. Maybe she has a clue but she sure as heck isn't going to make it easy on me.

I sigh. Clearly no musical help is coming. "You... you know I love you, right?"

She nods, her smile getting a little brighter. "Yeah. We're family."

I swallow hard. "I... After the last few days... well... I've..." I sound like an idiot again.

"Jeff," she says gently. "Just spit it out."

"Isabella Morales," I say, licking my lips. "I... I am in in love with you."

Her eyes widen and she takes a step back, her hand heading towards her mouth, her eyes wide in surprise.

My heart lurches and I'm afraid I've made a terrible mistake and my mouth just starts running of its own. "I know I am idiot and it took me forever to figure it out, but Sam reminded me about how we met, and all this musical madness got me thinking, and—"

"Oh, just shut up," Izzy says, cutting me off, and then she's in my arms and kissing me hard. The kiss is deep and passionate and electric, and I hear music playing and then the room is suddenly cool and I feel that urge to sing bubbling up.

I open my eyes and Izzy is looking around giggling. We're still in her living room but the walls are gone and we're in the middle of the forest, snow clinging to the pine and fir trees, the full moon illuminating us in a silver glow.

Snow is swirling around us and Izzy is dressed in an elegant silver gown that glints in the moonlight and I am dressed in an expensive tux.

We start dancing across her hardwood floor and we both sing:

Meet cute
Turns out we already met cute
Ten whole years ago
With a head bonk, we came together,

Izzy sings, *I ruined your pants*
And I sing, *And I ruined your sweater*
We both sing, *And ever since then we've been friends forever.*

Meet cute
Turns out we already met cute
All those years ago

We're back to the Fred and Giger dancing routine. I twirl her, she twirls me, and then we separate and Izzy sings:

I won't run off with your sister
Because, hey, you're my mister

And then I sing:

With you I'll be ever so gentle
And any day you want, we can watch Yentl

We come back together laughing and dancing and we both sing:

Meet cute
Turns out we already met cute
Ten whole years ago
Let's be ridiculous together, in all kinds of weather
When we're old and grey, in your arms I'll stay
Because...
Meet cute
Turns out we already met cute
Ten whole years ago

And then we're kissing again and all there is in the world for me is Izzy. It's very early on Christmas Eve and we spend every moment together until it's Christmas morning.

Izzy has been with my family and me for Christmas many times, but this time it's different. We're a couple now, and in the morning I'm actually happy to see my ex-fiancé now sister-in-law. My parents are beyond thrilled and the only thing anyone seems to have to say is, "What took you two so long?"

Life is not a musical, but sometimes I wish it were. There's a clarity of emotion that songs bring that words alone just can't touch.

Whatever happened to Izzy and me for those few crazy days hasn't happened again. We've asked around, as subtly as you can ask about such things, and no one else experienced it. It was just for the two of us. Perhaps a shared hallucination brought on by our love of musicals and our long friendship blossoming into something more. However you look at it, it was the very best Christmas present either of us could have asked for.

Life is not in technicolor anymore, but it's certainly a lot brighter than it used to be.

While I can't explain how it happened, I do know why. Sometimes love needs a little push, we certainly did.

And even if life isn't a musical, take it from Izzy and me and do your best to find the music in your life. It's there. You just have to listen for it.

BACKSTORY—MEET CUTE: THE MUSICAL

Holiday: Christmas

There's so much I could say about this one, but I don't know where to start.

I guess *Chicago* is a good place—the musical, not the city. The reason being, before *Chicago* I wasn't into musicals. At all, really. People breaking into song at a whim with emotions so powerful that prose can't contain them? No thank you.

But *Chicago* broke through all of that. I think it was because most of the musical numbers had a context that made it palatable and I could finally see the power of the genre.

I still prefer "aware" musicals, ones that give all the singing and dancing a proper context like *Chicago* does, but things changed for me musical-wise after *Chicago*.

Some other interesting things about this story. When writing for the *WMG Holiday Spectacular*, you only have a week to write the story after getting the brief.

One week.

This story has the lyrics to six songs in it and is fairly long to produce that quickly.

But, as often is the way with creative pursuits, the time pressure made this possible. Without it, I think I would have overthought it. I mean, this is a prose musical, what the hell was I thinking?

To be honest, this was an utter blast to write and just thinking about it puts a smile on my face.

Hopefully it puts a smile on your face too.

I've written a little more about this story in the Afterword.

PART 4

DEALING SECONDS

DEALING SECONDS

The lift was smooth and perfect, her hand darting past my snow-flecked overcoat into my suit pocket to snag my wallet right as she bumped into me in the middle of Grand Central Terminal in New York City.

I was turning around, looking up at the high arched ceiling of this place and felt the jolt of her bumping into me, and then my nose was filled with the scent of soap and jasmine tea. In her boots, she was just the right height so that her long chestnut brown hair tickled at my nose.

"I'm so sorry," she said, an appropriately embarrassed smile lighting up her heart-shaped face. "Are you okay?"

It was a two-pronged distraction attack. First the bump while the actual lift occurred, and then the distracting smile to erase any lingering feelings from the lift.

I took her face in and let my shy smile match hers. She had brown eyes the same shade as her hair, thick eyebrows, and a delicate up-turned nose, looking to be about twenty-five years old. She was wearing a long dark coat that hid whatever else she was wearing besides some fashionable knee-high brown boots.

We were in the middle of the cavernous Main Concourse, the air volume too much to warm properly, the echo of steps on the marble tile and voices from our fellow travelers all around us.

It was Black Friday, so the terminal was particularly busy as the consumeristic feeding frenzy got under way. Large elegant wreathes high on the walls marked the season.

"I'm..." I said, stammering a little. "Why... yes, I think I'm fine." I began patting at my overcoat absently, letting my hands wander near where my wallet had been. No reason not to enjoy this.

She was good. She reached out and touched my hand in a friendly but not overly intimate way. "Really. So sorry. I'm just... Well, I'm late, as usual, and if I don't get to work soon, I won't have a job."

Her hand was cool but soft and quite distracting even though I knew exactly what she was doing. I wouldn't have noticed the lift if I hadn't been expecting it.

"Oh yes," I said. "I'm fine. Just fine. I'm not from here. Where are the trains? Mine is on track thirty."

She smiled and it was a dazzling sight to behold. Her teeth weren't perfectly straight or perfectly white, which I liked, and that smile pushed up her cheeks, narrowed her bright eyes, and made me feel warm despite the cold room.

I had been playing the role of confused tourist and had been gawking when she ran into me. I was the third lift she had managed crossing the station, a routine she went through a couple of times a week. She was quite the talent.

"It's right over there," she said, pointing to the tunnel down to the trains. She glanced at her watch. "Best hurry."

She bustled off and I took a last breath in of her soap and jasmine scent, foolishly wishing that my part in this wasn't over.

IF WE REWIND THE SCENE A BIT, WHEN THE YOUNG LADY bumped into me, when her hand darted in and grabbed my wallet, my hand briefly dipped into the pocket of her long, dark coat.

My gawking confusion as I spun around looking at the arched ceiling of the Main Concourse of Grand Central Terminal was an act. Well, partially. The huge room is worth gawking at with its elegant marble, information booth in the center with that four-sided brass clock, and high arched ceiling depicting the 12 zodiac constellations. It's a cavern of a room with a constant swirl of people and noise.

My clothing was upscale, I was alone, and I looked confused enough so that I was just the kind of mark I knew that she was looking for.

She left with my wallet, which she knew about, and a miniature tracker and bug in her pocket, which she did not know about.

The name I had been given for her was Alice Smith, but I was quite sure that wasn't her actual name. I had been watching her for a week, studying her technique, planning this moment.

It was just a job. Five thousand dollars cash plus expenses which wasn't much for me at this point, but just the kind of job I took these days to keep my hand in the biz. The job came from an anonymous employer that filtered to me through one of my contacts.

I am a thief, just like Alice Smith. The acquisition of art and antiquities was my area of expertise but my skills ran the gamut. I had retired from big scores a few years ago after shaking a long-term FBI operation to catch me led by an agent named Molly Evers. I didn't need the money anymore and did this kind of thing just to keep things interesting.

But I'm not the most docile of tools and was often a bit too curious for my own good. I had scanned the plant, found its frequency, and could listen in myself and follow her if I wanted to. And after meeting her, I wanted to.

I know. I know. I was just asking for trouble.

We all have our weaknesses, and boredom is mine.

***

My wallet was also part of the game for me. The license looked real and identified me as one Carl Timmons from Chagrin Falls, Ohio. Seriously, there is a real town named Chargin in Ohio. There were a couple of credit cards, a picture of some kids that weren't mine, $143 in cash, and a slip of paper with a phone number that ended in 143.

My unknown employer paid for the fake ID and credit cards but the rest had been all me. I was curious if she would notice, if she would call, or if she would just take the cash and throw the rest away.

But that little bit of playfulness dropped away when I saw who was following her. Three tall, rather broad-shouldered men dressed in long black coats that carried themselves in that certain way that screamed ex-military, armed and dangerous, even when not armed.

Well, shit.

Despite myself, I followed, and I was reasonably well prepared because I believe in having plans, backup plans, and plans for when things go totally FUBAR. Funny how the later variety always seems to be needed. I think we are overoptimistic as a species, sometimes pathologically so. And despite my knowledge of this, I had been overly optimistic about this simple little job.

I TOSSED MY FEDORA TO A KID THAT WAS STARING AT ME, took off the fake glasses I had been wearing, peeled off the salt-and-pepper mustache, and waggled my eyebrows at the kid as his eyes got wide. I pulled out a black beanie and used it to cover my curly black hair. I took my coat off and reversed it, changing it from black to a dark brown. I put some sunglasses on, put an earbud in, slouched down from my six-foot-four height, and followed the men following the young lady.

You might be wondering if this was some kind of misguided sense of chivalry. If that smile and that soapy, jasmine smell had addled my brain. If boredom and loneliness had informed my decision. That if my mark today had been a balding middle-aged man, I might have made a different choice.

And, to be honest, I don't know. These were the circumstances I encountered, and this was the decision that I made. But it was one of those decisions that just clicked. There was no internal debate. There was no "thinking" about it. It was a gut thing and I just acted.

In retrospect, I will admit that the odds of me doing this for an intriguing woman were somewhat higher than for a middle-aged man. That said, I was really quite bored so it's anyone's guess.

After confirming that the tracker was registering on my phone, I gave them some space and followed those following Alice and we exited on to Lexington right where 43rd street runs into Lexington across from the Chrysler Building. From here you couldn't see its iconic Art Deco spire, but the hood ornament-type flourishes were visible high up where the spire formed.

When I got outside, I was greeted by a swirl of snow and a blast of cold air that carried the sounds of the ever-present honking cars and distant sirens, car tires hissing on the wet street since the snow wasn't accumulating yet.

I took a deep breath of the cold air, taking in the scent of the city which was a potent combination of car fumes, rotting garbage, and the clean smell of the snow. Distantly I could hear the sound of Salvation Army bells ringing as they started soliciting donations.

It was the day after Thanksgiving, now known as Black Friday and I tend to agree, it's a dark day when our overly consumeristic nature is beat into a frenzy and everyone is out for a deal. That made it a good day for Alice to lift a few wallets, but it made it a bad day to be in the city this close to Grand Central.

The group headed down the crowded sidewalk on Lexington and then took a right on 42nd, which was a bit odd considering the weather and that there was an entrance to Grand Central on 42nd.

I jumped to the obvious conclusion that Alice knew she was being followed. And then I jumped to the slightly less obvious conclusion that the dangerous-types following her wanted her to know she was being followed.

The first I got, but the second?

Was this some kind of snatch and grab and my part had been to get a tracker on her for insurance, or were the boys following her a complete coincidence?

I turned up the volume on the bug but it was no good. It was just echoing the sounds of the city with a lot of white noise from the swishing of her coat.

I didn't know what was going on, but I didn't like it at all. Now that there were pedestrians everywhere, I closed the distance a bit, but in the swirling snow and the crowd I couldn't spot Alice.

She was shorter than much of the crowd and I'm guessing she put a hat on against the weather because I couldn't see chestnut hair where my phone told me she was.

I followed along as we all headed down 42nd, checking on

my phone occasionally, but still not spotting Alice, but the three military dudes were easy to spot.

After crossing Fifth, the three mercenaries headed across 42nd while the tracker turned and headed up Fifth. Which was odd, unless...

I heard a louder voice in my earbud and cranked the volume. "...and she just gave it to me. I mean, glad to upgrade, but it's kinda cold."

I sighed and through the snow I spotted a jacketless woman with long chestnut brown hair heading up the steps to the New York Public Library. Those military-types, I think I'll start calling them the three stooges, were terrible at tailing someone and she must have figured out that I bugged her.

For those of you unfamiliar with New York City and more versed in pulp culture, when we're talking the main NYC library, the Schwarzman Building, think *Ghostbusters*. There are a series of steps, the first set flanked by statues of lions in repose, three arched entryways at the top of those steps with columns flanking, all of it done in exquisite marble.

It's a hell of a structure, not the type of thing anyone builds anymore and it deserves a pause to appreciate, and I needed a moment so I stopped right past one of those lions, the one named Fortitude, I believe.

Alice knew she was bugged. Alice was not stupid. Alice probably knew that I bugged her, putting me squarely in the "against her" camp.

Was I bored enough to get deeper? Intrigued enough? Daring enough?

The problem with me is I don't take well to that last question, the "daring" part. Doesn't matter that it was me asking, I reacted the same. I went in.

Just inside the library is Astor Hall, an ode to elegant marble with high, arched ceilings, grand stairways on either end, columns at the corners, candelabras perched on marble stands, and engraving in the marble wall recording whose huge piles of money created this place.

Any direction you look is worthy of a gawk. This library built as a monument to knowledge always took my breath away.

All that marble and those high ceilings made the space echoey and cool. Straight ahead were the exhibition halls and galleries, but I saw the last of the three stooges heading up the stairs to my left so I followed.

I took off the beanie and pulled out a green New York Jets baseball cap and settled it on my head. It wasn't much of a change, but anything at this point could be helpful.

This being Black Friday, the library wasn't that crowded and I was able to hang back and just keep the three stooges in sight. We ended up making the climb to the third floor and ended up in the magnificent reading room.

There was also a scene here in *Ghostbusters*, but let me attempt to describe it. The walls are marble, the floors brown tile with white marble accents. The room is lined with bookshelves about eight feet tall. Above that is a narrow walkway and more shelves of books. There are high, arched windows, the ceiling is done in carved wood with several large paintings of blue sky and clouds like the ceiling is open to the air. Cutting the long room in half is an ornate wooden enclosure with arched windows that the librarians hold court from.

In the room itself, there are two rows of long wooden tables on either side with lamps. People were sitting here hunched over tapping on computers, reading books, quite a few with headphones on. It's a large space so it's still a bit cool and the acrostics are a little softer than the entry hall but still pretty echoey.

Despite the consumeristic feed frenzy going on outside,

there were plenty of people in here but it didn't take long to spot Alice and the three stooges. They were back in a corner. Alice had her back to a bookshelf and the three of them had her penned in.

I settled the Jets hat on my head, pulled a fake police badge from an inner pocket (a real FUBAR pocket, if you will), and headed towards them.

I adjusted my walk, pulling my shoulders back and moving my hips like I was used to having a heavy belt hanging there.

The four of them were whispering, mostly the stooges, and I caught a few words from the guy in the middle, who had a deep voice that carried. I heard him say, "promise," "late," "won't be pleased." And as I drew close, I heard, "...will be consequences if the package is not delivered by Christmas."

As I got close, I spoke into my phone, my voice pitched to just reach them and my speech pattern sliding towards a Brooklyn accent. "Operator, yeah. This is NYPD Officer Murphy." I mumble a badge number. "Got a possible 10-34 in the main readin' room in the library on Lexington and 42nd. Send backup."

I pocketed the phone and the whispered conversation stopped.

"You boys havin' trouble findin' a book or somethin'?" I asked.

The middle one turned and I finally got a good look at his face. It was blocky and went well with his barely there neck and wide shoulders. He was almost as tall as me but probably outweighed me by a good fifty pounds.

"This is none of your—" he began, but I cut him off when I flashed my badge.

Alice was hard to see past all the wide shoulders and black coats. "Ma'am," I said. "You all right back there? Can you breathe with all that testosterone in the air?"

The blocky guy narrowed his eyes, his right hand reaching over to his left side where I'm sure he had a gun ready in a shoulder holster.

"Surely you ain't that dumb," I said. "You gonna shoot a cop on his day off with a room full of witness and plenty of cameras recordin' ya?"

His nostrils flared and I could see him weighing his options, his eyes darting around. He grunted, mumbled to the other two stooges, and they swept past me. Mr. Blockhead came last, his shoulder plowing into me painfully as he passed.

"You all right, ma'am?" I asked after they left.

Her eyes were wide and her chin was quivering. She was dressed in an oversized red sweater and a long black skirt. "I... I..." she mumbled, gave me a half nod, and pulled a phone out of the fancy black purse slung over her shoulder.

She poked at her phone and the phone in my hand rang, "Unknown Caller" popping up on the screen. Her chin stopped quivering and those brown eyes sharpened. "Why?" she asked, her voice quivering but with rage not fear.

My mouth opened but I had no words. She had figured me out awfully quickly and somehow had looked through the wallet, counted the money, seen the phone number, and figured out my little game all on the way over here while being pursued.

She was good.

She pulled my wallet out of her purse and walked up to me, her weight on the balls of her feet so she could bolt if she needed. She reached slowly past my overcoat into my suit jacket and slipped the wallet back into place all the while her eyes were locked with mine and her soapy, flowery scent filled my nose.

I didn't move, I didn't speak, although I was sure she must have heard my heart beating.

Her technique was all the more flawless in slow motion, her hand disturbing the fabric of my clothing as little as possible, her two fingers letting go of the wallet as soon as it was safe in my pocket.

Seeing some fine crow's feet around those expressive eyes, I upgraded my assessment of her age to early thirties, which made me feel much better about how my body was reacting to her presence, since it meant I was only about ten years older than her.

"There!" she said, her full lips forming a brief sneer before she stalked off, her boots hammering into the tile and echoing throughout the room.

I STOOD THERE STILL FEELING THE WARMTH OF HER closeness, still smelling her scent, my heart still hammering in my ears.

There was something here. Something I wasn't seeing. Something my hormones and boredom and loneliness were making it hard to see.

She wanted me to go after her. I knew that. Or at least part of me was screaming that at me. But this all was too pat, too easy, too well choreographed.

I needed to think. I sank down into the nearest empty chair, pulled out a deck of cards from yet another pocket, and started practicing false deals, both second dealing and bottom dealing where you pull the second card in the deck or the bottom card, respectively, and make it look like a normal deal.

In my mind, magicians are thieves and thieves are magicians. Both use skill and manipulate circumstances to do what doesn't seem possible. I had spent much of my life studying magic. Besides, it relaxed me and allowed me to play it all back in my mind a few times as the cards flew through my hands faster and faster, the quiet snick-snick of cards moving against each other calming.

I had followed Alice, studied Alice, learned enough about her to know what kind of target she liked and to be that target in the right place at the right time.

It wasn't a guaranteed thing, of course, but it was certainly in the realm of possibility. But, if we apply Occam's razor and go with the simpler explanation, then it becomes clear that she knew exactly what she was doing when she lifted my wallet.

Once the deck was dealt and I turned over the last card, the top card I had never moved, an ace of spades, I said, "Ah. That's it."

She gave me back my wallet and there was a reason for that. I pulled it out and found there was $122 in there and a different scrap of paper that had a phone number on it that ended in 122.

I smiled. Here I had thought I was toying with her but it turns out she was toying with me. This job had been a setup, but I had been the one that was set up, not her.

I smiled wider and dialed the number.

"Took you long enough," Alice said, amusement coloring her voice.

"What do you want?" I asked, my voice gruff.

"I want your help with something," she said, and I could hear the smile in her voice.

I should have hung up. I should have run away. But, seemingly without me thinking it, I said, "I'm listening."

***

HERE'S THE THING ABOUT A MAGIC TRICK, ONE THAT requires real skill—it doesn't matter if you know how it works, it's still impressive. Alice Smith had done a magic trick on me while she made me think I was doing a magic trick on her, and that's not easy.

"It's a simple job," she said as we strolled down a slushy sidewalk in Central Park, pacing ourselves so no one was close. "In and out."

The sun had come out, making the coating of fresh snow lying over the park bright and beautiful.

"Why me?" I asked. It seemed a much more important question than what the job was.

She shrugged. She had what appeared to be the same coat back on, her brown hair glistening in the sunlight. "My former partner and I have parted ways and this isn't a one-woman job."

She still smelled like soap and jasmine tea, and that combined with the fresh smell of the snow in the park was distracting me. I had been in love before, many years ago, but the secrets I had to keep was like a rot in our relationship.

"Why me?" I asked again.

She snorted and said, "You're Carlos Muller. Everyone in the business knows you are the best."

I stopped, my hands shoved into the pockets of my coat. I was still wearing the Jets baseball cap and sunglasses. "I work alone."

She stopped and turned and moved towards me, her motions slow and sensuous, accenting the clear athleticism of her body. I knew she was manipulating me but it was something like knowing how the trick worked, it didn't change the experience of it that much. She put her hand on my chest and said, "But do you really want to be alone?"

It wasn't much, but if felt intimate and it felt like a promise even though it probably wasn't one.

"From what I hear," she said, her voice low and husky, "you've got all the money you need and are in it for the fun. We could have a lot of fun together."

I smiled. I couldn't help it. "What's the job?" I asked.

We had wound around the park and she nodded towards some apartments rising above the trees along Central Park West. "There's a painting in that penthouse, and if I don't get it by Christmas, I'm a dead woman."

Besides studying magic, I've also studied acting. It's an important skill for someone in my line of work. If I hadn't, I would have gasped. She was nodding towards the building where one of my personas lived, in the penthouse, no less.

Some surprise showed, so I used it. "Wait," I said. "Those guys in the library weren't yours?"

She looked me up and down, one eyebrow raised. "Don't flatter yourself. I contracted you to plant the bug on me so we could meet, so I could be sure it was you. Those men were delivering a real message."

She sighed and her shoulders fell, her eyes wandering back to the building. "The painting is from the 1500s. 'The Adoration of the Shepherds' by Giorgione. It depicts shepherds recognizing the divinity of the baby Jesus. A classic of the Renaissance. My employer is serious about having this in his possession before Christmas. He's... well, he has some rather odd ideas about the piece. In any case, while the building is an unusually secure one, it should be straightforward enough, but I can't do it alone." She looked at me, those brown eyes no longer defiant. "Will you help me?"

I knew the painting well since I had stolen it years ago. Could this get any stranger?

"Why me?" I asked for a third time. "Sounds like an easy enough job. You don't need me."

She sighed, bit her lip, and nodded. "I... look, can I just be honest?"

I nodded but didn't say anything, keeping my face as neutral as possible. You have to be careful when a thief asks you if they can just be honest.

"I've been trying to track you down for years," she said, her eyes darting shyly away. "Call it professional curiosity. It's just luck that I found a way to catch your attention and I have this problem. These guys are serious—can you blame a girl for wanting the best?"

Her eyes met mine and I saw real fear there. But that didn't mean it was the fear I thought it was.

"No guarantees," I said. "But let's talk it through."

The smile that lit up her face made me feel like a young man again and a smile broke through my façade. And then she was hugging me and I was hugging her back and I knew I was in so much trouble but I just didn't care.

ALICE RENTED US A SUITE AT THE MANDARIN ORIENTAL Hotel not far from my penthouse. The living area had stunning views of Central Park and New York City, a view no less stunning because of my familiarity with it.

The sun was low and it had stayed cold enough that the trees in Central Park were flocked with delicate white. Lights were coming on and the distant honking of cars was mostly drowned out by jazz playing on the TV.

The room was all wood, with dark wood paneling and wooden floors. The glass dining room table was covered with schematics of my building. A laptop had search results on security systems. A gleaming room service cart was nearby piled with dirty dishes and there was a mostly empty bottle of wine on the table with splashes of red in the two wine glasses along with a steaming cup of jasmine tea near Alice.

She was still in that oversized red sweater and was slowly

working with a deck of cards, a long strand of Chestnut hair escaping her hasty ponytail, the glasses on her face making her look older in a way that fascinated me.

We needed a break and I was teaching her to deal the second card from the deck.

"It's called 'dealing seconds,'" I said. I had a deck too. I showed her the top card, which was a queen of diamonds, dealt the second card three times at a normal pace, and showed her the queen was still there.

I then slowed it way down and showed her that I was sliding off the top two cards just a bit, then sliding the bottom one out and the top one back. She fumbled with the cards and tried to copy me.

"It takes hundreds of hours to get good at it," I said by way of encouragement. Judging from the lift she executed earlier, she knew this kind of discipline well.

This was an awkward situation for me. I could just go get the damn painting and give it to her, but that would give away too much and I had a lot to lose. It was also clear that "taking care of her" like that would spoil any chance at something interesting.

But it wasn't just that. I was attached to the piece. My former mentor, a master thief named Alan Frank, had been obsessed with it and spent years planning to steal it from a museum. When another job we were doing went south and he left me for the cops, I got out on bail and stole it before he could and stashed it until I got out of jail.

Alan Frank was why I worked alone.

But breaking into my own building and stealing from myself? Could I actually do that? Was it worth my time?

Alice tried again, dealing out the top two cards and laughing nervously. "Do you think we can do it?" she asked.

I shrugged. "Plan everything," I said, turning my top card over and dealing seconds a few times slowly so she could see what I was doing. "Practice it." I then turned the top card back over and did it at a slow but reasonable pace and it was still hard to see. The human eye just wasn't built to catch it. "Plan for things to go wrong." I sped it back up. "Plan for things to go FUBAR." I turned the top card over and showed it was still the same. "And, yeah, we can do it."

She smiled, got up, yawned, and stretched in a way that was more than a little distracting. She padded over on bare feet, kissed me on the check, and said, "I'm really grateful for this," before walking into the bedroom and closing the door.

It seemed I was committed to stealing from myself.

***

THERE ARE A LOT OF OTHER TRICKS IN THE CARD mechanic's toolbox. You can do a false shuffle. A false cut. Deal from the middle. Palm cards.

It is a small area of magic and the only one I had really practiced. Because it takes time. It takes patience. It takes practice. And it's all real. There's no camera tricks. No stooges. Just physics and understanding how humans perceive things.

Same with acting. You have to practice, you have to understand human psychology, and it doesn't come easy.

But with both, belief comes into it. Part of you has to believe the act or the show won't be any good.

It was Christmas Eve and time was running out, and the first part of the job was mine. The lobby of my building was marble and elegant with a row of mailboxes and gleaming silver elevator doors. There was a festive Christmas tree setup in one corner and Frank Sinatra was crooning a scratchy Merry Christmas over the PA.

I came rushing in with an "In Time" delivery hat on, a red shirt, and a black jacket with the red logo on it.

Doing something like this and UPS or FedEx doesn't make sense. They know the delivery people. You need a lesser known service.

Danny Diaz stood behind the marble-topped counter in front of the door to the small security office dressed in a blue security guard's uniform. He was cursing at some scotch tape, several pieces stuck on his fingers, and a roll of red and green wrapping paper sat on the counter. Apparently he was one of those last minute shoppers.

Besides the "In Time" getup, I had some simple prosthetics that changed the shape of my face a bit.

Danny had a round friendly face and short salt-and pepper grey hair. He nodded a smile at me without really looking at me, ripped the tape off with his fingers with his teeth, and signed my handheld scanner.

"That time of year," I said, my voice lower than usual.

"I'll say," he said with a sigh. "Mr. Tenison is out for the holidays. I'll keep it here for him." He stashed it under the counter near the security gear and got back to wrapping.

<hr>

ALICE HAD SPENT SOME MONEY ON WHAT WAS IN THAT package. A lot of money. When I met her around the back of the building having changed coats, glasses, and hat, she was looking at her phone and said, "All good. The security system has been overridden."

She was dressed in jeans and a black turtleneck with a black overcoat. Her hair was pulled back and she had a few prosthetics that I had applied that made her face rounder and not so heart shaped. This was to fool facial recognition if the fancy device failed and video of us survived.

She tossed me the long plastic tube that was to contain the

canvas if we succeeded and I slung it across my back but then her face fell.

"What?" I asked.

"This could still go wrong," she said.

"We've spent weeks planning," I said and couldn't help but smile. I didn't know a lot about her, but I knew her, if you know what I mean. I knew her rhythms and what kind of jokes made her laugh. I knew the kinds of things that would make her pensive. I knew her nonverbal cues and what kinds of movies she liked. She felt like a friend, an actual friend, and while that's all it was, it was much more than I had had in a while. "Besides," I added, using the grin that almost always made her smile. "Would it any be fun if it couldn't?"

She smiled back and stepped up to me, rose onto her tiptoes, put her cool hand to the back of my neck, and pulled me down and kissed me. Hard.

Her lips were soft and cool. My heart sped up and my body responded eagerly and I kissed her back. It didn't last long, well... not long enough, anyway.

"What was that for?" I asked, shoving down thoughts of things beyond friendship with her.

"Just wanted to," she said with a smile. "Besides, it's almost Christmas and I knew that's what you wanted to ask Santa for." She poked at her phone, the lock on the service door clicked, and we were in.

THE BUILDING'S SECURITY SYSTEM HAD KNOWN FLAWS. AT least on the dark web the flaws were known. A couple of white hats had tried to point it out, but the big-time security company had laughed it off. It's why we could purchase gear for it. But the security to the penthouse, which I had overseen, had no such public knowledge of it.

Once inside, we took the stairs and climbed the twenty floors to the penthouse and I picked the lock to the emergency exit door while Alice kept watch.

Up here there was more marble, one elevator, and the two doors to the penthouse apartments. Apartment A, my place, had a keypad and this was my piece of the job. I had led Alice through some dark sections of town with some theater performed by some compatriots of mine so we could get information on the system.

No biometrics, just a touch-screen keypad with the actual electronics that controlled it ten feet away so there was no "hot wiring" opportunity. I, of course, knew the code, which changed algorithmically based on the day, but Alice didn't know that.

I blew some baby powder on the screen to reveal fingerprints. And yes, I have my own security people that wipe it down regularly, but I had been up here recently leaving some fingerprints to be found.

I took a picture of it and an app on my phone analyzed it, finding out where the most fingerprints were, indicating the digits used the most, analyzing the patterns trying to take an educated guess as the order they were used, and spitting out the most likely six-digit combinations.

Well, it looked like it did that, but it was just more theater. One of them, of course, was the correct one.

I handed Alice the phone while she read off the top picks and I punched them in.

The screen beeped after the first one.

"How many tries do we get?" she asked.

I shrugged. "Three, maybe four."

The second one failed.

The third one failed.

"You know this isn't very scientific," she said. "Six digits is a lot of permutations."

I grinned at her. "I've used software like this before. High-end AI. Besides, what's the worst that can happen?"

"The alarm goes off and we go to jail," she said.

"We planned for this," I said.

She nodded, read the next set of digits as I tapped them in, and the door clicked open.

THE PENTHOUSE WAS AIRY AND MODERN WITH OFF-WHITE walls, wooden floors, stainless-steel accents, and a lot of art hanging. It had a view similar to the Mandarin of Central Park and the city, just not quite as high.

"It's not here," Alice said after exploring the two bedrooms and ending up with me back in the living room.

I was staring at the full-sized reproduction of Renoir's "Luncheon of the Boating Party" that hung opposite the windows that overlooked Central Park. The canvas was large, over four feet tall and five and a half feet wide, larger than the painting we were after.

The reproduction lacked the texture and luster of the original, but it was still lovely. It depicted the casual gathering of friends under an awning, dishes scattered, a woman holding a small dog, the river in the distance. It embodied an atmosphere of leisure that I think we've mostly forgotten about.

"Fake," Alice said with some distain.

"Why were you so sure it was here?" I asked.

"Years," she said as she paced the living room, past the linen couch, the recliner, and the glass and stainless-steel dining room table. "Years of research."

She was taking this personally. If her life was on the line, that would explain it, but there was something different in her tone, in how she held herself. She was angry, not afraid.

"We took our shot," I said with a wry smile.

She stopped her pacing, her brown eyes sharp. "Not good enough."

I, of course, knew where the painting was and I had planned to "find" it once we got up here, but her change in tone stopped me.

"It has to be here," she said. She stopped next to me and stared at the Renoir reproduction. "This is the only wall big enough," she added, her voice low as if she was talking to herself.

She went to the wall and pulled on the reproduction but it was securely attached. She felt along the edge of it and an "ah-ha" escaped her.

She grabbed the edge of the painting, yanked it up about an inch, and there was a metallic click.

Something was wrong here and I knew it. I should have run but I was busy winding it all back in my mind. The odd job coming to me when I was bored enough to take it. Watching Alice who was clearly an accomplished pickpocket. The lift and bug plant at Grand Central. The three stooges following and threatening her. The bizarre coincidence that the painting she was after was in my possession. The flirting and the kiss before we came in here that put me off balance.

She went to the other end of the painting and yanked it up and there was another click. "Here it is," Alice whispered, mostly to herself. She pulled the reproduction down revealing an indent behind it that contained the Giorgione.

The painting depicted Joseph and Mary, their hands clasped in prayer, in front of a dark cave with the baby Jesus swaddled on the ground in front of them. Two shepherds were kneeling in front of them with a Venetian landscape off to the left.

The colors were shimmering and beautiful, the subtle undulations of the oil paints making it almost a living thing that changed as you moved, the entire effect stunning.

I took it in while this whole thing with Alice clicked together in my mind and knew that she had been second-dealing me the whole time, not a thing she had done had been what it seemed. She was a thief, that much was clear, but I no longer thought she was just a thief.

I wasn't surprised when she pulled a gun, pointed it at me, and said, "Carlos Muller, you are under arrest."

The door to the penthouse opened and three men in FBI jackets walked in, the three I have been referring to as the three stooges.

For once I didn't have any FUBAR contingencies prepared so I fell back on acting and put a smile on my face, and nodded. "Well, I guess I am. But we had fun didn't we, Alice?"

Her mouth pursed into a thin line. "It's Angela Waters," she said. "Special Agent Waters to you."

<hr>

AFTER A YEAR OF WEARING IT, I WAS RATHER USED TO THE orange jumpsuit. A stony-faced guard led me from my cell to a small conference room near the warden's office on Christmas Day and left me there alone for an hour.

The room was plain in the extreme with white walls, a round table, a few chairs, a whiteboard, and no windows. Even the small, sad, faux Christmas tree in the corner did nothing to liven it up.

I didn't know what was going on and I didn't bother to ask. I had been sentenced to five years, but I figured if I was a model prisoner I could get out a lot faster.

I took out a deck of cards from my jumpsuit pocket and

started practicing. First one-handed cuts and then a couple of techniques for false cuts.

You'd be amazed how far card tricks can get you in a place like this where boredom runs rampant. Dazzle the tough guys and you'll do okay.

I didn't look up when the door opened but I smelled soap and jasmine tea and I couldn't help but smile.

"Special Agent Angela Waters," I said. "I was wondering how long it would take you to come visit."

When I looked up, I wasn't disappointed. Her chestnut brown hair was pulled back into a ponytail and her brown eyes held the smile that wasn't on her face. She was dressed casually in jeans and blue sweater that hugged her athletic form.

"Why is that?" she asked.

I shrugged as she sat down at the small table across from me. "Those three weeks we planned, we were becoming friends, and maybe even..."

One of her thick eyebrows raised. "Really?"

"You used to be a thief like me until Agent Evers caught you, recruited you, and trained you," I said. "Evers had a bright career until she came after me, but I was always one step ahead and she overdid it and ended being forced out of the agency."

I paused, studying her lovely heart-shaped face. "I think you took that personally, but you, unlike her, did it right. You studied and studied before you made your play. You knew I was bored and retirement wasn't sitting well with me. You honed your pick-pocketing skills so it would be clear you were a thief. I bet you did most of it on your own time and even used your own funds so you could keep closing other cases."

She cocked her head to one side and studied me. "You've been doing some research."

I smiled. "I've got plenty of time."

She took the deck from in front of me, showed me the top

card, put it back, and dealt out about ten cards with graceful ease and then showed me the top card was still there.

I smiled—her technique was flawless. "Very good. Want to learn something else?"

She nodded and I showed her how to bottom deal. "It's a little trickier," I said. "If you don't create a little space between the bottom card and the card above it the deck will look weird and it will be obvious what you are doing."

We went a few rounds until she had the basics but still couldn't do it smoothly.

"I am curious about one thing," I said.

"What?" she asked.

"That kiss before we went into the building. You didn't need to do that. I was already hooked."

"Is there a question there?" she asked, a playful smile on her lips.

"Why?" I asked.

"I just wanted to," she said, echoing what she told me then. "And I figured it was my last chance."

I nodded and held her eyes. There was something else here, some reason she had come, but I had time and this was a lot more fun than I had had in a while.

"But, I was wrong," she finally said.

"About what?" I asked.

"About it being my last chance," she said, her voice low.

I blinked and I ran the possibilities through my mind. Was she still dealing me seconds, or had there been a genuine connection?

She reached into her briefcase and pulled out a glossy eight-by-ten of Van Gogh's "Irises."

"It's been stolen," she said.

"By whom?" I asked.

"We believe it was your mentor, Allan Frank," she said

It all clicked into place. "You need help catching him," I said.

Angela smiled and nodded.

"What's the deal?" I asked.

She pulled out a folder with a bunch of legal documents. "Cooperation on this matter. An ankle monitor. Restitution for your previous crimes. You know, the usual. After we get the Van Gogh back, you're a free man. Merry Christmas!"

I leaned forward and said, "But that could take years."

She nodded, leaning towards me. "And we'd have to work together. Closely."

"How do I know you are not still dealing seconds?" I asked.

She leaned back, took the deck of cards in her hand, flipped up the first one, which was the queen of hearts, and dealt it across the table deftly. It slid to a stop right in front of me.

I slowly flipped it over and it was the queen of hearts.

"You have my word," she said.

I just stared at her, keeping my face blank.

"Come on, Carlos," she said, her voice taunting. "You hated retirement anyway. Here's a way to get back in the game that doesn't end up with you behind bars. Your former mentor is not a good guy, he tends to leave bodies in his wake. You know it'll feel good to see him caught."

I still started.

She sighed. "Please," she said, leaning forward. "I'm out on a limb on this one and I really need you."

Angela knew me. She was working me. I didn't care. Any day on the outside working with her was better than the best day in here.

"Let's do it," I said.

BACKSTORY—DEALING SECONDS

Holidays: Black Friday to Christmas

This story combines several things very close to my heart: thieves with a moral compass (albeit skewed from the norm), magic, acting, and romance.

There's something about both thieves (the ones that use their smarts) and magicians as the protagonist opines about. They understand human nature in ways most of us don't and I find that fascinating.

One of the joys of a story like this is the research. Researching card tricks, New York City and its iconic locations, and artwork. All things that are lovely to learn about, but I just wouldn't go there without the needs of a story driving me.

I think it'd be fun to go really deep into some of these topics, like pickpocketing, the limits of human perception, card mechanics, and social engineering, and write a much longer story with a smart thief/magician where all the tricks are real.

I don't have the time right now, but maybe one of these days. If the idea appeals to you as a reader, let me know over at *Robert-JMcCarter.com/contact.*

PART 5

THE TINKERER'S LAST GIFT

THE TINKERER'S LAST GIFT

My father was a tinkerer.

Now that's a simple sentence full of weight, the "was" being, perhaps, the most important part of it. Most any sentence involving my father has a "was" in it. There are a few exceptions, like: My father's ashes *are* in my living room.

The same will happen for all of us, simple sentences stated about us will be dominated by "was" and not "is" or "are." In fact, given what brief sparks our lives are, the "is" and "are" are rare. This is reality, and it may be simple but it sure as hell isn't easy.

So, my father was a tinkerer. Let me give you an example. He spent a summer of weekends taking an Arduino microcontroller, a couple of cheap sensors, and some little solar panels and rigging our mailbox so it would blink with a red light when there was mail in it.

It was an admirable feat, the learning curve steep, and as a five-year-old following him around when he did it, I found it, and him, so fascinating.

There was a practical purpose there, you didn't have to

wonder if anything was in the mailbox, but it wasn't the kind of thing that seemed like it deserved that much attention.

And, really, it didn't. The tinkering was the whole point of it all.

I tell you all this so you will understand the strange feeling I had that cold winter morning when the package arrived. From him. My dead father. In that very same mailbox, the blinking red light beckoning me to trudge through the early morning snow and obey that beckoning light.

The package was a cube, about five inches on a side, wrapped neatly in brown butcher paper, and addressed by hand with a Sharpie, the blocky letters clearly made by my father's hand. The lines the Sharpie had made were faded, the paper had some water stains, and it looked old.

The return address read simply, "The Great Gig in the Sky." My father loved Pink Floyd and that song about death.

I could hear my heart beating in my head and sweat prickled the back of my neck, my breath sharp and shallow. I hardly knew where I was and had stumbled back into my house staring at the package with no memory of making the journey from the mailbox through the snow.

The box had weight to it, a heft that went beyond mere ounces. It felt weighty, important.

"Grant," my wife Mary called, breaking the spell. "What was in the mailbox?"

I was standing just inside our house, snow slowly melting off my boots and slushing on to the tiled entryway as I blinked dumbly trying to understand what was happening. I was so numb with shock that I had forgotten to stamp the snow off before coming in and hadn't closed the door.

The smell of baking cookies filled the air and the Christmas tree in the living room was fully decorated with a few presents under its cheerfully green boughs.

"Just junk mail," I called back, without even thinking about it as I closed the door.

Why had I said that? I had no idea right then, but have since figured it out. The package was from my father, my long-dead father, and I wanted it all to myself, at least for a little bit.

My father's old workshop—and now mine—was hidden behind a bookcase. Totally classic and he had done it himself. You had to pull on a leather-bound copy of *Journey to the Center of the Earth* to open in. He loved Verne.

I was back there with the package he sent from beyond the grave surrounded by his tinkerer's tools. Two oscilloscopes, soldering irons, a workbench with several vices, big and small, a big lighted magnifying glass, and shelves upon shelves of neatly categorized bins full of parts—a tinkerer needs a lot of parts.

The small room had no windows giving it this cave-like feeling and it smelled of 3-in-1 oil. It occupied the back part of the former garage which had been turned into an extra room about fifty years ago.

I sat on a stool in front of the scarred workbench, flicked on the magnifying glass, and put the package underneath it. I took my time, moving slowly, carefully. Not that I was afraid I would break something, but because this felt sacred somehow. I knew what was inside was important. It had to be, why else would he go through so much effort to deliver something to me years after his death?

I sat back and thought about it. Had it really been important that *this* package come to me after his death, or had it been just an expression of my father's restless energy, his need to create, to surprise? I think instead of becoming a high school science teacher, he would have preferred to be an archeologist. He adored the Indian Jones moves and *National Treasure*. I often thought that he wanted to be out there having daring adventures, not being the steady anchor his family needed.

I often felt the same about myself. Our daughter was married with her own daughter now, the house was paid off, and still I kept at the job that I felt so conflicted about. It was a good job. I was an electrical engineer—is it any wonder being raised by a tinkerer—but I was getting tired of the human parts of the job. I had no issues doing the engineering work, loved it, actually, but the endless meetings and office politics drained me more and more.

I looked at the package again and shook my head. "No," I said. This had to be important. This had to be something, not just tinkering for tinkering's sake.

I grabbed some tweezers and a thin metal ruler, put the package under the big magnifying glass, and started examining the ancient wrapping paper.

My father didn't call himself a "tinkerer." I think he and those like him at the turn of the century would have found the term rather anachronistic. "Maker" was the term they used, or "hacker," depending, but times have changed and what was old has become new again.

He came of age in the early aughts, and it was a heady time for technology. Smartphones were just around the corner, drones were buzzing in the sky, and building your own computer and overclocking the hell of it was the only way to go.

Climate change was being felt but it wasn't so bad you couldn't deny it, the housing bubble was building, but hadn't burst, the political landscape was changing rapidly, totalitarianism and fascism was starting to wake up but hadn't quite made itself known yet, and global pandemics weren't a regular occurrence.

It was a time when many tinkerers were tinkering and my father loved it.

Back in my workshop, I turned the package over under the magnifying glass. There was no tape, which probably wouldn't have held up over the decades, but I could see signs of glue holding the thick brown paper together.

The wrapping was neat and precise, wrapped like a Christmas present with a triangular fold of paper on each side.

I slipped the thin ruler underneath one side, gently pushing, trying to preserve the paper. This was my father—anything could be important. It was well glued, though, and the glue being much stronger than the paper, I felt panic when I heard the first sound of tearing. I pulled the ruler back and came at it from another angle, slowly working it, finding where the glue was weak, kind of like when I used to brush out my daughter's long hair when she was young. You would brush at the edge, only pulling a few hairs loose from her eternal knots, slowly working through to the harder part.

I switched from the ruler to a knife, an old one that was rather dull but could work its way through. I moved slowly, reverently, even. This was my father, so there had to be purpose behind it. But more than that, this was time travel, pure and simple. My father had created this decades ago and sent it forward in time to meet me here and now.

It wasn't lost on me that I was getting close to the age he was when he died. Was that on purpose? By design? But how could it be? No one knows when they will die.

I worked slowly, bent over the package, looking at it through the magnifying glass, the sound of my heart beating loud in my ears, close enough to the old paper that I caught a slightly musty scent.

I got through one end with minimal tearing and pulled up the flap and saw more paper. It was off-white with speckled bits of color, and I recognized it immediately. It was from my father's rather messy and somewhat short-lived paper-making phase. I delicately touched it. The paper was rough and there was something hard and unyielding underneath it.

I opened the flap all the way, gently shook the package, and the cube slid free of the paper. My father had been so precise in gluing the packaging that it hadn't stuck to the inner paper at all.

What I had before me was the same sized box but with different, handmade paper. I turned it over slowly, my mouth opening as I realized there were no seams, no edges. It was purely my father, and it was perfect.

So I left it sitting there on the workbench. This was not something I was going to rush. Not opening the package. Not the experience of it. And, especially, not all the complex feelings that were bubbling up.

My father's name was Gary. My childhood was pretty good, so he was "Dad" to me. Even after I was an adult, it took a while for him to become human to me. I didn't think of him as "Gary" until his mind started going and I awkwardly became the parent and he awkwardly became the child.

He was kind and rarely got angry, but, then again, he rarely showed emotions beyond his constant wonder with the world and how things worked. He was very childlike in his sense of wonder.

When the dementia hit and he became truly childlike was when he became truly human to me. That dulling of that sharp mind of his showed that he was actually and truly flesh and blood, as flawed as the rest of us.

I still grieve him becoming human in my eyes. There were, certainly, downsides to trying to live up to the incomplete, not-quite-human image of the man that raised me, but seeing his biology start tearing him apart still gives me nightmares.

Death is not easy, but when the mind goes before the body... it's not even in the same solar system as easy. By the time my father's dementia got bad, my mother was already gone. It was cancer that took her out. That meant that I, with the help of my wife, looked out for him, became the parents as he became the child.

Taking over his finances revealed a host of human weakness causing me to wonder how someone so smart in so many ways could be so dumb with money. Spoiler alert: it's because he was human.

Cleaning out his house after we had to move him into a facility, the house Mary and I now live in, revealed all these areas that he had pack-ratted full of unnecessary things. Even his hidden workshop was clogged with junk, even considering the kinds of things a tinkerer needs to keep around.

I blamed the dementia at the time, but in reflecting on the human man my father was, I can see now that this had always been a tendency of his. He accumulated things. Too many things. The waxing of his intellect didn't create that, it just amplified it.

The problem with an ending like my father's, with me being in the role I was in, is that it subsumed most of the good memories. After his death, I was traumatized and exhausted, left with dark memories of the man that had helped bring me into this world and raised me. While he still knew who I was, his wonder at the world was replaced by terror, everything seemed to frighten him, and he could barely put a sentence together. He hadn't just reverted back to being a child, he was a child living in an absolute nightmare.

Looking back, I now understand why I didn't tell my Mary about the package, why I hid away behind the secret bookshelf door activate by pulling on *Journey to the Center of the Earth*. I was desperate to reclaim my father at his best, to not be haunted by who he had been at the end of his life.

Möbius strips. The ouroboros—the symbol of a snake eating its own tail. The infinity symbol.

These are all variants of the same thing and symbols that endlessly fascinated my father, a fascination he passed on to me.

Stamped in black on the package covered in seamless home-made paper which sat on the small workbench in my father's (and now my) hidden workshop was one of those symbols. Actually, all three.

It was the image of a flattened snake that twisted around into an infinity symbol that was also a Möbius strip.

I hadn't noticed it that first night. It was two days later, after midnight, and I had snuck back here after Mary went to sleep. I felt bad about that. I wasn't lying, but I wasn't telling her about this, which was a hell of a thing to just not mention.

I had promised myself I would, multiple times, tried to do it once or twice, but just couldn't manage it.

This was something I wanted to have for myself, a moment alone with my father when he was at his best.

The symbol was stamped on. By a rubber stamp. Yet another tinkering phase my father went through, except I had never seen this stamp and I had the full collection.

I took a picture of it and gave it to google to search for, and while it came up with a lot of similar images, there were no matches.

Quietly, I found the tub with my father's rubber stamp

collection on one of the many shelves, pulled it down, and searched through it. I did find an ouroboros stamp and a Möbius strip stamp, but not one that combined the two.

I sat back down on the stool and took a deep breath and caught the smell of something floral underneath the perpetually oily smell of the workshop.

When I picked up the wrapped box, the thick, homemade, seamless paper noticeably rough, the scent got stronger. I brought it close, and it smelled like roses. That's what the red flecks in the paper were. Rose petals.

Roses symbolized love, add that to the Möbius/ouroboros symbol and maybe my father was telling me that love lasts forever. That love transcends the limits of our finite biology.

Maybe.

It was a good image and I felt emotions stirring. Strong emotions. The ones I hadn't felt since I sat with his recently vacated biology in the locked down memory unit of the facility he had just died in as I wept and wept.

Actually, it wasn't really weeping. That implies some restraint. This was full-body, ugly, snot-filled, heaving convulsions. The well-named "ugly crying."

I was sad that he was gone, that it was over even though the last few years had been hell. I was relieved and felt so very guilty about that. I was terrified to be in this world without my father, without any parents.

I was a grown man, married with a wife and a daughter, and yet I felt so very alone. My father had always been there for me —well... until his mind turned to Swiss cheese—and the world without him did not feel right. Actually it was worse than that, it felt fundamentally wrong that my father wasn't here anymore. Despite the evidence to the contrary and all the logic in the world, it didn't even feel possible that he was gone.

I hadn't cried much since then. If my father's death was the scale of crying for me, then nothing else had come close to reaching that level. Until this package from my father when he was well and whole traveled from the past, that is.

The tears came back in that hidden workshop. Not quite the same but more than I had cried, combined, since after his funeral.

I stared at the package, the shape distorted by my tears, and wept and wept.

I told Mary. I showed her the package with the Möbius/ouroboros symbol stamped on it. Let her smell the decades-old roses embedded in the seamless paper around the cube.

Not right away. I've been married long enough to know you don't wake up your partner in the middle of the night unless there is very a good reason. Especially your not-so-young-anymore partner who values her sleep. Even more especially since she recently retired as a school teacher after spending decades getting up earlier than is right.

Besides, I wanted to be with it by myself, feel the fresh tears without having to find words to describe them.

In the morning, I made her breakfast and brought it to her in bed while she was still reading.

"What's that?" she asked, her eyes finding the box sitting on the tray. Her sun-kissed blond hair had mostly ceded the territory to grey, but she was still beautiful, her green eyes sharp and inquisitive.

"Breakfast," I said.

She gave me a smile, a well-worn smile that said I knew exactly what she was talking about, a smile honed by years and years in the classroom with recalcitrant students.

"It's from my father," I added.

She blinked, put her phone down, and sat up straight, her mouth opening, but no words came out.

I took a deep breath, pulling in the scent of coffee to give me strength, and told her. Everything. It took a bit, and she sipped her coffee and ate her eggs and crunched on her toast while I did, her eyes flicking from the package to me and back, the whole time.

She knew my father. She was there for his entire disease, from the early days when he was hiding what was happening which resulted in some odd behavior, to the slow role reversal as we became the parents and he the child, all the way through to the traumatic end.

"Thank you for telling me," she said when I was done. "Now, open it."

I was sitting on the bed and just blinked at her. It was certainly an obvious next step, a necessary next step, but it was steeped in practicality when I, the engineer, was swimming in emotion.

"I know you," she said. "You want to savor this."

I nodded, still mute.

"It could be years before you open it," she said. "You never wanting to let go of the possibility of what might be in there. But I know your father too. He had this delivered to you—when was it?"

"Two days ago," I said, finally finding my voice.

"Two days ago," she echoed. "That was on purpose, that was done with intent. And today is Solstice, isn't it? Winter Solstice. Today, honey. He wanted you to open it today."

"He loved Winter Solstice," I said, the feeling of rightness in what she was saying warring with my emotions. "The shortest day of the year, the day when the sun returns, the holy day that

Christmas was set near, where in that religion the son of God returns."

She nodded. "You have my permission to do this by yourself. Or if you want, I will stand by you. But open it. Open it today."

"Wait," I said, getting up. "The packaging. I need the packaging."

This was my father we were talking about. Mary was right, the "when" was significant, as was the "how." I had slipped the package out of the brown butcher paper it was wrapped in, but I hadn't finished unfolding it. There was something there. I just knew it.

"There's nothing," Mary said, encased in a dark teal robe that made the green of her eyes stand out.

We were at the kitchen table, snow gently falling outside the window, the trees and houses of our neighborhood encased in soft white, the old heater working hard to keep the temperature up.

The butcher paper was out laid flat on our round wooden kitchen table. I had carefully worked through the glue on the other end.

But there was nothing. No writing besides the address. No hidden clues. No nothing.

This couldn't be.

"Maybe it's just packaging," she said.

I bit my lip and shook my head. "No."

She gave me a look, a narrow-eyed, appraising look. She thought I was on the wrong path and was weighing her words carefully.

She turned it over and pointed at the postage. The little label was clean, white, new, but the address and paper were old and faded, the blocky printing clearly my father's. "Someone held this for him. Sent it for him. The timing was important." She pointed at the inner box swathed in seamless homemade paper. "Open it."

I nodded but didn't move. My father, doing something this elaborate, was not going to have the packing be just packaging. Unless... unless his mind wasn't quite as sharp as it once was when he did this.

"What?" Mary asked.

I shook my head, shaking the feeling off. "There has to be something here," I said. "Really, there has to be."

She shrugged. "If there is, it's invisible."

A smile cracked my face. "You are brilliant," I said and kissed her before I surged up.

"What?" she asked.

"We need lemon juice and a blow dryer," I said. She still looked confused. "Invisible ink. He wrote something in invisible ink. We are going to 'National Treasure' this thing!"

IF EVER THERE WAS A MOVIE MADE JUST FOR MY FATHER, IT was *National Treasure*. Released in 2004, it features Nicholas Cage in the role of Benjamin Franklin Gates in a multigenerational treasure hunt in which the first major clue is hidden on the back of the Declaration of Independence, written in invisible ink.

The movie has everything. Action, adventure, clues, puzzles, villains, and history—albeit some of it was not quite accurate.

Viewing it was a yearly thing I did with my father on July Fourth, the date the Declaration was signed, of course. He was like a child watching it, delighting in each puzzle solved, each piece of cleverness, even though he had seen it at least fifty times. Afterwards, we would go find some fireworks to watch.

After his mind went and he was far enough gone to be in that facility, I showed up with a tablet on the Fourth of July ready to watch it, but he couldn't understand it. He couldn't follow it. And the PG-rated action terrified him.

That was when I knew I had lost him. But he was still with it when he created this package and there had to be something there.

To be sure, I check the dimension of the wrapping paper, and while it wasn't the same size, it had the exact same height to width ratio as the Declaration, slightly taller than it was wide.

And that was something. It would have been easier to make it square, it would have made more sense with the cube-shaped object inside. This gave me confidence that my father was fully there when he created this.

With Mary by my side, we squeezed lemon juice, gently brushed it on the paper with a Q-tip, and blew hot air on it with a pink blow dryer.

For a moment there, it felt like it was my father standing next to me, like he was feeding me the kind of trivia a history teacher would know about the Declaration of Independence, like he was whole and alive and well.

"I'm sorry," Mary said. The paper was just paper, nothing had happened, and the magic of the moment was broken.

"No," I said. "There has to be."

"Maybe it's been too long," she offered.

"No," I said again, still blowing hot air on the paper. I got it closer so it would produce more heat. This wasn't the founding document of our country, just brown paper, and if I burned it, I burned it.

I was staring so hard that I wasn't sure if I was imagining it or not, but I thought I saw a "S" and a "T" both written in my father's blocky style.

"Oh... my..." Mary said, her breath husky.

Unlike the movie, what appeared wasn't a set of numbers, a cipher, but just a few simple words.

DEEPEST NIGHT

BRINGS CLEAREST SIGHT

It was a message about the Winter Solstice. Clearly.

I stared at Mary, my jaw open. "You are right," I said. "We need to open this. Tonight."

***

UNWRAPPING THE HOMEMADE, ROSE PETAL INFUSED, Möbius/ouroboros stamped inner package was trickier. What if there were more clues on this paper? What if I cut right through it and ruined part of what my father prepared.

We were in the kitchen, the snow falling outside, big, heavy flakes. I could hear the distant rumble of the autonomous snowblower clearing our driveway for us. Our house was old and lacked the convenience of many modern houses, but I was glad these things finally worked well enough, so no one had to shovel snow, vacuum the floor, or fold the laundry.

The kind of tinkering that drove my father had entered the mainstream. I'm sorry he didn't get to see it.

"You have to pick a spot," Mary said. She was pacing behind me, and I was holding the cube. I knew that the Möbius/ouroboros symbol had to be on purpose. "Love lasts forever" was a good message, the seamless paper that had no beginning and no ending emphasized that message, but there was no removing it without creating edges.

There is magic in the Möbius strip. Take a strip of paper, twist it 180 degrees and tape it end-to-end and there you have it.

It no longer has a top or a bottom. There was magic like that in this wrapping. My father pulped paper, added rose petals, and carefully and skillfully formed it around this cube making it whole and continuous.

"If love lasts forever," I said. "Why do I have to break the foreverness of this paper?"

Mary sighed and slumped down on the wooden chair across from me. "Because *we* are not forever," she said.

I just sat there and blinked, my jaw dropping open again. I have a tendency to squirrel myself away, take on problems by myself, but most problems are better solved with someone else.

"Love lasts forever, but our lives don't," I said, letting the words come slowly, feeling them run back through my brain.

Mary nodded.

This wasn't a *National Treasure* type of clue. This was emotional, this was subjective, this was...

"This is not just for me," I said, the words rushing out of me now, powered by the excessive amount of coffee I had drunk, the bitter taste of it strong on my tongue. "He created this for you too. I would have never opened it in time. I would never have come up with that kind of interpretation."

She smiled, and even after all of these years there was a touch of shyness to it. "So... open it, dear," she said.

I nodded, but still moved carefully. I turned it over, so the Möbius/ouroboros symbol was on the bottom, pinched the paper on one of the edges, and using an exacto knife cut a small slit in it. I didn't want to cut through anything but the paper.

I had brought the lit magnifying glass from my workshop and peered under the paper.

"What do you see?" she asked.

"Plastic," I said. "It appears to be shrink-wrapped with something dark underneath. Maybe wood."

"Shrink-wrapped?" she asked.

I nodded. This wasn't a surprise. "The paper making process is a wet one and what is inside would have to have been protected."

"Great," she said, a playful smile on her lips. "So open it, Grant."

I nodded, took some scissors, and slipped them into the hole I had made and slowly cut about an inch and took another look.

I knew my slow, methodical approach was probably driving Mary crazy, but she didn't say anything which I really appreciated. I wasn't capable of rushing this. It wasn't in my nature, it wasn't the way I was trained, and I was still afraid of missing something.

I finished the cut and then made another one, forming a plus sign on the bottom of the handmade paper. The box slipped right out.

I carefully set aside the paper—it still formed a cube. I could take all the time I wanted to analyze it later.

What sat before us was a cube five inches on a side. There was wood underneath the shrink wrap on five sides, but one side was black, the side that had been under the Möbius/ouroboros symbol.

Mary stared at me, expectantly. She wanted to keep going, to pull the plastic off. I tried to imagine there being a secret message in the shrink-wrapping, but I couldn't picture it.

My father was fascinated with shrink-wrapping like any tinkerer would be. Here's plastic, something that is processed with heat that shrinks when you apply heat. Not a deep mystery, but one his mind couldn't resist.

I took the cube and turned it over, looking at it more closely. The wood was stained dark, the box well made—woodworking was another thing my father tinkered with. The edges were crisp right angles, and on the bottom, opposite the black square, the Möbius/ouroboros symbol had been laser etched into the wood. I compared it to the stamp on the homemade paper and it appeared to be the exact same design and the same size.

"What if it doesn't work?" I asked.

"Work?" Mary asked. "What do you mean 'work'?"

I blinked, staring into her lovely eyes. Something had made me think the box had a function. I hefted the box. It was heavier than it needed to be. There was no seam which there would be if you could pull off the top. I tapped on the black end and it was hard, harder than plastic.

My subconscious had put it together and I nodded. "There's something in the box and it doesn't appear to open. My guess, it's the guts of an old smartphone. You know how he was always tinkering with them."

Smartphones changed everything in the aughts. The first iPhone came out in 2007 and suddenly everyone had a real and powerful computer in their pocket. Components got smaller and cheaper, screens got better, tools for creating apps got easier.

Every one of them had GPS, Wi-Fi, an accelerometer, and more. The mass manufacturing of smartphones led to all kinds of technology, much of it wearable and small.

"But..." Mary began. "It's been sitting for how many years? Will the batteries still be good? How do you charge it?"

"In those days..." I began, trying to remember what I knew about lithium-ion batteries. "Two to three years when used. But if it wasn't used...? They don't actually fare that well. They do better if kept charged."

"But... this is your father," she said.

I nodded. "Even alkaline only have about a ten-year shelf life."

"Maybe this is not what you think it is," she said gently. "Let's pull the plastic off and see." She slowly pulled the cube from my hands. I let her, my mind was stuck on the battery problem. She pinched the side of the plastic like I had done with the homemade paper and snipped a small hole with the scissors. She was being very careful, which I was glad to see, but I watched her every move.

She cut a plus sign, just like I had, and slipped the cube out of its third layer of wrapping. She set it in front of me.

I nodded and said, "Thank you." After all these years she can see when I'm diving headlong into analysis paralysis.

She smiled. "What's next?"

I had no idea.

IF THIS DEVICE WAS MEANT TO BE USED ON WINTER Solstice, this Winter Solstice, it seemed to me there had to be electronics involved. It was a sealed cube. There were no seams, nothing to press, nothing to twist. Having electronics involved wasn't a sure thing, but given my father and when the package was delivered, this seemed probable.

I was back in my hidden workshop. Mary had told me she needed the kitchen and sent me off. This is what decades of marriage will do for you. She knew I was going to have to figure this out and I absolutely wouldn't resort to cutting it open or doing anything so crude as that. She also knew she didn't want to sit around for hours and stare at me while I did that.

I put the cube under the magnifying glass. The wooden portion was hardwood, I'm not sure what type. It was simple but very well made, the edges fitting perfectly together. The top was black and felt like glass.

I rummaged around one of the bins and found a twenty-year-old smartphone. The top looked exactly like that, except it was a square.

No one made square phones. Ever. I had a tablet out there,

so I talked to it, and it confirmed that there had never been a square smartphone, especially not five inches square.

There were, though, those foldable smartphones, but none of them were ever that wide.

I had it do more searches, running through archived versions of the internet, and found plenty of matches in the right year. LCD screens of all kinds of sizes were made, of course. The closest matches were LCD screens made for aviation systems.

So the guts weren't a phone, but it didn't mean it wasn't some kind of electronics like a Raspberry Pi single-board computer. My father was always messing with them, but it had been years since I had looked at one. I rummaged around again and found one and confirmed that they were easily small enough to fit in the cube.

That left us with the question of power.

"No batteries," I said aloud, my mouth getting ahead of my brain. "There are no batteries."

My father would have understood the issue. Old batteries can leak, can damage things, can make a huge mess. He wouldn't have risked putting batteries in it, which could only mean...

I shook my head. It was so obvious. The cube had to get power wirelessly. There was a single standard back in those days called Qi. To get technical, it used resonant inductive coupling, to get less technical it used a magnetic field to transmit energy. It was used primarily for smartphones but the technology was adaptable.

I pulled out the bin marked chargers and found an old Qi charger, a round plastic puck around four inches in diameter. I then had to find the right USB cable and the right transformer, but I got it hooked up and plugged it in.

I put that old cell phone on it to test it and the phone woke up and gave me the battery charging symbol. The lithium-ion batteries were so old in it that it wouldn't hold a charge, but at least I knew that it worked.

I pulled the old phone off and put the cube on and... nothing. It just sat there inert.

What could that mean?

Raspberry Pi has a boot sequence and, for that matter, so does the LCD screen. I guess it would be possible to engineer those out, but not easily and that was likely beyond my father's skill level.

I read some articles about resonant inductive coupling, about how the sender and the receiver communicate when the charger looks for a resonance change coming from the receiver.

It's very simple, not a complicated protocol like Wi-Fi or Bluetooth, but fairly technical. Suffice it to say that the receiver, by changing how it receives the energy, can communicate with the transmitter. And the transmitter, by changing how it transmits the energy, can communicate with the receiver. This way the receiver only charges its battery until it is full.

But there isn't a battery here.

Since the tablet was fired up, I had it do another era-based search and found a lithium, non-rechargeable battery with a twenty-year shelf life, which we were just outside of. And some Nickel Iron (Ni-Fe) batteries with thirty-year or more life expectancies.

But Ni-Fe was out. They were large, required watering, and not appropriate here. And non-rechargeable lithium seemed out too. Even using a trickle of a charge they would have run low by now.

I was starting to think about drilling a small hole in the cube, so I could get a camera and light in there and find out more about what was in it, but that felt like cheating, like taking a Rubik's cube apart and putting it back together to solve it.

The space of the hidden workshop was feeling small, I

needed to move, to get some air, to clear my head so I could think. I turned off the magnifying glass and flicked the light switch off, plunging the room into darkness. In the darkened space, I saw that there was a dim blue light where the cube was sitting.

I flicked the overhead light back on and felt the hope that had started to build pop like a soap bubble. The light wasn't coming from the cube, but from the Qi charging puck.

I walked over and removed the cube to get a good look at it and the light turned red. That soap bubble of hope reformed when I put the cube back on and the light turned back to blue.

Of course. These had a simple visual cue, the light turning from red to blue, to tell you when it was charging. But the cube wasn't turning on. Why?

"Capacitor," I said, my subconscious once again operating my mouth.

My father would have known that a battery wouldn't have lasted but he could have used the next best thing. A capacitor.

A capacitor is, quite literally, like a battery in that it stores electrical energy. The primary difference is that batteries store energy in chemical form and capacitors store energy in an electric field.

A super capacitor holds enough energy to substitute effectively as a battery, and since there is no chemistry involved, you don't have any shelf-life concerns.

I shook my head, a huge smile on my face. My father wasn't a trained electrical engineer, but he sure thought like one. The guts of the cube was probably a Raspberry Pi single-board computer, a square aviation LCD display, a few super capacitors and some support circuitry, and a Qi charging receiver likely scavenged from an old phone.

The current coming from the charger probably wasn't enough to turn the cube on, so it was waiting for the super capacitor to charge up first, but I could do something about that. I used the first Qi charger I could find and the first transformer I could find with the right USB connection. A better charger, a higher wattage transformer would speed this up.

Tunelessly humming like my father used to do in this very same shop, I got to work.

TIME WAS THE NEXT ISSUE.

If this cube that time traveled from the past was going to turn on for Winter Solstice, it had to know what the date was to know when it was Winter Solstice. But the cube had sat inert, without power for somewhere around twenty years and it could not know what time it was.

I paced in the small, confined area of the hidden workshop as the cube sat on the upgraded Qi charger, the blue light indicating it had found a receiver and was charging it. It was still inert, but I was pretty sure I was on the right track.

Typically, computers get the correct time from the internet, the same way phones get the time from cell towers. But protocols change. The internet of today is different from the internet of my father's day. The security protocols have changed numerous times and even if I got an old Wi-Fi router up and running, the cube wouldn't be able communicate with anything.

Maybe it's a manual thing. Maybe when the cube boots up it will just ask me the time, but that doesn't feel right. If my father wanted this thing to do whatever it's supposed to do at a specific date and time he wouldn't have left it to chance.

For a moment, it's like my father is with me, pacing the three short steps in either direction, surrounded by his tools in his secret workshop, the unfinished cube on the workbench as he tried to figure this thing out.

How does a computer determine what time it is without the internet?

"GPS!" I said with a smile.

Time is an absolutely essential piece of how the Global Positioning System works. Each GPS satellite has multiple atomic clocks that add very precise time data to the signal. If it had a GPS receiver, that would give the cube the ability to know what time it was and where it was and thus what time zone.

GPS dates back to the 1970s and became fully operation in 1993. It was decades later that he was building this, but it was reasonable to conclude that GPS would be available twenty years later. And it was, in fact, reasonable. The GPS network was still in use.

This left me with nothing to do, which felt wrong, somehow. Was powering this up the only mystery my father left me to solve? That didn't seem right. But maybe this wasn't about solving mysteries for the fun of it. Maybe there was a different intent.

There had to be, didn't there? My father obviously put a lot of time into this. Having this feel a little like a "National Treasure" adventure was certainly a bonus, but it couldn't be the purpose.

I sat on the stool and stared at the cube. If I was doing something like this for my daughter, or my grandchildren what would I want to say?

I love you, certainly. Maybe impart some hard-earned wisdom about mortality and the gift that every day is. How important it is to do your best whether you win or lose. How if you keep learning, keep getting better at something, the aging process is not quite so difficult.

And those are all fine things to say, but there's a problem with it. Wisdom boiled down to just a few words often turns into cliché and is rather ineffective. Wisdom is earned more than taught. Being a teacher for so long, my father could certainly come up with a good lecture when he wanted to, but that didn't feel like it.

And I knew my father loved me. We had a good relationship up until his mind started to go and he wasn't capable of having a good relationship, not even with himself.

There was more, something specific to my father, but my mind wouldn't go there. It was a thought right at the edge of consciousness, a thought about my father in particular, about what he would want to say to me, or at least what I would hope he would want to say, but I couldn't isolate it.

Right then, the cube beeped and the screen came to life.

WE ALL WANT MAGIC IN OUR LIVES, OR SOMETHING THAT feels like magic. Something that transcends the mundane and pulls us out and to another place. Something that lets us forget the everyday difficulties of being human, of making a living, of the challenges of our biology as we grow older.

I think, in some ways, that is what my father sought, and I after him. How do you create something that is more than the sum of its parts?

But that feeling doesn't last. Look at the latest tech gadget that feels like a miracle for a while before it becomes commonplace and we want another miraculous gadget.

When my father's cube came to life, the one that he built and created for this moment, I felt the magic. The dark magic of biology had taken his mind away before his body, but now this artifact from the past, from when he was whole, felt more like magic to me than any tech gadget I had ever experienced, even those I helped to create in my job.

There wasn't a lot to see yet, just a pulsing white dot at the center of the screen. I fiddled with my watch until it showed the seconds ticking by—it didn't feel right to talk to it—and sure enough the dot was pulsing every second.

There hadn't been a boot sequence, not that I saw, but this might be it. Or it might be something else. Maybe there was more mystery.

I stared at it for about a minute, which was way too long for a boot sequence. I grabbed a role of masking tape, tore off a small piece, and placed it at the edge of the dot and gave it another minute.

No change. The pulse was every second and it wasn't getting bigger or moving at all.

I gave it another two minutes. No change. Definitely not a boot sequence. I rotated the cube, keeping it in contact with the Qi charger, and didn't see anything but lovely hardwood. I was afraid to take it off the charger, but maybe this was just that, a charging indicator, just like the LED on the Qi charging puck.

Another five minutes and I started feeling a little crazy. The magic of it coming to life was now washed away in worry that I had missed something.

Was it charging? Was it waiting? Was it signaling me that it needed to do something?

If my theory of it using GPS to determine the time was correct, then being in this windowless room might be an issue. For GPS to get an accurate read, it needs to receive signals from four satellites and that is harder to do inside.

I couldn't take it outside. There was several feet of snow on the ground with more falling, but I could get it close to a window which would help with the signal. But that would mean removing it from the charger, and I didn't want to do that.

I understood the electronics involved well enough to know it shouldn't make a difference. If the super capacitor couldn't power it for long enough to move it, then it would just turn off and this would all start over. But this pulsing white dot on an ancient low-res LCD screen was a signal from the past, from my long-dead father, and I was desperate to keep it alive.

"Fine," I said. I would move it *and* keep it alive.

IF I COULDN'T MACGYVER A PORTABLE CHARGING SOLUTION for my father's cube, then I had no right calling myself a tinkerer, much less an engineer.

Those shows, the ones in 1985 and 2016, were a Tinkerer's dream. Every week MacGyver would have to "MacGyver" his way out of a difficult situation using his encyclopedic knowledge of engineering, applied physics, and weaponry.

On that scale, this wasn't even a challenge.

A device like the Qi charger runs on DC, direct current. A battery, which I would need to use, provides DC, so you think it would be easy, just hook the battery to the charging puck. Nope. The puck is looking for a certain voltage and amperage, and while it's possible with a few components to provide that, I was in too much of a rush, so I used a battery, a spare for our AI dishwasher, an inverter to turn the DC into AC, and a transformer plugged in to another Qi charging puck, all on a small rolling kitchen cart.

It wasn't elegant or pretty, but it was quick, which made it a "MacGyver" kind of thing.

So, the cart had the new setup with the second Qi charging puck. I had it close to my workbench and carefully moved the old charging puck and my father's cube to the cart. It kept pulsing. The Qi puck still had the blue light showing me it was charging.

I slowly moved the two pucks close together. There are

better systems now, but for these, the charging device had to be centered over the puck.

This was no bomb, the stakes in terms of life and death, were low, but that is not the way it felt.

I sat there on the workbench stool staring at the arrangement. This cube was, for me, a powerful artifact, a magic object. It had the potential to transform my relationship with what happened at the end of my father's life. Like any true talisman, it could make it so much better or so much worse.

What if this pulsing was all that it does? What if my father created this too late in his disease and this was all he could manage?

A wave of grief flowed through me, like a sudden rogue wave flowing much farther up the beach than the others. This was a possibility, and it would just emphasize how terrible his disease was, how much it took away.

Or it could be something truly magical and bring me back to where my father was whole and healthy with a sharp mind and a quick wit. It could change the past and make it so my last experience of my father wasn't the worst.

I was stuck and I knew it. This wasn't a decision I was capable of. The personal stakes were too high.

I spoke to the tablet, "Can you tell Mary I need her help."

"You are so adorable," Mary said standing next to me in the hidden workshop staring at the cube. I had just caught her up on my dilemma. She had just taken a shower and smelled like a cloud of soap, bringing much needed freshness into the confined space.

"Adorable?" I asked.

She nodded. "Yes."

"Why?" I asked, and I got a glimmer of what she was doing and couldn't help but be grateful. She was distracting me, giving my mind something else to work on, for at least a moment.

"Like all fathers and sons, your relationship was complicated, but you loved him so much," she said. "And I know you want this to be something amazing, something that will make the tender spots in your heart not so tender anymore."

"But...?" I prompted. This started out as distraction but now it was feeling a lot more pointed.

"But," she said with a small smile. "That's not possible. Your father's end will always be a tender spot, will always be difficult to revisit." She paused and took a deep breath. "My father died gently and unexpectedly in his sleep, basically the complete opposite of yours, and it's still a tender spot for me."

I nodded and bit my lip.

She took my hands. "But that tenderness is love, Grant. It's love or it wouldn't feel that way."

I nodded again, feeling a much bigger wave of emotion crash over me. Love for Mary and her presence and wisdom. Grief that my father was gone, that he had to die in the first place, which still feels fundamentally wrong even though it is a fundamental fact of life.

"Do you trust me?" she asked.

She was still ahead of me and was planning something, and I had no idea what it was. But there is only one answer to give when your wife of thirty-six years ask you if you trust them, so I said, "Of course."

She nodded once, let go of my hands, grabbed the cube, and moved it from one charging puck to the other.

I stood there staring, gape jawed, the one-second pulse continuing unabated.

While I still stood there, Mary started to slowly push the cart out of the hidden workshop into the living room.

Dishy was busy cleaning up from dinner, her multiple arms gathering dishes from the kitchen table. This wasn't an anthropomorphized robot that the 20th century like to imagine, but a utilitarian box on wheels that looked much like the last century's dish washer but with the aforementioned wheels and multiple arms that reached out and loaded dishes into its body.

We called it Dishy, not very imaginative. This was a new version and we were beta testers, a perk of my job.

I always watched Dishy, because that was the price of the perk, but that night I watched her like a hawk. The old house that had once been my father's and my grandparents' before him was small, our dining table in the kitchen. We had moved it in front of the sliding glass doors that lead outside to give my father's cube better access to GPS signals.

That was five hours ago and it had continued to pulse steadily every one second with no change. A couple of hours ago I had switched it from battery power to being plugged in. It made me nervous, but I managed to do it myself this time.

"How late are we going to go with this?" Mary asked, standing next to me as one of Dishy's arms reached for a glass of water near the cube.

I leaned closer, readying myself to leap forward if Dishy did not recognize the cube as something that should stay put. "What?" I asked. I had heard Mary but my brain hadn't registered the question.

"How late are we going to go?" she asked.

I shook my head. "You can go to bed whenever you like."

Dishy grabbed the glass and left the cube and I let out a sigh of relief.

"Not what I asked, honey," she said gently.

My brain caught up with her questions and I looked into her blue eyes, compassion decorating her lovely face. My stomach was tight, and I had hardly been able to eat.

I looked at my watch. I had reconfigured it to show the current time and a countdown to the official start of winter. We had six hours and twenty-seven minutes to go.

"Until winter is here," I said.

She smiled and nodded her head. "Kitchen," she said. "Brew two cups of coffee, half-caf."

"I'm not going to take it apart," I said. I had been thinking it but hadn't really meant to say it.

"No?" Mary asked, not missing a beat. It's hard to explain how useful it can be to have someone in your life that really understands you and really loves you.

"No," I said. "I have ideas how he did this and I'm probably right on most of it, but I don't want to know exactly what's in there."

"Why?" she asked.

"A magic trick is usually not so magical when you understand how it works," I said.

She nodded and was quiet for a moment as we both stared at the cube, and then she said, "You are still hoping for magic."

It wasn't a question. I nodded in answer anyway.

"More magic than this already is?" she asked, her voice hushed. "More magic than a gift from your father who has been gone for eighteen years?"

I nodded again. "Just a little more would be nice."

She grabbed my hand and squeezed it and we both watched Dishy finish cleaning up and then park itself under the kitchen countertop to start the washing cycle.

THE PULSE OF THE CUBE WAS BECOMING SO NORMAL, SO regular, that it was like my own heartbeat. Something that was there, something I knew about, but I wasn't very conscious of it.

It was approaching midnight, 45 minutes until the official start of winter, and the boredom of this vigil was starting to make me numb to it all. My butt was, literally, numb from long hours in one of the wooden chairs that go with the old table that goes with this old house.

Distractions were not welcome. Mary had a tablet and was flipping through, reading the news, but I had stayed staring at the cube for hours, except for one brief bathroom break. The magic was long gone, and I was too tired to even hope anymore, but this was a vigil now. I wasn't going to leave this cube.

Well... eventually I would fall asleep. I'm much too old for this kind of thing, all-nighters are for the young. And what then? What if this wasn't tied to the exact moment of Winter Solstice? What if some of the hardware was fried and this blinking, unchanging dot on the square LCD screen was all it could do?

"You're like him, you know," Mary said.

I glanced at her, and she was staring at me. I hadn't realized she had stopped reading. "What?" I asked, coming back from the near fugue state I had been in.

"Your father," she said, nodding at the cube. "You are like him. He would have acted like you are in this circumstance."

"Are you saying I'm stubborn?" I asked, doing my best to smile through the fatigue.

She smiled and that did more than coffee would have to wake me up. "That's a good thing, Grant. If you'll recall, I turned you down at least six times before we finally went on a date."

I really smiled then, but it didn't last. The dark side of my father's stubbornness came to mind. "He was so stubborn at the end," I said. "So fixated on everything being just so. Even when he couldn't put a sentence together, things had to be all in the right place or he was a nervous mess. Do you think I'll be like that?"

She pursed her lips, her eyes searching mine. "I hope not," she said. "You have the genetic markers, like your father did, but this is a different time, the science has progressed some, and you have taken much better care of yourself than he did."

"But there are no guarantees," I said, my eyes traveling back to the cube. "No guarantees."

"Would life be any fun if there were?" she asked.

Mary and I had survived several pandemics, a war, seemingly endless political upheaval, and the brunt of the climate crisis, but we had had some fun amidst it all. You have to find the fun, it's not just handed to you.

"You are the fun," I said. "So I'd be okay with a guarantee or two."

She smiled, but it wasn't a full smile, more like she was amusing me or not really amused by me.

"Whatever happens, this doesn't change much," she said, nodding at the cube.

That really woke me up and I sat up straight. "What do you mean?" I said, keeping my tone neutral. The last thing I needed to do was alienate my supportive wife on this matter, but she was straying into dangerous territory for me.

"What do you think I mean?" she asked. Well, at least she knew it was dangerous territory.

I shrugged and pointed at the cube sitting on the charging puck on the table with the blinking dot. "It won't bring my father back. I know that... that... I'm... I'm hoping for..." I ended in another shrug. I couldn't find the words.

"You are hoping for...?" she prompted.

"A... a different last moment," I said. "Since this got here, I feel him like I haven't in years, like the old him is here, like this is something we are doing together."

Mary was just looking at me, her face neutral, but I felt my cheeks flush hot.

"I know it's silly," I said. "I know it's—"

She got up and I stopped my babbling mid-sentence. She walked over, took my hand, pulled me up into a fierce hug, and whispered, "It's not silly. Not at all."

I was facing away from the cube, and suddenly she stiffened in my arms. "Are you okay?" I asked.

"The cube," she said, pulling away.

I turned and it wasn't just that blinking dot anymore. Well, the dot was still there, still pulsing every second, but above it was a symbol. Two roughly rectangular shapes with a third similar shape sitting on top of them.

It almost looked like a lowercase "n" but the vertical rectangles were much fatter than the horizontal rectangle.

This symbol was just above the center off the screen, just above the pulsing dot.

"That's... that's..." Mary said excitedly. "That's Stonehenge. The dot is the rising sun, still below the horizon. This is real, Grant. This is real."

<hr>

LONG AFTER MY MOTHER DIED, WHEN IT BECAME CLEAR what was happening to my father, I took him to England, to Stonehenge, on Winter Solstice.

It was just the two of us, and while the travel was hard on him, he was like a kid at Stonehenge. It's maybe a bit of a stretch to call the people that built this ancient monument tinkerers, but isn't that what they were doing?

They had been studying the movement of the sun, the planets, and the stars, and they placed these enormously heavy rocks in a way that showed they understood it all very well.

Maybe not tinkering, this was a level or two above that, but it was the same kind of energy.

My father had been fascinated with Stonehenge. Read every book he could find, watched every documentary on it—the good ones and the cheesy ones alike.

That's why when the symbol appeared on the cube from the past, I was confused. We went to Stonehenge *after* the disease had made itself known.

I just stared at it, but Mary was busy talking to her tablet. "Find a live feed of Stonehenge," she said. Her mouth dropped open and she slowly turned the tablet so I could see it.

The sun hadn't risen yet, but the ancient rocks were lit by the coming dawn which wasn't going to be long.

"He did it," Mary said, her cheeks flush with excitement. "He did it."

A few thoughts flitted through my head. First, that Mary hadn't believed this would turn into anything and had been trying to cushion my inevitable. Second, the dissonance of the timing with our trip to Stonehenge after his disease was diagnosed and out in the open. Third, was this feeling that my father was there standing next to me, pushing his glasses up on his nose and grinning like a little boy at all of this because his decades-in-the-making plan was actually happening.

"Add a countdown to sunrise at Stonehenge," Mary told the tablet, and it displayed five minutes and thirty-four seconds and started counting down.

I glanced at my watch and saw that winter had arrived, but that wasn't the timing my father was using.

"Say something," Mary said.

"I... I think I need a moment," I said and wandered out of the kitchen.

OF COURSE I ENDED UP IN THE WORKSHOP HIDDEN BEHIND the bookshelf opened by Verne's *Journey to the Center of the Earth*. I knew I didn't have much time, that if there was more, the cube would activate when the sun rose at Stonehenge, but I needed a moment.

Mary didn't follow me. I'm quite sure she wanted to, but she knew me well enough to know I needed some space.

"Well done, Dad," I said. I felt like he was with me, so it only seemed right to talk to him. "This is your best invention yet. A smart time capsule. Amazing."

I paced the small space, my eyes grazing over the many tubs, the workbench, the neatly arranged tools. In truth this space was too small for a proper workshop, but there was something special about that constraint. It forced you to pick and choose, to focus, to get things done and clean up.

"I don't know if there is more," I said, breathing in the perpetual oily smell of the space. "Maybe you just built this as a gift for me when we started talking about going to Stonehenge. Maybe after you started feeling your mind change, you came up with this plan to send it to me long after you were gone. It doesn't matter."

I stopped and pulled up the stool and leaned on the work-bench. It was made of fiberboard, designed to be easy to replace when it became too worn, but I never had. Some of the stains and burns were my doing, but many of them were my father's. I ran my hand along a particularly long gouge wondering how it had gotten there, what forgotten history it recorded.

"If there is more, it doesn't matter," I said. "But that you did it does. Thank you, Dad. Thank you for teaching me to take things apart and put them back together, urging me to always understand how things worked. Thank you for being the best father you could be. Thank you for loving me."

The wave of emotion I was feeling crested and then froze. There were tears that needed to be cried, but not quite yet. There was grief that needed to be revisited and wounds that needed to be treated again. But not yet.

I finally understood that it didn't matter if there was more. This cube was a demonstration of my father's love and an embodiment of who he was. There was no losing the magic there.

It was all magic.

I nodded once, smiled, and went out to receive the tinkerer's last gift.

BACKSTORY—THE TINKERER'S
LAST GIFT

Holiday: Winter Solstice

There's a few stories in this collection that I wrote for the Holiday Spectacular and never submitted, and this is one.

Why, you might ask, would I write a story for a particular publication and not submit it? There are lots of reasons, but in this case the story was simply too long and didn't meet the requirements.

Some stories are like that, they need some room to breathe and refuse to occupy the space allotted to them. It's actually a good thing when that happens. The relationship between writer and story, at least in my experience, is a dance, a cooperative effort, not me as the writer demanding the story be what I want it to be.

I feel like it's my job to find the story, not the story's job to be anything but what it is.

I'm also aware that this is not a story I would have written when I was younger. It's slow and contemplative and more than a little wistful, things that age seems to bring.

This is, also, a fairly personal story but not really in any direct way—or, at least, not in that many direct ways beyond its general geekiness. It's mostly the feel of it that feels personal, if you know what I mean.

This story received an honorable mention in the Writers of the Future contest.

PART 6
A GRAVE KIND OF LOVE

A GRAVE KIND OF LOVE

WE MET AT THE GRAVEYARD AMONG THE GRASS AND granite... where most ghosts happen to meet, shortly after midnight, when the ghosts gather. She was standing there off by herself, her jade-green eyes watching the play some of the ghosts were putting on, *Romeo and Juliet,* her hands clutching her stomach.

The moon was full, and Thanksgiving was just past, the living in the city of Tucson madly preparing for Christmas by shopping until they dropped and spending until they were spent. Some more Christmassy things were planned for these ghostly midnight gatherings, the Midnight Circle, but tonight it was a Shakespearean tragedy, something to cheer up the dourest of ghosts after the most family of holidays. He dies. She dies. Lessons are learned. Tragedy works great when you are dead.

There was something about her, the way she watched the other ghosts put on the play of love gone wrong, that made me think it spoke to her in a specific way, like she was seeing it for the first time or with new eyes.

She was beautiful, long black hair the color of midnight on a mountain framing her round face. She was young, maybe seventeen, a few pimples splashed on her high cheekbones and one on her slightly upturned nose. Her simple outfit, jeans and a light-green blouse, let her natural beauty shine forth.

She was a new ghost—the pimples gave it away; she hadn't figured out how to alter her form yet. And I'd never seen her before and I would have remembered seeing her.

This rendition of the play was altered slightly. After the two young lovers died, the ghosts playing them let their forms go diffuse, looking altogether more ghostly as the living imagine us to be, and rose up into the air holding hands while they watched the shock of their death unfold upon the Capulets and the Montagues.

After the prince uttered "For never was a story of more woe. Than this of Juliet and her Romeo," and everyone left the grassy area the players had used as stage, after the props melted into the grass, they floated down together, beatific smiles on their faces and kissed.

Turning the tragedy into a kind of happily ever afterlife story. A bit of a risk with this crowd, but it was well received since we all want to have a happy afterlife.

"Pretty sweet, right?" I said, having slowly maneuvered through the crowd of ghosts until I was next to her.

"Huh?" She seemed startled, as if I were waking her from a dream, her arms still clutching her stomach.

"Those two," I said, nodding to the ghosts that played Romeo and Juliet, "Jesús and Lela are really in love. Met in Mexico City a while back when Jesús went back home. Nice to see people of color in the roles, don't you think?"

She smiled, just a tiny thing, like white people often do at such comments, and nodded her head.

"My name is Trisha," I said, extending my hand, "and I died when a semi jackknifed on I-17."

She blinked twice, turned, and walked away from me.

The ritual is standard here among this graveyard in Tucson, Arizona. You state your name and how you died. It is a bit of a morbid ritual, but since we are all dead anyway, why not?

I didn't chase her, not my style, but I was bummed. Not many dead teenagers hanging around the graveyard. Most that don't move on and are actually ghosts don't tend to do well, and end up being those lost moaning vaporous clichés you see in the movies.

This girl, if she didn't find a friend, was going to end up that way too. And yes, I had an awful crush on her, and yes, this was not the first. Despite dying over twenty years ago and having experienced more dead than alive, much of me was still very much the teenager I was when I died.

It's not like I expected her to swoon and fall into my arms. She looked like she identified as female, but I had no idea if she was straight, gay, or asexual, but a friend "my age" would be nice, you know.

And truth be told here, we don't have bodies, and while there are intimacies, to be sure, there is no sex. All that messy biology may be behind us, but we still have all those messy emotions.

***

HER NAME IS TIFFANY. ACK! WHAT A TERRIBLE NAME, IT makes her sound like one of those insufferable rich girls that have privilege problems and expects the world to bow down before her because Mommy and Daddy gave her everything from the moment she was born.

But that's my mind, my immigrant heritage, and my blue-collar upbringing, not my heart. My heart wants Tiffany. Actually, my heart wants Tiff—it can't handle her full name even in its squishy, crushy state.

Tiff drowned. In a pool. With her high and drunk high school friends too messed up to think to dive into the pool and save her.

She died a whole week ago and I gotta tell you, I should know better than to get involved with some newbie ghost who doesn't have a single clue. But the heart... the heart.

All of this info took me two seconds to find out. While we can watch all the TV and movies we like (except 3D, of course, with the stupid glasses), the gossiping here is about ten times worse than high school. We literally have nothing to do but to talk to each other and tell stories.

Well... we can go haunt our living relatives (did that, so dangerous) or stars, say Sarah Michelle Gellar (so boring... really, I tried it) but stories are what drive our community and keep us all sane.

Anyway, the next day I found Tiff walking the graveyard alone, her arms wrapped around her stomach, her ghostly form getting diffuse along the edges, taking her one step closer to that moaning, terrorized, clichéd ghost state.

I "ran" up to her. The quotes are around "ran" because any biological-type actions are done consciously. Earlier when I said she was walking, she wasn't. She was hovering along, her feet nothing more than wisps of brown, another bad sign. "Hi again," I said, a smile on my face. "I'm Trisha, sorry if that 'how I died' thing was too much last night."

She shook her head. "No. I'm just... You know..."

"Freaked out? Thought you'd be in heaven or something? Never thought you'd die so young? Wish you could go back and redo just one itty bitty moment and change it all?"

"How do you know?" Her arms loosened just a touch and that was a good sign.

"'Cause everyone here has a regret like that, at least one, if not, like, ten thousand and one."

She pursed her full lips and nodded.

I'm writing this like it was just some "casual" encounter. I did just "run" up to her *after* making sure my form was good, my long black hair was pulled back into a ponytail, my calf-high boots perfect, my jeans formfitting, and after having practiced a thousand ways to say hello, finding none worth a damn, and telling my stupid heart to shut the hell up.

"Do you know why everyone does that 'I died' crap?" She shivered even though without the biology she can't be cold.

"No one ever told me, but I have a theory."

She nodded, her green eyes really looking at me, and my poor "heart" getting all mushy on me.

"It's because we've got to accept what has happened to us and acknowledging it every time we meet someone helps with that."

She nodded like I was brilliant or something and I was wishing I was alive so I could attack her right this moment. But then I remembered what it had actually been like to be me and be alive and certain facts that would likely send her running, and let it go. The lack of an endocrine system helped with that letting go stuff.

I extended my hand to her. "So, my name is Trisha and I died in a traffic accident."

She stared at my hand for a while and finally took it. I adjusted my form to meet hers where it was at, meaning I got a bit fuzzy around the edges, so I could feel the ghostly numb feeling of her hand in mine. If I hadn't done it right, our hands would have just gone through each other.

"My name is Tiffany, and I... I drowned."

"Good job, Tiff." I should have asked her if she hated the nickname, but a "no" wouldn't have worked.

"I... I've got a few questions. If... if you don't mind."

I smiled because having those gorgeous green eyes focused on me was the only thing I really wanted.

THE GENTLE FLASHING OF A CHRISTMAS TREE ILLUMINATED Tiff's high cheekbones and full lips as we talked like girlfriends talk. We had been talking all day and it was about 11 p.m., I could feel midnight coming and the nightly gathering of the ghosts.

The tree was tall and symmetrical, a fir or a spruce—I can never tell the difference—with tinsel and a star on top and hundreds of blue and white ornaments. It stood in the center of the graveyard where we put on our nightly plays and told stories.

The tree had that slightly translucent quality you see with an experienced ghost. Almost solid, but not quite.

"Say hi to my friend Tiff, Blinky," I called to the tree.

The tree didn't speak but it bowed its star and waved a few ornament laden branches which softly tinkled as the ornaments collided.

"What!?" Tiff asked, grabbing my arm and doing it right. She didn't hold onto it long, but I really wanted her to.

"All the set pieces for *Romeo and Juliet*, you noticed some of them were a bit transparent, right?"

She nodded, her smooth forehead furrowing.

"They were ghosts."

Her mouth opened, because I had lectured her endlessly about good ghostly hygiene, which boils down to that if you look like a human you will feel more human. "Blinky and a few of his friends have mastered transforming into inanimate objects safely. All the big set pieces are them."

She was in awe staring at Blinky and I was in awe staring at her.

"So they don't go into the Bar... Bardie..."

"Bardo," I offered. "That's where those moaning, regretful, stuck in the past, wispy-ass ghosts are."

As if on cue one floated through the graveyard and the ghosts made room for him saying kind words like "We miss you Gene." "Love you, man, let's hit a movie, okay." The bardo brains are all so far gone such a simple thing isn't likely to work, but you never know.

"Bardo. You said it was a Buddhist thing, right?" she asked.

I nodded. "Except everyone here misuses the term. In Buddhism it's the place you must travel through between death and rebirth when you get to face all your crap. A ghost in the bardo is not on its way to rebirth, just lost in its crap."

She nodded, and our conversation turned to other topics and I was glad. I wasn't quite ready to tell her of my own experience with the bardo. We talked more of what ghosts can and cannot do until her curiosity landed her where every teenager's conversation (living or dead) ended up.

"So... no sex?" she asked, her voice low, her eyes darting around to make sure no one was close. We were "sitting" on a granite tombstone, her form much better. She was easy to coach and learning fast.

I nodded my head and bit my lip. "No. But there are... well... things." I nodded over to a group of three ghosts. Jesús and Lela who had played *Romeo and Juliet* last night, and a third man named JJ. The three of them were together. A lot. It made me wonder if they were having a group thing... or getting ready to have a group thing... or thinking about a group thing.

"What kind of things?" Tiff asked.

I frowned, because while I liked playing the role of mentor, I wanted to do the things, not talk about the things. Being a bit of a romantic, I've come to the conclusion that just like in life, the afterlife is better with someone else.

She was staring at me and I couldn't help but smile. I leaned a bit closer and whispered to her. "It's kissing, but...."

"But what?" Tiff asked, a slight squeal in her voice.

"No body... No barriers. A kiss on this side is... *everything*." I leaned back and watched her mind turn it over.

"Have you!?"

I shook my head. I did get close to this one girl, but... she got sucked back into her old life and ended up in the bardo and is still there. I hadn't dared try again until I saw Tiff's emerald eyes.

Her face darkened and she wrapped her arms around her abdomen again, her eyes going to a nearby granite headstone that had a small Christmas tree set up at its base.

"What is it?" I asked gently, putting my arm on her shoulder.

"He... I..." she muttered and walked off.

"WHAT SHE NEEDS RIGHT NOW IS A FRIEND," a gentle baritone said, interrupting my in-depth self-flagellation session.

I had been gazing longingly in the direction Tiff had flown off, running the conversation back in my mind, trying to figure out what I had screwed up.

"Shit! Banquo," I said, turning to the big-bellied, bald man, that was kind of like the father of the graveyard. He showed up like Yoda did in a Star Wars movie and dispensed cryptic advice. "You scared me half to death."

His eyebrow raised, and his lips curled up in amusement. "You know what I mean."

"And so do you, Trisha," he shot back.

I nodded and looked back the way she had gone. "You know what sucks, Banquo?" I didn't give him a chance to reply and forged on. "It sucks that I was a teenager when I died. If I had just been a little older, I think all of this would be easier. I wouldn't be stuck in the never-ending crush cycle of doom."

He just laughed at me, loud and booming. It turned heads and Blinky the tree leaned toward us like he wanted to hear better. "Love makes teenagers of us all," Banquo said.

That quote sounded like Shakespeare—Banquo's the one that knows all the plays and puts them together—but I just didn't feel like asking him.

"And think of poor Emily," he continued, "she died at age four and has been here longer than most anyone."

I rolled my eyes, the only possible response that was appropriate to all of that Yoda-like, parental BS.

"A friend, huh?" I asked after I was done being a teenager.

"You know this, Trisha."

"What I don't know is where she went."

Banquo closed his eyes and took a deep breath, his belly swelling up noticeably. No one had better form than he did, his slacks and his button-down shirt wrinkled perfectly and moved as he did. These things take work when you don't have a body. He also had mad psychic skills. All us ghosts became way more intuitive the day we died, but he's next level.

"A pool," he finally said. "She's by a pool."

"Where she died," I said, knowing it in my heart.

"Yes. She really does need you."

Not thinking, I flew off in the direction she had gone, determined to be that friend and leave all the crushy stuff behind.

THE HOUSE MADE ME FEEL UNCOMFORTABLE AS I FLEW IN. It wasn't a monster house or a rich house, but it was nice house with fresh beige paint and a big pool out back, complete with a slide for the kids and a pool house with a bathroom and a place to store all the toys.

These folks loved their pool time, and in Tucson I sure get that, but wealth to me means a "I got mine so you can go jump" kind of privilege. I wasn't officially born in this country, but I am as American as you can be, getting here before I could crawl.

It didn't take long to spot Tiff, she was in the water lying on the bottom of the pool, her form going diffuse as she raced toward that hellish clichéd ghost place, the bardo.

Sitting next to the pool was a middle-aged woman with raven-black hair and a few extra pounds perched on a lounge chair crying her eyes out.

Inside standing at the patio door was a boy, athletic and handsome, with blond hair staring at the crying woman.

I didn't need to have my ghost-enhanced intuition to see what was going on. The woman was Tiff's mother, the boy was her boyfriend, and this was his house, his parents unable to refuse Tiff's mom access to the place her daughter died. All three of them were stuck in the tragedy that had happened here.

And that's to be expected, the grief normal. It's not easy losing someone you love and it's not easy dying.

But what Tiff was doing was not good for her, not at all. Much more of this and she would be gone, lost to the bardo. She needed a friend, and how.

I went down into the water and said, "Come on, girl. You just got to see what Blinky is going to do for tonight's Midnight Circle."

She didn't respond, her eyes vacant, her mind slipping into the regret of her young life and how it ended. As I leaned close, I could hear the pounding beat of trance-dance music and the rowdy laughter of drunk people, her memory so strong I could sense it.

I tried to take her hand, but it was too wisped out. I'd be unstable if I followed her there. And I knew where she was going. I'd spent ten years in the bardo myself. Ten years that felt like ten thousand.

Shit!

I shouted and pleaded and cried, but she couldn't hear me or see me as her form got more diffuse, seeming to melt into the blue water around her.

I needed to do something shocking, something that would break through to her and I could only think of one thing.

I kissed her.

Stupid, I know. I was risking my afterlife and all my secrets, but I had to do something.

I let my form go wispy until I could hear my brother taunting me as we sped down the rain-soaked highway, dark-green pine trees flashing by in our headlights as we headed back south.

Give it back, Arnold, I shouted.

He was in the front passenger's seat and had just taken my lipstick.

No, Trevor. You just look like a freak in this shit.

I surged up and said, *My name is Trisha.*

Well, you don't look like no Trisha.

My father opened his mouth to speak, glancing over at us and lost precious seconds of reaction time and didn't see the jackknifing semi soon enough. There was screaming and the deafening sound of crunching metal and shattering glass and...

We connected, Tiff and I, the intimacy of a flesh-and-blood kiss amplified a hundred times. I could feel her, I knew her, and she knew me. My secret. My past. My shame.

I felt my ghostly form reverting back to "Trevor," the boy I never really felt I was. Gangly and awkward. Shy. Never comfortable in my own skin.

I got a hold of her and flew her up, straight out of the pool and into the night until the neighborhood was a speck, kissing her the whole way, letting my life pour into her as hers poured into me.

She was the youngest of four and mercilessly teased by her older brothers. She had terrible acne and thought herself ugly. She loved the boy who had been too drunk to save her and had just found out, she had just told him, that she had gotten pregnant. It hadn't gone well, full of shouting and blaming and they'd overdone it.

She loved pancakes and Adele. She was terrible at math and thought that made her stupid. She...

Up there, high in the Tucson night sky, she pushed away from me, her form now returning back to normal.

"You're a boy," she gasped.

And I was, looking like Trevor not Trisha.

"I never felt like I was," I said. It seemed lame to say it that way. I felt all the judgments of the world and all my own judgments that I wasn't like everyone else.

I couldn't read the look on her face. Disgust? Confusion? Fear? A mixture? None of the above?

And then she flew away, but back toward the graveyard and not toward her boyfriend's house. Relieved, I just slumped into my shame, hearing the taunts of my brother, the screeching of metal, knowing that the three of us died that day and it was my fault.

"I got you, Trisha," Banquo said, suddenly there, enfolding me in his arms.

There under the full moon, my death so fresh, full of shame for being seen looking like a boy, I cried and cried as he said

"Trisha" over and over again until it drowned out my brother's taunts and my female form came back.

I STAYED AWAY FROM TIFFANY AFTER THAT. AND DIDN'T think of her as "Tiff" anymore. She is a white-bread white girl, and I am a Latina who was born a Latino. No room there, no matter what my heart said. I am Trisha and I wasn't Trevor for anyone while I was alive and certainly not while I was dead. Saving her robbed me of my female form briefly. It wouldn't happen again.

I felt for her, my heart now knew her, all that vague crush inspired imaginings filled in with the hard facts I had learned when we kissed. And my heart still wanted her. But my heart wanted me to be Trisha more.

So I stayed away as December crawled by, as the ghosts started rehearsing for a stage adaptation of *Scrooged*, written by Banquo of course.

I attended Christmas Eve Mass, hovering over my mother as she lit candles for her long-dead husband, son, and me.

I saw Tiffany, of course. Talking to other ghosts and seeming to be in good spirits, but she was always looking away when I looked at her.

Whenever the shadow of shame started creeping in, I just remembered Banquo's voice saying "Trisha" over and over again until it passed.

I am Trisha.

In my heart I always was. Now I can look the way I feel. And if that means I'm alone, then—

"You are coming, aren't you?"

I jumped. Banquo had a way of sneaking up on you.

I saw the compassion in his face and had to look away. He

knew my secret, but that fact hadn't spread through the grave-yard like wildfire. It looked like both he and Tiffany were keeping my secret, and for that I was grateful.

"Coming?" I asked dumbly, buying time.

"*Scrooged*. We're about to start. It'll be Christmas when we end." He nodded up toward the Midnight Circle area where most of the ghosts had already gathered. I could see Blinky and his gang swooping around as a miniature Santa with his sleigh and reindeer as a warm-up act.

I shook my head and looked down.

"Please, Trisha. It would mean a lot to me."

He held out his hand and I took it. After what he did for me, how could I refuse him?

THE *SCROOGED* PLAY WAS FANTASTIC. GHOSTS GETTING TO play ghosts is just a hoot. Banquo played the role of the narrator, the old guy with the big book, and half the graveyard was in it at one point or another.

At the end, after the players had returned to the circle and Blinky and his crew were back to looking like people, Banquo strode out into the middle.

"We have a tradition here, that a new ghost gets the floor whenever they are ready to tell us their story," he said, his voice deep and resonant, the kind of voice that could reach the back of a theater. "It is a rite of passage, and tonight we'll hear from one of our newest members."

His mischievous green eyes caught mine for a moment and then he looked away. "Tiffany, if you please."

Everyone clapped and there were a few calls like "How'd you die?" and "Make it good!"

She walked out holding her stomach, but when she got to the center, she took a deep breath and let her hands fall to her sides.

"Hi. My name is Tiffany, but some of my friends call me Tiff." She looked straight at me and smiled when she said "Tiff." "I drowned in my boyfriend's pool pregnant with our unborn child."

She told of her life and her death, haltingly but with great courage. Things I had learned when I kissed her. The ghosts were rapt and applauded and hollered when she was done, her pale cheeks lighting up red. She had a story for sure, and a difficult passage. That'll get you respect around here.

And then she walked straight up to me as everyone dispersed.

"I'm sorry," she said, quietly. "I needed some time."

I nodded, not able to speak.

"I... I've thought a lot about this and..."

She looked away, her arms going to her stomach, and I felt like I was going to just die. Right there. I probably would have if I hadn't already been dead.

"You..." she began again. "I mean... I can't believe what you..."

And then she took my face in her hands and kissed me and she didn't need to speak anymore. That ghostly super-kiss said it all, and so much better without our regrets front and center. The kiss said that I had been there when she needed someone. That I was her friend. That me being a girl in a boy's body who happened to like girls could take a bit to get used to. That now she didn't care. That although there was a lot to get over and adjust to, she wanted to explore this afterlife with me. That...

Well, you get the picture.

Pretty silly that the best kiss of my life came after I was dead, but I'll take it.

Behind us a group of ghosts started singing Christmas carols at the top of their lungs. There were some good singers there, but some just had their enthusiasm.

Our lips parted and we held each other and watched. Banquo's baritone was front and center as he and the rest of the singers beamed at us. Our hands clasped together, we went and joined them and sang our hearts out. After all, what could be better for a transgender Catholic girl ghost past the crush stage and fully in love on an early Christmas morning.

BACKSTORY—A GRAVE KIND
OF LOVE

Holidays: Just after Thanksgiving to Christmas

I think an essential part of a writer's job is to put yourself in other people's shoes. You can't, after all, write stories filled with people just like you. Well... I guess you can, but that, frankly, sounds like a horror story.

This was my attempt, in part, to try to feel like what it might be to be someone very different. And I was also trying to write a holiday romance between two ghosts.

Just like "Emily Loves Christmas, Emily Loves Murder," "A More Adventurous Afterlife," and "Ghosted," this story takes place in my ghost world. There are, to date, six novel-length books and many short stories written in that world. You can find out more at *ShuffledOff.com*.

This story was originally published as part of the 2019 *WMG Holiday Spectacular*. It was reprinted in *Joyous Christmas* and *Pulphouse Fiction Magazine: Issue #21*.

PART 7
A GHOST IN TIME

A GHOST IN TIME

December 21, 1952

She was humming, just simply humming. No real tune, the sound of it one of plain contentment.

It was late December, but still she was outside behind a modest home hanging laundry on the line and humming while she did. The air was cool, there was a bite to it when the wind kicked up, but it wasn't that cold.

She looked familiar, her long plaited hair, her bright green eyes, her aquiline nose, and strong cheekbones bringing back fond memories. I had seen her at this age in pictures but never in person. Her name was Abigayle Trendall and she was my grandmother.

I could hear the distant sounds of a radio broadcast coming from inside the dwelling and the muffled shouts of children fighting or playing. I never had any of my own so I wasn't always good at telling the difference.

I had never ghosted back in time before and the sensations of it struck me. The scene I was seeing was heightened in a way, the colors so bright, the sounds so clear, that made it almost seem surreal. But it wasn't like being in virtual, the experience had the weight of reality brought home by tiny details like the bits of rust on the poles that anchored the laundry lines, the dirt and wear on Grandmother's clothing, the utter richness and mundanity of all the detail.

Some sensations were distant, like the feel of the cool air and the smell of the fresh laundry, but others were heightened like my eyes had never seen so clearly and my ears had never been so sharp.

Grandmother paused after clipping a sheet to the line and fiddled with her clothing. She wore wool slacks that fit her tall frame well and a fashionable coat, both in navy blue, the ensemble rather nice for the task at hand. She sighed and looked up at the sun, a small, relaxed smile on her face.

It was a moment of contentment or maybe hope, when just being outside, just letting the sun shine on her was enough.

There were three lines strung across the yard, dead grass underneath her feet. She had sheets on the two outside lines creating a little private space for her between them.

She wasn't old, just shy of forty, but her face had the fine lines that showed she was one of those that smoked cigarettes and loved the sun. Crow's feet and frown lines were prominent as well as deepening wrinkles on her forehead that hinted at worry. Her long brown hair was plaited back and shot with streaks of blonde, which was the kiss of the sun, and just a few streaks of grey, the kiss of time.

To me she looked so young and so beautiful.

When she sighed again and tilted her head down and opened her eyes, she was looking right at me.

For a moment I was worried that she could see me, that she could detect my presence here. But the sunshine was bright and what little disturbance my consciousness created in this time would not be visible.

A smile lit up her face and she suddenly seemed even younger. "There you are," she said.

My heart sped up but I resisted the temptation to panic. I was here, at least at a quantum level my consciousness was, but I was also not here. My body was back in the t-chamber and I was just an observer of that which was.

I turned around, as much as any disembodied consciousness can, and saw that there was another woman behind me, a smile lighting up her face. She was short to my grandmother's tallness with black hair that hung to her shoulders dressed in jeans and a dark peacoat that was too big for her. She looked to be around forty, but her face was rounder and lacked the fine weathering of tobacco and sun, pale compared to the face of my grandmother. She had brown eyes that were at once soulful and intense.

They were in that corridor of privateness, the sheets flapping on either side of them, their eyes locked in a way that spoke volumes.

It didn't feel right to be between them so I moved to the side and watched.

"It's solstice," the second woman said with a smile that looked at once happy and sad. "Winter solstice."

I knew of her, this second woman, but did not know her name. That was one of the things I was here to find out.

"The sun shall return," my grandmother said.

"And so I have returned," the dark-haired woman said.

They stood there staring and it felt like something was passing between them, like unseen electricity sparking through the air, or perhaps feelings and words carried by something other than language.

The breeze kicked up and the flapping of the freshly hung laundry drowned out any other sounds and it no longer seemed like they were in the backyard of a simple house in a dense neighborhood on a winter's day. It felt like in all the world there was just the two of them.

The woman with the dark hair licked her lips like she was hungry or maybe thirsty.

"Thank you for coming," Grandmother said. "I am sorry I couldn't get away. Little Terry is sick again. That girl is always sick, it seems, and the doctors are baffled."

My ears perked up at the mention of my mother. I knew some of those shouts from the home were hers. She died when I was only five and I longed to see what she was like as a child, but that was not why I was here.

"I understand," the other woman said, taking a tentative step forward, but from the pained look on her face, I wasn't sure that she did. "This is our twenty-fourth time doing this together. Twenty-four is the number of family and..." She trailed off, her lips pursing and her nostrils flaring as she blinked back tears.

The air was thick with need and longing and I felt embarrassed to be there. But the number twenty-four was key for me. It meant the first time they did this was in 1929.

"I prepared," Abigayle said, looking away and reaching down to the laundry basket full of damp clothing and bedding and pulled out a small glass mason jar with a red fluid, some seven-day candles that were about halfway burned down, and two old pillows.

"I brought fire," the other woman said, pulling out a lighter. It was silver and etched on the side was a dot with a circle around it, the astronomical symbol of the sun. "And food, gifts from the earth." She hefted the paper lunch bag in her hand.

"You always bring the fire, Terry," my grandmother said with a smile, her cheeks flushing red, her voice almost apologetic.

I felt a flood of relief. I now knew the woman's name and it was so obvious. My mother had been named after this woman.

Terry didn't blush at what my grandmother had said, she

only smiled and nodded like this was something she knew about herself.

They both moved slowly, tentatively, as they arranged the cushions, put the candles and the jar of wine between them, laid out some cheese and crackers on a clean white cloth napkin, and sat down facing each other.

"We shall not be disturbed?" Terry asked, the tone of it making it sound like a half question.

My grandmother nodded to the house, which was shielded from them by the gently flapping, large white sheets. "College Football is on the radio. Even little Terry likes it and she's doing okay today."

Terry nodded and glanced at her watch. "It's 2:42. One minute until the sun starts returning to us." There was a sadness in how she said it, this clandestine meeting, the two of them hiding in plain sight.

"Then, let us give thanks," my grandmother said, her tone deepening, the rhythm of her words steady. "We do not worship the sun like those long ago, but we celebrate its return. The sun is life and its return signals that the depths of winter are here but that the joy of spring and new life shall come."

I knew the words and mouthed them along with her. She had taught me these words when I was young, when she taught me about the Roman's Saturnalia, the Hopi's Soyal, the Lohri festival in India, the Santo Tomás Festival in Guatemala, and more.

She taught me how Christmas was placed at this time of year to redirect the "pagan" celebrations of the returning of the sun to the then burgeoning religion.

"And we give thanks," Terry said, her tone matching Grandmother's, "for each day we have under the sun, for the gift of light and the gift of life. We give thanks for that which makes our very existence possible and celebrate the return of the sun in this, the northern hemisphere, while acknowledging the perfect balance of it as this is the longest day of the year in the southern hemisphere."

Grandmother thought that important too, while this was our shortest day, for others it was the longest. While winter was coming on in force for us, it was summer that was descending for others. This was nature. This was balance. This was what was real.

Terry went to light the seven-day candle closest to her, but the candle was burned down and the lighter could not reach it. Grandmother fished in the laundry basket and handed Terry one of those long stick matches for lighting fires. Their fingers touched briefly, a small shudder passed through my grandmother.

Terry used her lighter and the long match, lit her candle, and gave the burning match to Grandmother who lit her candle.

Together they said, "We welcome back the sun and the warmth and life it brings."

They shared the mason jar and drank wine, they ate, they marked the returning of the sun with their simple ritual, but there was a restraint there that I was surprised by.

A few minutes after solstice was over, the energy of the ceremony seemed to dissipate and my grandmother slumped a little and asked her companion, "How is your life?"

Terry smiled but it was a little twisted, like there was glass in her mouth. "The psychologists, in their infinite wisdom, have declared homosexuality as a mental disorder and my family has disowned me."

Grandmother blinked and looked down.

"Do you think it is a mental disorder?" Terry asked, her voice low, her face puckered like she had eaten something sour. "Do you think your feelings for me are a... disorder?"

Grandmother didn't look up but said, "How can love ever be a disorder?"

A sob escaped Terry. They were both looking down, Terry picking at the dried and dead grass as the wind kicked up and flapped the cloth around them making it seem like they were far away and all alone.

"You do love me," Terry finally said.

"Yes," grandmother said, not looking up. "And I love Gary and my children. I—"

"Do not worry my sweet Abby," Terry said, cutting her off. "I will never ask you to leave them. Not for me. Not for us."

There was silence between them, excited shouts rising from the house and the sounds of cars on the nearby road, piercing the illusion of their isolation.

"But I can't keep doing this," Terry said, now staring at my grandmother who finally looked up.

"No?" Grandmother asked.

Terry shook her head. "No." She moved the plate and the candles that were between them and scooted close to Grandmother and took her hands and squeezed them.

"I cannot touch you but once a year when the sun returns," Terry said. "It is not enough."

My grandmother's cheeks flushed red but she held Terry's eyes.

"Just like the sun returns every year," Terry said. "My thoughts always return to you and my love is as eternal as that sun which is now returning to us."

Grandmother sniffed and nodded. "But...?" she prompted.

"This is love," Terry said. "We know that."

My grandmother gently nodded her head.

"But because of this world it is also a wound," Terry said, and she looked away. "Seeing you, touching you, feels so good. It heals me. Leaving you reopens the wound and it is worse each year."

The wind died down and the football game inside must have gotten boring because there was a sudden, thick silence.

Terry leaned over and kissed my grandmother. It was tentative at first, but then my grandmother put her hand on Terry's neck and drew her close. There was a passion there as strong as the sun that was returning and I had to hold my own tears back.

I have had a long life. I have loved. But I have never loved like this. I don't think many do.

The kiss lasted a long time and a whole book of feelings was carried on it. The wind kicked back up, the sheets flapping around them, and without a word, Terry got up and walked away without looking back.

It was clear by her straight back and the set of her shoulders that she would not be returning.

Silent tears flowed down my grandmother's cheeks.

I stayed with her even though she couldn't know I was here and I couldn't comfort her. The t-chamber had limits, the fabric of reality had limits, and I knew no one else could come back within fifty meters and fifty minutes of my trip here. This was the privacy I could give her.

When the tears became wracking sobs, I couldn't stay and triggered my exit.

DECEMBER 22, 1929

The bedroom was dark, the waning gibbous moon casting a silver glow over everything through the window.

My eyes didn't need to adjust, since I didn't actually have eyes, the quantum machinery of the t-chamber casting my awareness further back in time this time. To the first winter solstice celebration for Abigayle and Terry.

We were in a converted attic space, the off-white plastered ceiling steep. The floor was rough wood with old throw rugs covering over it and I imagined that it would creak when you walked on it.

At first I thought I was at the wrong place or that I hadn't specified the right date, but then there was a giggle and the flaring of a match.

"It's time," Terry said, the lit match casting her face in its warm glow. The last time I had seen her she had been nearly forty, now she was fifteen. Her complexion was so smooth, her face heavier and rounder, but her brown eyes still so intense.

They sat on pillows on a patch of bare wood, a tapered candle between them as well as a mason jar with what had to be wine, some bits of Swiss cheese, some soda crackers, and two fresh seven-day candles. Terry touched the match to the tapered candle and they almost looked like ghosts themselves in the flickering pool of light, the rest of the room hidden in darkness.

They were both dressed in night shirts and swaddled in thick robes with slippers on their feet. My grandmother's hair was more blonde than brown and spilled over her shoulders. Terry's hair was black as the night and long too.

"Are you going to cast a spell on me?" my grandmother asked with a nervous giggle.

It was odd to see her as a girl. She was in her seventies when I was born. I again felt like an unwelcome voyeur, that I shouldn't be here.

"You can count on it," Terry said, her voice bold and a bit loud.

"Shhhh!" Grandmother hissed. "Don't wake anyone up."

Terry looked around like someone was watching and then giggled, covering her mouth and muffling the sound.

It was dark and I was worried my presence would be noticed. It doesn't happen all the time but sometimes ghosts in time are seen, our spectral presences felt. But the two young women were much too focused on each other for that.

When she recovered, Terry handed grandmother a slip of paper and took one herself and whispered, "My aunt says we must follow this, exactly. We must start right before the moment of solstice and be doing it while the sun starts to return to us."

"What if we don't?" grandmother asked.

Terry shrugged and it was a brief, imprecise gesture. "Then the magic won't happen, I guess."

I watched as they awkwardly did the same ceremony they would do for the last time in twenty-three years. Their words slow and stilted, first my young grandmother and then Terry. They toasted the return of the sun with the wine, sharing the jar and laughing. They ate the cheese and crackers, naming them the gifts of the earth and the sun. And then sat there staring at each other.

"So when does the magic happen?" grandmother asked.

"Now," Terry whispered, her voice husky in a way that seemed comical to me because of their youth. She leaned over and kissed my grandmother and it wasn't the kiss I had witnessed in 1952. It was shyer, sloppier, much more tentative at first, but it was powered by the passion of youth.

My grandmother pulled away, putting her hand to her lips. "You don't kiss like Gary does," she whispered.

"Damn right," Terry said, hunger in her eyes.

"We shouldn't," grandmother said, but she licked her lips and stared at Terry's lips.

"You feel it, Abigayle Trendall," Terry said quietly. "I know you do."

Grandmother bit her lip and looked away. Even in the dim

light I could see that her young cheeks were flushing red. "You shall be the death of me, Terry Grandon," she said.

That was it. That was her name. That's what I needed.

I should have triggered the end to this ghosting back in time. I should have left. This was a private moment, the most private of moments.

I knew that t-chamber wouldn't let me stay if things got too heated. This was one of the first modifications to the device as this technology was used in the same way as many new technologies had been, to indulge in our endless fascination with sex.

Despite the intimacy of the moment, I couldn't leave. Not yet.

"But it will be a pleasant death," Terry said, leaning close to her.

"Do you promise?" grandmother asked, smiling in a way that looked entirely too mature for her age.

"I do," Terry said, licking her lips. "Do you promise?"

Grandmother nodded. "I do."

They were young women exploring, teasing, but it sounded strangely like a wedding ceremony.

They kissed again and the youthful passion of it was overwhelming. That was enough. I left.

DECEMBER 21, 2006

This was the hardest jump of all. This is the one that was forbidden. This was the one that was destined.

My grandmother was old, her face as wrinkled as a dried-up apple, her years of smoking and sunning having more than caught up to her. Her green eyes were dim and it was hard to tell exactly where she was in her mind. She was doing a kind of time traveling herself.

She was sitting in an old blue recliner dressed in a brown robe that could not hide how thin she had become. She was in her bland room in the care facility she lived in, facing the window staring out at the courtyard watching the last bits of fading light, the sun having gone to bed extra early this day.

We were in a locked down memory unit and grandmother belonged there.

"Solstice is here," she said, her voice like the whisper of fall leaves in the wind. "The sun is returning. But she never did."

A young man squatted next to the chair holding her warm hand with its paper-thin skin. He was just seventeen, tall and lanky, dressed in jeans and a light blue button-down shirt that if you looked closely you could tell was a woman's shirt. His hair was dark brown and curly, falling past his ears.

"What was her name?" my grandmother asked, turning to the young man. "Can you tell me, Allan? What was her name? She should be here with me."

Grandmother's hair was still long and plaited into a braid but it was pure white with tendrils of it having escaped the braid to frame her weathered face.

"Call me Ali," the boy who did not want to be a boy said. He had asked more times than he could count for his grandmother to call him that.

I knew this scene and I could hear the words coming before either one of them said them. I felt for the old woman whose memory was a fleeting series of soap bubbles that popped at the slight provocation. I felt even more for the young man who didn't feel at home in his own body.

I felt for him, because I used to be him.

And that was why this was forbidden. You were not allowed to be a ghost in your own presence. The t-chamber did its best to detect such things, but this was sixty-four years ago before I had transitioned, before the gene therapy that saved me from the disease that took my mother so young.

"I just want to remember her name," grandmother said. "I just want to see her lovely face one last time." She took a deep breath and it came out in a shuddering exhale. "It was a different era, you understand that, don't you, Ali? I... I..." She trailed off her dim eyes going distant.

The younger me blinked, surprised that Grandmother had used that name.

"Of course," he said.

"You don't think me terrible, do you?" she asked.

"Of course not. It could not have been easy so long ago."

"As it is not easy now for you," Grandmother said. Her eyes went back to the darkening courtyard and my younger self looked at his watch and said, "It's almost time. I have everything. We can do it just like you taught me."

Ali unzipped a backpack and pulled out the jar, candles, lighter, and slips of paper.

"I... I need to remember her name," Grandmother said. "How could I have forgotten her name?"

This was the moment of destiny. This was why ghosting back to yourself was forbidden. You can alter the timeline. You can create a paradox.

But as the ghost in the room, I was relaxed and unworried. This had already happened when I was young and on the cusp of a change that terrified me just slightly less than not making that change.

As Ali pulled up a stool and arranged things on the windowsill in front of Grandmother, I prepared. It was an odd thing. I had no idea how to do it but I knew it had already been done.

Ali sat next to the old woman and held her hand. When he stilled, I moved close and I...

I don't know how to explain this. I was a ghost, a presence, I had no body and I could not touch my younger self, but that is what I thought about doing, putting my hands on the young Ali's head. Touching me in the past.

I have only written about two trips back in time, but I visited many winter solstices with Abigayle and Terry and I had done a lot of research. I poured that knowledge into the younger me.

At first I felt like nothing, but still I persisted trying to feel what I imagined it would feel like.

Ali shook his head, his overlong bangs falling into his eyes. "What...?" he began.

And then I felt it. I don't know how to describe it besides saying I felt a connection. It was like looking into the eyes of someone you loved. I felt the younger me more viscerally than just a memory and the information flowed.

"Her name..." Ali began to say, his words tentative and a bit slurred like he was in a trance.

"Yes?" Grandmother asked, suddenly more energy in her voice, like she could feel me too and knew this moment was coming.

The younger me swallowed, took a deep breath, and said, "Her name is Terry Grandon and you celebrated your first winter solstice together in 1929 in your bedroom in the attic. The ceremony came from Terry's aunt."

Grandmother blinked and then her eyes welled up with tears. "Yes. Yes. Of course. Damn this mind of mine. I named your mother after her, although your grandfather never knew. How could I forget that? But why didn't she ever come back?"

I stayed like that and poured what I knew into my past-self knowing that this would be hard on Ali. It would be over fifty years until the technology to do this would be created and there would be an explanation. And another fifteen years waiting for my chance to use it.

I poured everything I knew about Abigayle and Terry into Ali, and just one other thing. I let young Ali know that there was a way out of the confusion he was feeling—that it was going to be the hardest thing he would ever do. That soon he would give in and start thinking of himself as a her and follow the difficult steps after that and everything would change for her.

It was a strange experience. I was the older Ali pouring what I could into the younger Ali and remembering what it felt like at the same time.

Matter can't travel through time but energy can. Consciousness can. Spirit can. Ghosts have been seen throughout the centuries. We are those ghosts. And while I remember the confusion as to what was happening as my mind was flooded with thoughts and ideas, I also remember the warmth of it. It felt like I was home, for the very first time.

It changed everything.

I stayed and watched as they welcomed the sun back with the same ceremony Abigayle and Terry had first done in 1929. I said the words I knew so well with them. I too celebrated the return of the sun, so glad for a few more moments with my long-dead grandmother even in her greatly diminished state.

I watched the shift in Ali as she stopped fighting being a her and relaxed into what she was. She smiled and, although I knew better than anyone how far she had to go, it was one of those smiles that says you are glad to be alive and makes those that see it feel the same way.

I watched as she used the information I had fed her and found some old pictures of Terry on her phone. I cried with them as Ali told her that Terry had died suddenly of a brain aneurysm in 1954, two years after grandmother had last seen her and that's why grandmother could not find her in the seventies when she went searching for her. I wept tears of joy as the younger me told her grandmother why she wanted to be called Ali.

This interaction between me and my younger self was a temporal paradox, a causal loop to be specific, forbidden and feared. Much like the realities that the world wasn't ready for what my grandmother and I dealt with.

Grandmother's lucidity soon faded, her eyes dimming, and she said to young Ali, "I believe it's solstice today."

"Yes it is, Grandmother," Ali said, and I was so proud of my younger self for not fighting Grandmother's confusion, not taking on a battle that could not be won and had no benefit.

"I used to celebrate winter solstice with the most lovely woman," Grandmother said.

Ali nodded and smiled. "Yes. You have told me about her," she said. "Her name was Terry Grandon and you loved her very, very much."

Grandmother smiled and suddenly all the wrinkles didn't matter and I saw the much younger woman between the clean sheets sighing and looking up at the sun. I saw that sweet moment of contentment and anticipation returning to her.

She wasn't grieving what couldn't have been, what the world wouldn't yet let be. She was just in that sublime moment of love, celebrating her favorite holiday of the year and remembering someone so very dear to her.

BACKSTORY—A GHOST IN TIME

Holiday: Winter Solstice

Those of you that have read much of my writing know I write a lot of ghost stories, and here I wrote of a different type of ghost, and provided a different explanation for ghosts.

I have also written a volume of time travel stories and this is a different kind of time travel story being so quiet and contemplative.

It's also a different kind of holiday story, revolving around the Winter Solstice like a few other of these.

And, if you've read much of my work you also know I write about grief a lot. I feel it is one of the most integral and universal parts of the human experience and one we aren't that good at talking about.

All of those things came together to create this quiet time travel, ghost, holiday story.

This story was previously published in *Finding Time: Twelve Meticulously Crafted Time Travel Stories.*

PART 8

A HOLLOW EARTH THANKSGIVING

ONE

NOVEMBER 25, 1889

THE MELANCHOLIA THAT DESCENDED ON ME WAS QUITE surprising.

I, Marco Walker, had achieved what few men or women of adventure ever had. I was living in the hollow earth, spending my time under the unblinking central sun, daily discovering things in this strange, dangerous, verdant, volcano-filled land that I had never imagined even a few short months ago.

Gustave Eiffel at the behest of the Hollow Earth Society had sent me down here to rescue Jules Verne who had gotten stranded during his quest to retrieve the golden Scepter of Khufu. This prize was desperately needed to make the finances of the Society whole again and keep the hollow earth a secret. Funds had run dry after Eiffel's daring drilling of a direct path to the hollow earth while he built his marvelous tower above it.

And rescue the hardy Verne, I had, and fallen in love with this strange world within a world.

In the months since, I had slowly established a livable space here, a raised hut that could keep me safe from the plentiful cockroaches that were a foot long and the ubiquitous and always voracious rats that weighed at startling thirty-five pounds or more.

I had found food beyond the French Army rations I was supplied with and even a kind of friendship with Nekta, the highly intelligent creature that lives down here that must be descended from those that the legends of the Yeti and Sasquatch are based upon.

The central sun never moves, so there is no night, and my work here is exhausting, but this is what I live for. And given that I had passed forty years of age, a most feared marker for men of spirit and adventure, and found myself still full of vigor and on this unmatchable adventure, I had nothing to complain about and no reason for melancholia.

It was not the isolation. I have always more needed the open sky and a bounty of unknowns to keep me happy. And besides, I had Nekta to keep me company occasionally and had recently taught her how to play checkers, of which she was quite the natural, besting me more often than not.

My raised hut was in a verdant swath of grassland below one of the great volcanic mountains that dominate this land with thick forest on each side.

That morning, I spent time sitting in my modest hut rereading my journal trying to discover the source of this dreaded melancholia, flipping from page to page, reading of my adventures and the marvels that I had found. But there was nothing until I noticed the date. November 25, 1889. It was nearly Thanksgiving and I had forgotten.

THESE ARE MY PERSONAL JOURNALS, NOT WHAT I HAVE BEEN sending to the surface as part of my work for the Hollow Earth Society. My journals and plant sample go up and supplies come down in Eiffel's most clever contraption he calls *"La Taupe"* or "The Mole." It is an extremely claustrophobic, coal-powered and clockwork-driven contraption that both dug the tunnel through the Earth's crust and conveyed me here. Nekta is not part of those journals as they did not warn me of intelligent life down here and I await a frank discussion with Monsieurs Eiffel and Verne before revealing anything about her.

And since I must not assume what will survive of these journals, I will take pains to describe this most unique environment that I find myself in.

First. We are on the inside of the earth so the land curves up and there is no horizon per se.

That said, because of the extraordinarily dense metal called gravitinium in the middle of the Earth's crust, one's sense of gravity is perfectly normal here.

Second. The atmosphere is much thicker than on the outside and very moist. While there is no horizon, when there is a view, the concave curve of the land disappears into the mist in a most spectacular way.

Third. The central sun at the center of the earth while small is quite close, leaving the temperature warm and fairly constant. And since the sun never moves, it affects everything. No nocturnal animals. Plants that need full sunlight have to be taller than their competitors. And this land, which acts as something like a terrarium, is extraordinary fecund and verdant.

My raised hut sits near the mouth of the tunnel Eiffel's Mole dug through the Earth's crust in a swath of grassy land, a valley below an extraordinarily tall mountain, at least the height of Everest I estimate. Not more than a century or two ago, that mountain was an active volcano and burned away the forest along this swath of land. Tall trees stand as sentinels on either side of the grassy swath but none have invaded yet.

After realizing what I needed was to celebrate Thanksgiving, I gathered my pack, my machete, and my trusty Colt revolver and set out to gather what humble foods I could to create myself a Thanksgiving feast. For this year there was much to be thankful for.

First, I hiked into the foothills of the mountain, careful to watch the skies for the vicious pterodactyls and the ground for the huge feline I had encountered up here previously. By a small creek I dug up some tubers that tasted like a cross between a potato and a turnip. One was enough seeing how a single one of these weighed at least three pounds.

I put it in my pack and followed the creek until I found the bushes I sought with bright red berries the size of a grape. These were not cranberries, to be sure, but they were tart and the closest match I was likely to find. I could cook them with some of my precious sugar and make something worth eating.

From some deciduous trees clinging to the mountain I gathered some nuts. They were rather bitter but edible when roasted.

Very sadly, there would be not pumpkin pie, but my feast was shaping up. Mashed tubers. Tart berry sauce. Some hard bread from the French Army rations. And while I heard the sound of many birds in the jungle and saw them flying overhead from time to time, I had seen no large fowl as of yet. The fresh meat I ate most was the ubiquitous and vicious rat, which was not as unpleasant as it sounds.

Once I made it safely back to my raised hut and thought about the solitary Thanksgiving feast I would prepare with these foodstuffs, my melancholia returned, and much worse than before.

A feast is meant to be shared, especially this one that occurs on this very American holiday. Even though I had spent much of my time away from my country of origin, ever since the ending of the Civil War which I fought in as a young man, I have found it to be the most laudable of holidays and have partaken of it no matter where my adventures took me.

I have celebrated with James Chapman in South Africa. With John Muir in the wilds of Alaska. But celebrating it alone seemed to be wrong and not in keeping with the wonderful spirit of the day.

It was after that dreaded Civil War that Sarah Josepha Hale was able to convince Abraham Lincoln that our torn nation needed a national day of thanks. And of that I could most hardily agree. I may have been considered a young man when I fought in that war, but I was still in my teens, and at the end of the war where our fine country fought itself, I was not young in spirit in the least. After a strife like that a nation and her people need to give thanks for what it has. As did I.

And I have found that no matter where I am in the world, that if I but explain the rationale behind the holiday, that I have many merry companions in giving thanks.

At this, I thought of Nekta and my melancholia lifted. Most assuredly she could understand the need for feasting and giving thanks!

She lived in the forest, exactly where I did not know, but once while high on the mountain, I had seen a tendril of smoke in a small open area of the forest some miles to the east. I was a well-experienced explorer and tracker so I could surely find her and then I would share this holiday with her.

It was too late in my "day" to set out, but I attacked the rest of my chores with a vigor I had not had in weeks.

TWO
NOVEMBER 26, 1889

I set off after breakfasting with a pack containing several days' rations, my trusty Colt Peacemaker on my hip, my machete—you can go nowhere in the hollow earth without one—and the telescoping metal cane that Gustave Eiffel had told me to keep close at all times down here.

I eyed the gray sky above me. I could not see far, being in this valley as I was, but I could discern no building storm. A fine rain had fallen an hour ago and the air smelled moist and was very refreshing.

The hollow Earth has terrifically violent thunderstorms and this metal cane has drawn the lightning away from me and saved my life. It was scarred now and the handle was warped a bit, but a better companion for this land there could not be.

I paused at the edge of the valley, the verdant grasses, ferns, and occasional bushes growing higher than my waist. I had found some grasses that yielded a nutty grain that was edible and reminded me of barley but had yet to fashion a bread worth eating.

My pause was not because I feared death itself, for I had

danced with it many times. Nor was it because I was no longer sure of my mission; it was to celebrate Thanksgiving with another. I paused, as is wise when facing the unknown, and checked in with my head and my heart to make sure this was the best path forward for me.

I gazed at the line of trees in front of me. The trunks were six feet or more across with smooth gray bark. The mighty trees were three hundred feet tall and quite straight with small leaves that were not present until the tops of the tree where they sought direct contact with the light of the central sun.

I could feel it in my gut, that most potent mixture of excitement and fear. This was my path, of that there could be no doubt. I took a deep breath and strode in.

My mission was much harder than it might seem at first. I had seen Nekta exit the jungle more than once. I had tracked her in the grassy valley before we met when she was watching me. And she always exited the forest in a different spot.

While I knew roughly where her encampment was likely to be, there was no trail I could follow and no landmark to guide me.

Under the canopy of the forest, things changed suddenly and dramatically. While the light of the central sun is blunted by the moist air, in the forest it is suddenly like the twilight that never comes in this land.

The grasses are gone but the oversized ferns remain as well as a collection of bushes, mosses and other small plants that can thrive in the dim light.

The monstrous gray trees have thick vines dangling down that use the trees' height to spread themselves out and I see some rather normal-looking monkeys using these to climb the massive trees as I enter, squeaking in their play. There are also other smaller trees. These with a dark rough bark and huge pale-green leaves designed for the scant light. It is these smaller trees that I have been harvesting to build with.

I have sometimes called this a forest and at other times a jungle. In truth, it will take a skilled naturalist to determine the proper nomenclature. It was verdant, to be sure, but the trees were placed well apart and the bare, fertile ground was often visible.

The air was slightly moist and smelled strongly of that most glorious perfume that only occurs in an ancient forest. It was the scent of plants decomposing, of the forest renewing itself, of the plentiful moisture the plants held. It was the smell of life itself.

I, of course, wore the stinking concoction Verne had taught me about and Nekta had helped me refine to keep the cockroaches and other insects away, but I had been wearing it long enough that my nose could smell beyond its fetid bouquet.

And while the light was dim, the wind high above would move the leaves and a shaft of brilliant white light would come spiking down from time to time adding unexpected brilliance to the dark space.

The sound of birdsong was plentiful and that of the playing monkeys, but no other sounds greeted my ears. None of the roars that I had heard before from far away.

I stood still and let my ears take in the sound and let my eyes adjust to the dim light and felt the melancholia completely lift.

So it was with great relief that I strode into the forest seeking someone to give thanks with.

With my compass as guide—yes it still works in this strange land, the Earth's magnetic field intact down here—I headed east deeper into the forest. I walked slowly with care as if I had entered a stranger's house, not wanting to disturb anything without their permission.

My plan was simple. While Nekta used a different path out of the forest each time she came to visit me, near her home there must be signs of her. I was of a mind to penetrate deep in the forest until I found such sign or until it felt like half the "day" had passed me by.

This might sound like a sure recipe for boredom to you, but not to me. For the forest was endlessly fascinating.

The land itself was rarely flat, sloping from higher to lower across my path. There were volcanic rocks—dark and craggy basalt—bursting out of the ground. And, most interestingly, there were signs of animal life. Tracks. Scat. Endless birdsong, monkey grunts, and other sounds not so easily defined.

I am an explorer not a naturalist, but still it is not lost on me how similar the fauna of the hollow earth is to its counterpart on the outside. How very similar and how very different. There is a much smaller variety of flora, most of it is significantly larger than on the outside, and some of the adaptations clearly for the unmoving central sun, but it was all quite familiar.

And the fauna is similar too. For example, along the edge of the forest I found the prints of a large cloven-hooved creature which I thought might be wild boar. And, as with most things here, an unusually large specimen.

I crossed babbling creeks full of cool, fresh water. I climbed rocky outcroppings and sat and watched and listened and made notes in my journal of landmarks in case I would need them to exit this forest. I found open areas, blistered and burned, where the most violent thunderstorms of this land made themselves known. There, I took off my Stetson and I let the light of the central sun shine on me, quite surprised to find that I had missed it.

After an hour or two of this, I began to think my fear of the strange sounds I had heard were overwrought. But I held them close, nonetheless. Long experience had taught me that the unknown was, by its very nature, always full of surprises.

It was as I took a drink from another creek that the hair on the back of my neck raised. It was nothing I heard or saw or smelled, but something much more primal than that. I was being hunted.

And I was as unknown to the hunter as this land was to me. So it was being careful. What sense I had of it was so subtle that I could not tell you exactly what had given it away, but something had.

It was trying to determine what kind of danger I was. And while I wrote early that I did not fear death, that did not mean that I desired it. Death comes to all men and women, the great and the common alike. I've seen enough of it to know that one day it will come for me despite my skill and care. And yet I was determined that this would not be the day. That I would not become another creature's Thanksgiving feast.

Smokey fires kept the rats at bay. The salve featuring the stinking flower that grows here keeps the giant cockroaches, mosquitoes, and other insects away. But I knew there were predators that were not so easily deterred. The monstrously huge feline that Nekta and I faced, the pterodactyls that flew in the sodden sky, whatever roared deep in the jungle, and whatever predator stalked me now.

While I had been cataloging hiding spots as I walked, I began to make a much more earnest inventory. Which trees had a handy vine dangling down that I could use to get off the ground.

Which pile of boulders had likely hiding places where I

would rather face rats or insects than whatever this clever thing was.

This was a land of plenty if one was merely hungry. But this creature sought the unknown prey, sought the thrill of the hunt, sought me.

And I had to give it its due and a large measure respect. In the quarter of an hour since I knew I was being hunted, I had only heard the quiet crack of a twig two times to further give it away. It seemed the large roars where not of great concern for if they were the kinds of creatures I suspected, I was a mere morsel for them and they would seek bigger prey. No, it was this thing that hunted me that caused Nekta to warn me away from this forest.

I could turn and try to make it back out of the forest, but this creature was far too clever. I could climb a tree and gain the high ground waiting for it to reveal itself, but that left me open to it gathering its kin or other dangers.

So after a brief time, where I checked my trusty Colt and refreshed myself with a sip from my canteen, I did what it least expected. I ran.

MY PLAN WAS SIMPLE. ACT LIKE SCARED PREY SO MY stalker acted like a victorious predator and reveal itself.

Yes, this would give me scant moments to defend myself, but I was betting that whatever this creature was, it did not understand the power of gunpowder and lead. And I would rather know my danger and face it than to be worn down over time.

As I ran, I finally heard and saw signs of the predator and, much to my surprise and more than a little chagrin, it was not one creature hunting me but many.

Those snaps of twigs had been a ruse of these clever beasts designed to convince me that there was only one.

I did not see them clearly, just flashes of dark gray fur running fast on both my flanks. The beasts were big, about four or five feet tall and there had to be at least five of them.

While my trusty Colt was up to the task of two or three, what I faced was beyond its capability. Six rounds was not enough to dispatch five or more wild beasts in motion.

As they ran, as I ran, my views of them were fleeting but because of their speed and long legs I did not think they could climb. So I holstered my Colt keeping my machete in hand and looked for a tree I could climb.

I soon found one of the great gray-barked ones with a dangling vine that should work. I changed my course which was greeted with a sharp bark and I knew this was a pack of canines that hunted me and they knew my intent and what it meant to their meal.

I redoubled my efforts and ran as fast as I could, as did they. And while they were much faster than I, I didn't have far to go. I heard them close behind me, the sound of their rapid, excited breath making my skin crawl, but I made it to the tree which had a large boulder in front of it. I used my momentum and ran up the boulder, tossed my machete behind me, hoping to slow my pursuers, grabbed the vine, yanked myself up, and started climbing. To my great relief the thick vine was as strong as it looked and I pulled myself clear just as multiple jaws snapped where my feet had just been.

I did not look back, not yet. Perhaps these beasts had strong hooked claws like the fox and could climb some after all. Perhaps I had misjudged them with my fleeting impressions. In any case, I wanted to be far up the tree before looking at my pursuers.

I was approximately twelve feet off the ground when the vine twisted suddenly around to the other side of the tree putting me in a most awkward position. To my considerable delight, I then found something odd. A groove had been hewn into the side of the tree that was a perfect handhold and would take me to where the vine was easily reachable again.

I did not question my good fortune, but used the notch and pulled myself up, my breath coming fast, my heart beating hard, feeling that bright sense of aliveness one feels when facing imminent death.

After the Civil War, while I had had more than my fill of killing, I have to admit that I found myself enamored with the experience of surviving. There is no other moment when I feel more alive, more awake, more free. It is what drove me into the wilds of the world and ultimately what led me to accept Gustave Eiffel's offer and, despite my rather violent claustrophobia, allowed him to lock me in his rumbling, stinking, coffin of a Mole for two days for the harrowing journey down to this place.

So as I climbed, I feared but I also reveled in the fearsome creatures getting further away below me.

And they were none too pleased. Snarling and barking, yips of disappointment accompanying my climb.

Still I hadn't looked but there could be no doubt that these were the hollow earth's canines and fierce and exceptionally intelligent hunters they were.

There were several more well placed grooves carved into the smooth bark and I grew more curious about it. Soon I came to the biggest surprise of all, a grouping of rare branches over a hundred feet up the tree where a low platform had been built of smaller branches and secured to the tree with some fibrous plant like jute. It was not a roomy platform or comfortable, but it was easily big enough for me.

With survival assured—at least for the moment—I studied the forest from this new perspective and drank from my canteen truly thankful to be alive.

THERE WERE EIGHT OF THEM, THESE HOLLOW EARTH canines that had chased me up a tree. They were big, about four feet tall at the shoulder and weighing somewhere on the order of 175 pounds. Their build seemed to be that of the greyhound with thin torsos, long powerful legs, and short, course fur a mottled gray. But their head and their upright ears reminded me more of wolves.

They had protested for a time, but had quickly settled down and were resting much as I was, perhaps deciding if I was worth the wait.

While they were of interest, this platform and what it meant was of much greater interest.

My simple plan to penetrate the forest until I found signs of Nekta's passage had been destined for failure now that I found this. Nekta did not walk on the forest floor. Nekta traveled up in the trees.

For it wasn't only a platform up here, but a thick, living vine that was wrapped around the trunk. This vine joined the top of a tree maybe a hundred and fifty feet distant with the middle of this tree. The vine was oversized like most other things in the hollow earth, four or five inches in diameter with large leaves spaced frequently.

Looking at the arrangement I was quite sure that Nekta had the strength to climb this, and perhaps I did too but not for too many lengths like this. But as I studied it, I noticed that high in this tree another vine reached to about the midpoint of that other tree.

I smiled at her cleverness and her dedication, for it must have taken years to cultivate the forest and grow the vines thus. I cannot imagine that these vines joined these trees like this naturally. But it was the most perfect, if slow and a bit arduous, way to travel in safety.

I knew these hollow earth canines would not be making a meal of me as I continued climbing the tree to reach that higher vine.

I AM NOT A YOUNG MAN ANYMORE AND WHILE I AM STILL strong, I am not as strong as Nekta or built like the monkeys I have seen using these vines.

I had the example of Jules Verne, who at sixty-one came down here and recovered the Scepter of Khufu and would have made it out of here without aid if not for the damnable rats and the injuries he received from their repeated attacks. So I knew there was much more adventuring that I could do. But if the truth be told, I don't think Jules Verne spent his time several hundred feet in the air clinging to a vine and moving hand over hand down them in an imitation of what simians do so easily.

As I dangled and sweated, I felt the heavy weight of all my years, and quickly.

The canines merrily tagged along watching me as if I were their entertainment before their meal. They were waiting for me to slip and fall. And that just might be a more pleasant ending, letting the fall kill me before the beasts consumed me.

Two hours and some dozen traversals later, I sat in another platform halfway up another tree snacking on some French Army rations—quite good as these things go—contemplating my melancholia and the desire to celebrate Thanksgiving with another being.

My impulse was similar to the pilgrims at Plymouth Rock, to celebrate the season—even if there are no seasons in the hollow earth—with those native to this realm.

But things did not turn out well for those natives and history has shown that the pilgrims did not have the best of intentions. While the spirit of the holiday is most wholesome, I was wrong to try to bring it to Nekta. We could communicate, after a fashion. She knew a smattering of French and I had taught her more. She had taught me some of her strange words that came from languages I could not recognize, but a concept as abstract as a day of thanksgiving would be difficult to convey at this point and would benefit me and not her.

While my melancholia did not return, this realization deepened my fatigue. I set about trying to find a way to sleep on the platform. I could not lie down comfortably, but I could bind myself to the trunk of the tree with rope from my pack and let my tired body rest.

I set about doing this as my canine companions below settled in too.

THREE
NOVEMBER 27, 1889

I FIND THAT THE SLEEP AFTER A CLOSE BRUSH WITH DEATH to be exceedingly sweet. Even sitting on a hard platform made of branches high in the air while bound to a large tree with a length of rope.

I did not dream but was cradled in the sweet succor of nothingness. No worries, no cares, just the deepest of sleep. It is a skill I acquired in that terrible war and has served me well. I can sleep easily and deeply and I can awaken quickly.

And that is what happened here. Through the darkness of unconsciousness, I heard a plaintive whining, high-pitched and filled with such need that it tugged at my heart. No creature should be this bereft.

I opened my eyes to the eternal twilight of the forest, my nose greeted by the loamy scent of it and my eyes seeing no movement. With some difficulty because of their mottled gray fur, I could spot my sleeping companions below and they were not moving.

And yes, they were in truth hunting me, but in my mind, I had begun to think of them as companions, as souls whose lives had merit and value. I had no desire to kill them, only a desire to not be killed.

I heard the whining again. It was coming from deeper in the forest. I untied my bonds and stowed the rope. Flexing my shoulders and feeling the deep soreness yesterday's activities had earned me. My companions noticed too, the largest one—the alpha, I presume—raising itself and giving a low, menacing growl.

I moved into a crouch, for some reason feeling that this development would require me to move and quickly, and just watched. I saw ferns move, heard a twig snap, and then another whine, this time closer.

Now that I heard it clearly, the whine was that of a canine. What was this? Was it the ruse of some clever creature come seeking a meal out of those that sought a meal out of me?

I watched and waited, feeling my heart speed up and my body preparing to respond even though I was over a hundred feet above whatever was about to happen.

It did not take long, perhaps two minutes, but it felt much longer. Soon another canine emerged from behind a dense grouping of ferns, this one thin and looked old, its short fur lighter, its gait marred by a bad limp. It was clearly injured.

The alpha did not hesitate, a growl rumbling out of it as it leapt forward and attacked the other canine. This was not as I expected. In my mind I was likening these creatures to the outer earth's wolves who tend to be very caring of their injured pack-mates. Was this just a canine from another pack injured and desperate for help? Or where these canine so very different from wolves?

Whatever was happening here, I could not idly stand by and let this poor creature be slain by one of its own. I pulled my Colt out and I fired into the air.

The sound of it was out of place in this grand forest, almost obscene. There was silence for a moment while the beings that heard it tried to fathom its import. The alpha jumped back from the injured canine which was motionless on the forest floor. It swiveled its head, its upright ears seeking the source.

The forest was completely quiet, all birds had ceased their singing and all monkeys had stopped their calls. There was no breeze to speak of and everything was utterly still.

I did not let the alpha wonder at the source of the noise. I aimed carefully and fired again, letting my shout join the noise of the gun.

"Git!" I yelled, the sound of my voice and the gunshot echoing through the trees.

The alpha jumped but remained uninjured, my bullet finding its mark a few feet to the left of him.

"Git!" I yelled again and fired again, this time the bullet kicking up dirt quite close to him.

They were confused and I could not blame them and I had no intention of letting that confusion abate. I kept firing, landing bullets close to multiple canines until my gun was empty and they were yelping and running away deep into the forest.

I BELIEVE IN MY INSTINCTS. IN FACING LIFE AND DEATH ON my own terms. In listening to my heart and my mind. What man, woman, or creature is complete without the balancing influence of both heart and mind.

My mind told me I was insane, but my heart would brook no argument and I soon found myself with that injured canine sewing it up and then binding its wounds and fashioning something of a litter out of some particularly large ferns and some ready branches from one of the smaller trees.

The beast was skinny, emaciated even, but it was wiry and

strong and had very long legs. It tried to rouse itself as I sewed, but the gash on its shoulder where the alpha's teeth had sunk into it was just too much. The smallest of growls rumbled out of her and then she lapsed into unconsciousness.

Yes, it was a she and I was no longer convinced of her age. She just might be young, only her injuries and frailties making her look old. Because of the difference in the coloring of her coat, it seemed she was not of the same pack as the ones that hunted me.

Once the litter was ready, I paused. Perhaps this creature did this knowing that the other pack would dispatch it quickly. Perhaps the alpha considered this a kindness. I had delivered such kindness to animals with my Colt on numerous occasions.

But my heart would not listen so I used my mind to keep myself safe and a good thing that was, for the rats smelled the blood and came crawling out of the forest before we were ready to be off.

My machete had been dropped quite some distance from here and all I had was my Colt and my telescoping metal cane. So I put both to good use. I drew the cane out until it was a good three feet long and made sure its end was still sharp. While I had only faced these rats in ones and twos, this was group of a dozen or more and I would be hard-pressed to defend the injured canine and survive myself.

I must remind you that these rats weighed forty pounds and were armed with long sharp claws and deadly fangs. They were quite different than any rat on the outside.

The cane, once adjusted, made a passable sword and I used it as such, dashing to and fro and stabbing the greasy brown fur of these beasts and feeling not one bit of pity as they squealed in agony.

My Colt I saved for grave need when two or more were upon me as I danced around the injured canine. At one point, I heard her growl and saw her try to get up and join the fray. It did my heart good to see that the noble creature still had fight left in her.

Their numbers were great but I was fighting for something besides my own survival and that animated me with a vigor of a man of many fewer years and I soon dispatched them finding myself covered in sweat and having received two bites to my left leg. Nothing serious, just two more bites added to the many I have received in my tenure here in the hollow earth.

With the rats vanquished, I finished my preparations, using my rope to secure the canine to the litter and creating a crude harness that wrapped around my chest. We set off back toward my home with the briefest of detours to retrieve my machete.

I won't bore you with the details and travails of my journey home with my heavy burden. Suffice it to say that many more rats died and I had to apply a liberal portion of Verne's stinking salve to kept the enormous cockroaches away from us. I have written about these beasts multiple times and do not wish to try your patience.

I will say that when we broke free of the twilight of the forest, I was never so glad to see the hazy yellow ball of the central sun hanging in the eternally gray sky straight above us.

"Things are looking up now, *Chienne*," I said as I took a breath, removing my hat, and wiping my sweaty brow with a handkerchief.

I will admit that "chienne" was not a clever word for the creature I was dragging behind me. Chienne is merely the French word for a female dog. But, the word being French, it did have some magic to it, much better than calling her "dog."

It also had the benefit of being a single syllable and despite all those letters in French being fairly simple to pronounce. In English you might spell it as "Shenn."

Chienne did not move and for a moment I feared my efforts had been for naught, but I studied her nearly inert form and saw her chest rise and fall. I had gazed on her enough that I was now reminded of the hound our family had when I was a boy and life was simple. The memory harkened to a simpler and innocent time and the feeling was quite welcome.

My mind still told me that this might not be the right thing, that I would have to be very careful to earn her trust and not fall victim to those sharp teeth and strong jaw. But Thanksgiving would be here in just a matter of hours and my heart would have it no other way.

FOUR
NOVEMBER 28, 1889

THIS HAS BEEN A THANKSGIVING LIKE NO OTHER. Difficult and trying, and I am far short on sleep, but it has been most rewarding.

Using the pulley system I have setup at the hut, I got the unconscious Chienne into the raised shelter which is eight feet off the ground and tended her and her wounds all night, sleeping only here and there for I had much to do.

I skinned and dressed the rat that had attacked us on the way in and set a pot boiling on my cook fire that is down on the ground and put some bone broth on for my new companion and some fresh meat roasting for me.

I harvested grass to make a bed for her and to give her a place to relieve herself that was easy to clean up. I redressed her wounds, splint her front right leg which was likely fractured, and applied some healing salve from my stores and then, finally, dressed my own bites properly.

She first awoke shortly after my clever calendar clock ticked over to a new day, this special day. The ground rumbled, which it often does when a large and distant volcano erupts, and she raised her head and saw me, letting out the fiercest growl she was capable of in her weakness, which was not much, her fierce yellow eyes fixed upon me. But then her nose began to work as the scent of the meat and broth reached her.

I was ready with some cooled broth in a plain brown ceramic bowl and eased it across the crude wood floor to her with the cane.

My hut is fairly generously sized, twelve feet to a side, for soon there will be others down here with me. I lack the tools to mill lumber so all is made out of the trunks or branches of smaller trees, an oiled canvas tarp serving as the roof, metal from a damaged Mole creating a sturdy lightning rod which has seen much use.

There are windows on all sides, propped open since there was no storm. It was a crude but hardy shelter, but to her it must have been most strange.

Her thirst won out and she lapped some of the bone broth her eyes never leaving me. After she had her fill, she lay down, her eyes open and staring at me but they did not stay open long and she was soon sleeping.

THIS WAS OUR DAY. I WOULD GO OUT AND TEND TO THINGS when she slept and feed her broth and bits of meat when she awoke.

I ate bits and pieces but had no feast. Tending for this noble creature was the only feast I needed.

I slept in snatches after restringing my hammock to be high off the floor, too high for the lame canine to reach me.

Each time she awoke and saw me, she stared at me with those yellow eyes and growled.

Each time I tended to her needs, I thought I saw those eyes soften just a touch.

If you have seen war, like I have, you know what thankfulness truly is. It is another day living and breathing. It is another day where you do not have to take a life. It is the simple comforts of food and shelter and being of use to another being.

I have watched my beloved Thanksgiving change, where people give thanks for their bounty but not their burdens and their troubles, which to my mind misses the point. If you but find thankfulness in your heart for that which you do not desire, does not life become all the sweeter for it? Can not each day be a gift then?

My companion for this Thanksgiving may just be an injured, wild, and distrustful canine in this hollow earth far from my home and the home of the holiday that I cherish so much, but I could not have asked for a more satisfying celebration of it.

I do not know if Chienne and I will become friends. I do even not know if I will be able to heal her fully and let her return to her home.

This is not what matters. We do not control the fates, we can only do our best with what they bring us. And the fates brought me Chienne and I could not be more thankful.

BACKSTORY—A HOLLOW EARTH THANKSGIVING

Holiday: Thanksgiving

Thanksgiving is my favorite winter holiday. Hands down. Probably because it's about great food and being with people you love without the pressures of gift giving and the other trappings some of these winter holidays come with. And, of course, it's about giving thanks, which is always something worth doing.

I know families can be challenging, even on Thanksgiving, and at times it can feel like more of a burden than many of us want. But what if you found yourself alone on your favorite holiday? Really and truly alone.

This story was written in November of 2020 during the COVID pandemic and the isolated feeling of Thanksgiving that year definitely influenced the story. It's not surprising that I was drawn to writing about my most isolated character.

These hollow earth stories are fun to write because they are truly old-fashioned adventure yarns. They are also rather challenging to write because of the old-fashioned part. Reproducing Marco's voice, which is very different from my own, and trying to be honest to the era is challenging and that makes it super rewarding.

This story first appeared in the 2021 WMG Holiday Spectacular. It has since been reprinted in *A Weird Holiday Season: A Holiday Anthology* and has a stand-alone edition. There are three of these hollow earth stories out with one more in the works and you can find out more at: *RobertJMcCarter.com/HollowEarth*

PART 9
GHOSTED

GHOSTED

I've been ghosted.

I know, kind of ironic considering that I am a ghost, but there you have it.

I met the woman of my dreams, fell hard, made a terrible mistake, and now she's just gone, probably in danger, and it's all my fault.

But I'm getting ahead of myself. Let me start at the beginning, it all began at an amazing Thanksgiving feast.

Carol and I bumped into each other at the Fraklin Family Thanksgiving Extravaganza—that's what they called it. They even had sweatshirts emblazoned with it.

Most of you reading this are probably alive so you might not think that "bumping" into someone is special or unusual and that's because you all still have a body and it happens as a matter of course. Bumping into someone when you're a ghost? It's a million-to-one kind of thing, which I'll explain in a minute.

The Fraklin Family Thanksgiving Extravaganza was a highly sought after event in the graveyard. The Fraklin family was large so there would be upwards of thirty people in attendance, a number of them very good cooks, and one of them a chef, so the food was to die for.

Not that we could eat it, since we were already dead, but if you were going to be a ghostly voyeur at a Thanksgiving feast, well, this was the one.

The entire affair on the afterlife side was organized and rather bureaucratic. You had to apply for a spot, get approved, and then be there for your appointed window, not one minute before or one minute after.

You are probably wondering how someone might stop you when you are a ghost and can fly through walls, and it all comes down to culture and civility. The afterlife is long and it's a good idea to do your best to get along with your fellow earthbound spirits.

But I got a slot, the coveted "carving of the turkey" slot. Me and six other ghosts crowded around Henry Franklin as he ritualistically stroked the knife over the sharpening stick as he prepared for his sacred duty.

Henry was in his sixties dressed in a bowtie with bright green eyes and ruddy cheeks. He had on the sweatshirt, of course, but that wasn't formal enough for him and he had a button-down shirt on underneath with the bowtie sticking out.

Henry had a considerable girth and he was growing his grey beard out for the upcoming Franklin Christmas Extravaganza where he would aptly play the role of Santa. He wasn't the oldest here, but this was his house and he was clearly the patriarch.

He finished honing the knife with broad, dramatic strokes, took a step forward towards the huge and perfectly roasted turkey on the end of the long table in front of him, and all chatter stopped and all eyes were on him.

Henry's son Ethan, the chef, had prepared the turkey, and even though I was a ghost and couldn't take a bite or even smell it, it looked so golden brown, so juicy, so delicious, that my mouth almost watered.

There were thirty-one living onlookers, all wearing that sweatshirt, whose mouths were watering, ranging in age from eighty-eight to two. Well, the two-year-old was asleep, but you get the picture.

This long table looked like it was out of a magazine or part of a movie set, like the cornucopia of the gods had spilled forth dishes ranging from sweet potato pie to homemade cranberry sauce to stuffing to gravy. This was the feast of the year at the Franklin house and the carving of the turkey was the starting gun for the festivities.

Henry put the knife to the turkey and there were a few sharp intakes of breath, but this was just a feint to throw off the younger ones—the adults knew how this dance went. He stood up straight and said, "But first we must pray and give thanks." He nodded to his daughter, Paige, who was a Methodist minister. "If you will do us the honors, dear."

It was then that I backed up—I wanted to get a better view of the carving—and bumped into someone.

Now, I've been dead long enough to know that such things don't happen, but I was so focused on the festivities that I had almost forgotten that I was dead, my memories of Thanksgivings past filling in the blanks of my limited ghostly senses, the memory of past aromas making it seem more real.

"Excuse me," I said, looking to my side and seeing a woman standing there.

The woman I bumped into was not old and not young, her

round face decorated with a few fine wrinkles. It was her eyes that captured me. They were blue, decorated with delicate crow's feet and showed untold depth of both joy and sorrow. I couldn't help myself, I started. There was just something about her.

Her long black hair cascaded over her shoulders and she wore a silky blue dress that matched her eyes perfectly. She was beautiful, but not in the perfectly symmetrical way that movie stars are, she was beautiful in a well-worn, practical kind of way, if that makes any sense. Or let me put it this way, she was beautiful in a way that both caught my attention and seemed right, somehow, right for me.

And at first I didn't notice and didn't care whether she was living or dead, just that she was new and I didn't know her.

Paige was praying, giving thanks for the feast, all living eyes were closed. Sometimes, I think maybe that was part of the magic of that bump, that it happened in a moment of gratitude during a day built for gratitude.

"Excuse me," she said, almost at the same time as I did, and we both laughed.

And just when I noticed that she was slightly transparent, and dead like me, surprise blossomed on her face at the same time I'm sure it showed on mine.

Let me explain. We are ghosts, and although we look like we have bodies, we most certainly do not. We are ethereal, we are gossamer, we are less substantial than a light breeze.

Normally when you run into another ghost you go right through them, although there is often a slight tingling sensation.

Technically, we are localized emanations of electromagnetic energy emitting at very high frequencies.

Yeah. This is science, not my area but other ghosts have explained it better. It's how this "typewriter for ghosts" I am telling you this story with works. It detects those very high-level emanations and lets me communicate with you directly.

And that's the key to this little miracle at the Fraklin Family Thanksgiving Extravaganza. Ghosts can touch, if they work at it, and match their frequencies. Each ghost, quite naturally, operates at a frequency that is uniquely theirs, one that can change with time, mood, or effort.

So bumping into another ghost accidently was a million-to-one. Bumping into someone as beautiful as this ghost, a ghost I had never met? I can't even hazard a guess at the odds.

"That was..." I began.

"Unexpected," she finished.

As Paige continued to pray, I felt something I hadn't felt since I was alive. Intrigued. Delighted. And most of all, hopeful.

THE FRANKLIN TURKEY WAS BEING CARVED, BUT I DIDN'T care. Distantly I could hear the chatter of the living, the clatter of silverware against china, some laugher, and the toddler starting to fuss, but none of that mattered.

"Umm..." I began, suddenly remembering not only what it had been like to be alive, but what it had been like to be a teenager. "Well... I..."

The woman smiled and by God she was even more beautiful, her cheeks rising and her blue eyes sparking. "My name is Carol," she said extending her hand and initiating the greeting ritual of ghosts everywhere. "Carol Franklin, and I died while on safari in Kenya when I was bit by a black mamba snake."

I blinked in reaction, but not having eyes it was just a holdover from my long lost biology. I knew what was next, but I couldn't beat that death story. At least the mystery of her presence was solved. She was family and not part of the bureaucratic nonsense I went through to get in.

"Right," I said. "My name is Barry O'Neil. I died in a traffic accident."

We shook hands and surprise once again blossomed on her face, echoing exactly what I was feeling. There was no adjusting frequencies, there was no trying. We could just touch.

And sure, it was that very numb, barely there feeling of touch us dead are afforded, but somehow it felt like more.

"Nice to meet you, Barry," she said.

"Very nice to meet you, Carol," I said.

And then we just stood there staring at each other while the feasting commenced and I didn't feel self-conscious or care one little bit how I looked. As long as I could look at Carol's lovely face, everything was OK by me.

I had found another ghost in this huge world that ran on the same frequency as I did, nothing else seemed to matter.

I REALLY CAN'T TELL YOU A THING ABOUT WHAT HAPPENED at the Fraklin Family Thanksgiving Extravaganza after I met Carol. There was only her. There was only our conversation. There was only me wanting to touch her again to confirm the miracle of our matching frequencies.

"I was a reporter," she said some minutes later, once I was able to ask a salient question. "I was doing a piece on climate change in Africa, how alternating droughts and floods are having an outsized effect on the people there, how it's only going to get worse. What did you do?"

I couldn't match this woman. Not her looks. Not how she died. Not what she did for a living. She was out of my league by a mile. All I had was that matching frequency thing so I just stuck with the humble truth.

"I was a 'package delivery driver' for UPS," I said with a

shrug. "I was working when I died. I'm usually dressed in that boring UPS brown, but I dressed up for the occasion."

Ghosts, of course, don't wear clothing, but with effort and practice we can alter our appearance, but most ghosts tend to default to what they most commonly wore. I had lightened my usual brown button-down shirt, removed the logo, and added a tie.

"Nice," she said. "I dressed up too."

"I noticed," I said, and she looked away shyly. Didn't she know she was gorgeous? And if she didn't, that made her even more attractive.

"Times up, Barry," a brawny ghost named Kent said. "Next shift is coming in. Head on out. You got thirty seconds. No closer than a hundred yards from the Franklin property."

Kent was kind of a bouncer. Each ghost has different aptitudes, and if I didn't leave he would remove me and there wasn't a thing I could do about it.

My mouth opened and I tried to find some words, any words, to express what I was feeling to Carol, but I found myself mute.

"It was really nice meeting you, Barry," she said extending her hand.

I took it and it was effortless, again. "Can we...? I mean..." I stammered.

"I'd like that," she said. "How about I find you for Solstice?"

"You can..." I began.

She nodded, and with a "pop" was three feet away, and then with another "pop" she was right next to me. Some ghosts are good at traveling instantly from point to point and you can pop to a destination or a person, and she was clearly very good at it. I had tried but couldn't do it, at all. But at least she had my number, in a manner of speaking.

Kent was hovering, literally, close by. My time was almost up. "Great," I said. "I'll find us something special."

She smiled and nodded, her eyes crinkling up again and said, "Looking forward to it."

It had never seemed so long between Thanksgiving and Solstice. Seriously. I've had years pass quicker.

My promise to find "something special" for Solstice haunted me. In the moment, I forgot that I do the same thing every Solstice. I watch over my living nephew George, which seemed rather mundane to me and not proper second date material.

I asked around the graveyard about Carol Franklin but no one knew much. One ghost, a real old-timer who used to be a mailman, remembered the name. Told me she was a cousin and not from here.

That left me with three plus weeks to worry and wonder and worry some more.

When Solstice came, I "changed" into my tie—really just focused on it for a while until my outsides matched my vision what I wanted to look like—and flew off to my usual Solstice celebration. I waited for Carol on the roof of a seventies-era single-story cinder-block home in an older neighborhood.

It looked like it was a cold evening with a few flurries of snow lazily floating down, some sticking to the branches of the bare deciduous trees showing promises of winter to come.

I was there by 5 p.m. and it wasn't until six that I started to worry. We hadn't set a time. When was she planning to be here? What if she had met a more interesting ghost, our matching frequencies be damned?

At eight, I was getting rather restless and started pacing the roof. At nine, I felt bad about not being in the house with my nephew, but I knew the real fun wouldn't start until after eleven. By ten I was so nervous I couldn't maintain my "fancy" outfit, and if you could have seen me it would have looked like a slightly transparent UPS guy was pacing back and forth on the roof.

I began to doubt myself, an old habit that survived my death. I wasn't a very impressive person.

I had driven a big panel van for a living, going door to door delivering packages. I was nearly forty when I died and I still played D&D on Sundays with my nephew and some friends. I had been hooked on video games. I wasn't athletic unless you call being a decent disc golf player being athletic. I had been engaged once, but never married. No kids. What did I have to offer a globe-trotting reporter?

"Is this about me?" a feminine voice softly asked.

I'm not proud of it, but I jumped. Like I had just seen a ghost —which I had—and let out a very unmanly squeak. I had been so lost in my thoughts that I hadn't heard her pop in.

"Yes," I said, with a grin that I am sure looked sheepish.

"You were afraid I wouldn't show?" she asked.

I nodded but didn't dare say a thing.

"That's cute," she said, her cheeks flushing just a touch red. She looked around and asked, "Where are we?"

"My nephew's house," I said. It was after eleven and I could feel midnight approaching. We all can feel midnight, it's when the dead feel the most alive. "I... well... it's just what I do on Solstice, not that special. I would understand if you—"

Her smile cut me off as she walked across the roof towards me. "I'm sure it will be fine." She held her hand out towards me palm up, the invitation clear.

I put my hand against hers without a thought of frequencies or electromagnetic radiation and... it worked! Our hands met and I could feel her. Again. Effortlessly.

"That is..." I began.

"Amazing," she finished.

THEY WERE READY FOR US IN THE HOUSE.

The lights were off and about a dozen candles were lit and incense was burning. My nephew George, his girlfriend Tasha, and George's best friend Oliver sat on the floor huddled around a Ouija board in the center of the modest living room. Generic new age style music softly played.

"What...?" Carol began.

I smiled and saw this with fresh eyes. Sure this was normal to me, but not to anyone else.

"My nephew," I said nodding at the dark-haired young man with glasses. "He loves magic. Was a Houdini freak. We got drunk one night and he made me promise that if I died I would find a way to contact him like Houdini promised his wife."

Her mouth was open and I laughed because now she was the one that couldn't find any words.

This was back before the SECI chamber, this typewriter for ghosts had just been invented, but no one really knew about it. Back before the world changed when the living didn't actually know the dead were here, didn't have proof.

"How do they know," she asked. "I mean, you know, tonight is..."

As I mentioned, ghosts feel most alive at midnight, and the night we feel most alive all year is Winter Solstice, the longest night of the year. I know Halloween and Día de Muertos get all the press, but the longest night of the year is more powerful for the dead.

"His father died five years before I did," I said. "Really ripped him up. He got interested in the occult, starting messing with the Ouija boards and reading the weirdest books." I shrugged. "Grief is strange, affects us all in different ways. I never tried to stop him. He had read something about the Winter

Solstice and ghosts told me if I died that he would be listening for me every Solstice."

"Are you ready?" George asked the other two.

They gave solemn nods.

"Will he... Is he...?" Oliver stammered. He had curly red hair and a round face with pronounced smile lines.

"It's real," Tasha whispered, her black hair woven into dark locks, the flickering candlelight illuminating her dark eyes. "I swear it. Uncle Barry has been here the last three years."

George nodded solemnly.

"Wait..." Carol said. "Do you...? Can you...?"

I smiled and nodded. "George picked the right night. I don't know how, but it actually works."

She smiled and suddenly it was like the room wasn't dark but the sun was shining brightly. She clapped her hands like an excited little girl and asked, "Can I help? Please, Barry. Let me help!"

I'M ASSUMING YOU ARE FAMILIAR WITH A OUIJA BOARD. It consists of a plastic pointer shaped like a rounded arrowhead that everyone lightly puts their fingers on, that slides around a board pointing out letters, numbers, or simple phrases like "yes" or "no."

It was created so the dead could talk to the living, not that many people really believed it.

That Solstice the three living had their fingers on the pointer as well as us two ghosts.

There was a lot of questions for Oliver's sake to prove the ghosts guiding this were real. Oliver held his fingers up behind his back and asked the board what the number was.

We got it right three times, but he still wasn't buying it, thinking it was a trick.

The best question and answer of the night was when George asked, "Should Tasha and I get married?"

The answer Carol and I guided them to was, "You rolled a 20 with her, G."

It was D&D speak, which we had played together for years, for "you got luck."

But in the end Oliver still wasn't convinced, so he said, "Hands off everyone. If your uncle is really here, if he's really guiding this, let him move it. By himself."

Carol just stared at me. "Can you do that?" she asked.

"Never tried," I said. "But I feel strong. Why not?"

It was Winter Solstice. It was almost midnight. So I put my hands gently on the pointer and tried to move it.

The pointer didn't do anything, of course. We ghosts are very high-frequency localized electromagnetic emanations. How the hell are we supposed to move something purely physical?

Guiding the living must be a different thing. Intent, perhaps a bit of a psychic connection with my nephew, something like that. But this plastic pointer, even though it had felt-tipped feet to slide smoothly over the board, no way.

"You can do it," Carol said encouragingly.

And all the science stuff wasn't known yet. That came with this typewriter for ghosts so I really didn't know any better and only had movies and TV shows to fuel my imagination.

So I focused. I concentrated. I imagined.

This wasn't logic, this was gut, pure and simple.

"See," Oliver said with a snide nod of his head. "It's all in our heads. You all just guessed."

"Three times we guessed how many fingers you were holding up in each hand?" Tasha asked. "Really?"

But Oliver said exactly what I needed to hear. He made me mad.

So I tried again. I focused for all I was worth and it moved. I have no idea how, but it worked. The pointer moved about a quarter of an inch.

In retrospect, I think it was the moment, the day and time of the year when ghosts feel the strongest, my giddy hope-filled attitude with Carol by my side, and George and Tasha's intense desire to see it happen.

George and Tasha were ecstatic, Oliver was still in denial claiming a "seismic event" but it didn't matter. Carol was hugging me and I could feel it. Not just the barely there sense of touch, but I could feel my heart, my emotional heart, waking up as if it had been asleep for a long, long time.

Long after the Ouija board session had ended and the living had gone home or gone to sleep, Carol and I sat up on the roof of that simple cinder-block home and talked.

About everything.

My childhood fear of swimming. Her alcoholic parents and rather difficult childhood. More details on our deaths. She told me about her ill-fated marriage and divorce. I told her about my fiancé and how she cheated on me on the most cliched way, with my best friend.

We talked about movies and music. Our conversation ranged from the mundane to the mystical, from the best way to eat an apple to what lies after our time as earthbound spirits.

All of it was a delight, but most delightful was that we held hands. For hours. And it was always effortless.

As the horizon started to lighten, going from black towards a deep purple, the coming dawn made itself know, I asked, "What's next?"

"Next?" she asked, sounding sleepy or distracted. Our conversation had ebbed and we had lapsed into a companionable silence.

"For us," I said, feeling my nonexistent stomach twist up, afraid that tonight hadn't been enough, that she was way out of my league and had far more interesting people to spend her afterlife with.

"Christmas?" she asked.

It wasn't the answer I wanted, because at this point I never wanted to be away from her. We connected both literally and metaphorically in a way that I had never experienced. But I smiled and said, "Where?"

"Rockefeller Center," she said. "New York. 10 p.m. sharp. Can you make it?"

I was a little confused as to why she wouldn't just pop to me and pop us both there, but the first blush of love doesn't leave much room for such analytical thoughts.

"Of course," I said. "It's a date."

INTIMACY FOR THE DEAD IS DIFFERENT THAN FOR THE living. Obvious, right?

Not emotional intimacy, that's the same, but physical intimacy. There is no flesh, there isn't much of a sense of touch, but there are a couple of things.

Holding hands is roughly equivalent to the dead as it is the living, but kissing? Now that's something different. That is going "all the way" by ghostly standards.

I've never experienced it myself, but I've heard stories, and by the time Christmas rolled around and I had spent two days flying halfway across the country to New York City to see Carol, I wanted nothing more than to kiss her, to feel that legendary connection.

I was also terrified of it. I suspected the stories that circulated the graveyard were a bit overblown, but if half of it was true, kissing for ghosts was way more intimate than anything the living ever did, because when ghosts kissed they were witness to each other's memories, something akin to a Vulcan mind meld.

I was there at 10 p.m. sharp, hovering about the iconic ice rink in front of the majestic Rockefeller Center building staring at the 80-foot-tall spruce decorated to the nines with colorful, twinkling Christmas lights and a blazing white star on top.

It was just me and about twenty-thousand other ghosts.

I had, actually, gotten there at 5 p.m. and was blown away by how many ghosts there were. Way more than the living. Some pretending to ice skate. Some flying around the star "dressed" as angels, and a least a hundred ghostly Santa Clauses ho-ho-ho-ing around, not to mention dozens of elves and a few ghosts that managed to appear like reindeer with shiny red noses.

I was a small-town boy. Never made it to NYC while alive and hadn't even thought at how many earth-bound spirits might be in a place like this.

I knew I didn't need to look for Carol, since she could pop right to me, but I did. All evening. All night. Until just before midnight when she finally popped in, but it wasn't what I expected. She was a mess.

Being a "mess" as a ghost is a whole different thing than for the living. Mussed hair and wrinkled clothing take work and skill when you are dead. A ghost out of sorts will be more transparent, the edges of their form fuzzy.

This is what Carol looked like, still in that blue dress but clearly not herself.

"I'm sorry, Barry," she said before I could get a word out. "I can't tonight. There is something I need to... I can't." She looked around, her eyes widening at the floating swarm of ghosts we were a part of. "Can we try again on New Year's? I want to try again. Find somewhere beautiful and quiet and I'll come to you."

I barely got a nod out, and then with a "pop" she was gone.

FOR OUR NEW YEAR'S DATE, I CHOSE A PLACE ABOUT A quarter mile east of Chicago on Lake Michigan. You still had that big city vibe, we'd be able to see some nice fireworks and have the glittering lights of the city as a festive decoration, but there were no people, no ghosts, no no one, just the water that I was hovering just above.

It was beautiful in a stark way. The skyscrapers lining the lake tall and majestic with a constant stream of cars, their headlights slowly moving in either direction in front of the buildings along the shoreline.

There were quite a few boats out, more lights bobbing in the gentle waves of the lake—some living must have had the same idea that I did.

I was just far enough away so that the noise of the city was distant, like a pleasant white noise.

I was more nervous than at Christmas. What was that about? Was there something about her that would get in the way of this? Was there something wrong with her?

There are dangers to being an earthbound spirit. Those moaning, terrifying ghosts that the living write about are based on fact. Those are ghosts that are lost, that are living in a hell of their own making reliving the worst parts of their lives over and over.

The prevailing thought is that we ghosts are here for a reason and that reason is to deal with our unfinished business before "moving on." But if you get caught in your past, get swamped by your regrets, there is no moving on for you—there is only reliving the worst part of your life. Forever.

All of this was running through my mind when I heard a "pop" and Carol was standing in front of me dressed in the blue dress that matched her eyes so perfectly, her ghostly form crisp and barely transparent.

I held my hand up in front of me, palm up. She didn't speak but smiled and stepped over the water to me, put her hand up and touched her palm to mine.

It was still there. Our frequencies still matched, and I was so relieved.

"I'm sorry about Christmas," she said.

I shook my head. "You are here now. That is all that matters."

After our hands parted, Carol looked around, seemingly noticing our surroundings for the first time. "Where are we... Oh my. This is nice. And we can't, thankfully, feel the cold."

"I feel very warm," I said, and then felt silly. I was smitten and my mouth seemed to have a mind of its own.

"Me too," she said, walking over to me, looping her arm in mine as we both gazed at the city.

I wanted to ask her about Christmas, about what happened, but this was early days of our relationship and I let it go.

We started talking and it was easy, once again. About our past, both living and dead. About our interests, both mundane and profound.

It was so easy that it was like we had known each other for years and years and time slipped by and midnight approached, and while we had some companionable silences, it never felt awkward or forced.

When fireworks started blossoming above the Chicago skyline, I pulled her close and said, "I have feelings for you, Carol Franklin."

She swallowed, a very conscious gesture for a ghost, and nodded. "I have feelings for you, Barry O'Neil."

As the fireworks got more intense, the water around us reflecting the bright pops of blue, white, red, and gold, I pulled her close.

This was it. This was the moment. I could feel it. My afterlife would never be the same.

Our eyes met and are lips grew closer.

There wasn't a rush. We had our whole afterlives in front of us, but I wanted this more than I had wanted anything, ever.

As the fireworks crescendoed in explosions so bright and so colorful it was like we were up in the sky amongst the fireworks, our lips nearly met, and...

And Carol pulled away and in the sudden darkness said, "I'm sorry, Barry. I can't."

"What?" I asked, disoriented by the sudden change in the mood, the relative darkness, the strange twist this night had taken.

"It's not you," she said. "I... I lied to you. I am not what I seem."

"What do you mean?" I asked, managing to get a whole sentence out in my confusion.

Her form went fuzzy and I knew she wasn't in a good place again. She shook her head and said, "I was trying to be a reporter, I was, but I was just the manager of one of those mailbox stores. I had sold a few articles, just silly stuff about fashion and entertainment—no one would buy what I wrote about Africa."

She began pacing over the water and wouldn't meet my eyes.

Was this what happened on Christmas? Did she get worked up about this before she came to me?

"I've never been to Kenya," she said. "Or anywhere, really. I was in Canada once, but that's it. No one wanted to hear about what I had found out, so I blogged about it, posted it on social media, but everyone just wants pictures, just wants to press the like button on those stupid 'look at my wonderful life' posts."

She walked over to me and finally met my eyes and what I saw was a bit unsettling. Her eyes were too wide and her beauty had somehow twisted until it was a bit scary. "A black mamba didn't bite me," she said. "I got drunk at a bar, very drunk, drinking black mamba cocktails. It had been a bad day. I was fired, ran into my ex-husband, and received three, count them three, article rejections all at once." She started pacing again, her form getting more diffuse. "When I got home I was so worked up I took a couple of sleeping pills. I just needed to escape. They did nothing, so I took a few more... and then a few more..."

When she looked back at me, she was crying and it actually looked like mascara had run down her face, making her look a lot more like the living imagine we look.

"I killed myself," she said. "On accident, kind of. But I did it. If we kiss, you'll really see me, and I was nothing. You are amazing, Barry. So kind. You moved that Ouija board thing. I'm nothing. I'm sorry I lied to you. I'm sorry I let this go on so long. I'm... I'm just sorry."

She stared at me like I should say something, and I wanted to, but this was a lot. I was still processing. I knew I should say something like "It's all right" or "I don't care" but my tongue was tied.

Her cheeks turned red and her tears started flowing faster, and then with a "pop" she was gone and I was left alone amongst the waves suddenly feeling very, very cold even though I was a ghost and ghosts couldn't feel the cold.

It's been a very busy month and a half since New Year's.

I think about Carol all the time. I spent the first week of the new year waiting for her to come back, to come find me, to give me a chance to explain.

I spent the whole week thinking about what I should have said, what I would have said if I had had a little time. I feel deep shame for my lack of caring words when they were so needed, but that is not helpful. Shame is bad for the living, but it's even worse for the dead. Shame is the easiest way to lose yourself and become one of those moaning ghosts reliving the worst of their past, stuck in a hell of their own making.

I was more worried about Carol's shame and what I might have done to make that worse.

After that first week, I figured something out, something important, and I needed to tell Carol about it, but it was clear she wasn't coming back, that she had ghosted me, so I got busy. I had important things to learn.

Word had begun to spread among the dead about this new device created in Tucson that allowed ghosts to write their own stories. Given our inability to use technology, you'd be surprised how fast and how far word spreads among the dead. It's like gossip in a small town, faster than you'd think possible.

They were calling it a "SECI Chamber" and SECI stood for "Search of Extracorporeal Intelligence," an obvious nod to SETI and the Search for Extraterrestrial Intelligence. Word was that it was harder than hell to use and that you had to be adept at touch to use it.

Well, I had moved a physical object, hadn't I? And if I could write, then I could do something that might help Carol.

So off to Tucson I went and, to make a long story short, I can use the SECI Chamber and this story I've been telling you is my way of learning how to use it.

The next thing I needed to do was to learn how to pop, so when I'm not here practicing on the SECI Chamber, which, by the way, is very hard to use and not at all like typing, I've found a friendly graveyard and a ghost named Banquo, one of those teacherly types, and have been learning to pop.

Well... I've been learning the fundamentals of popping, been practicing it all that I can, but I haven't actually done it. Not yet.

But today is Valentine's Day, a day to celebrate love, a day to celebrate two hearts finding their match. Maybe there's some magic to it. Maybe the vibe of it will give me the boost I need so I'll be able to pop to Carol.

I have a backup plan, and that is I will beg and whine until Banquo pops me to Carol, which is doable if I describe her vividly enough for him to visualize her clearly, but I really want to do this on my own.

Wish me luck. I'll come back and let you know how it goes.

I won't go into the hours of concentration it took me to pop to Carol. That is a small and rather inconsequential detail in this story, except for one thing. It was very hard and I wanted this badly enough to pull it off.

But when I popped to Carol, it wasn't what I was expecting. At all.

It was night and we were in the backyard of a single-story house that felt abandoned. The large maple trees had shed their leaves long ago and looked skeletal, the yard was covered in snow with bits of weeds sticking up.

Without our flesh, ghosts are rather intuitive, and I was pretty sure this was Carol's childhood home. From what I knew of her past and her parents' addictions, this was not a good place for her to be.

It was dark and Carol was sitting on the swing of a rusty swing set, a stiff breeze causing it to move and squeak rhythmically. Carol was floating back and forth with the swing in a pretty convincing way.

She was still dressed in her blue dress but it looked darker, almost black, and she was rather transparent, her form wispy along the edges.

At first I thought she was lost, her eyes seemed vacant.

I had no thoughts of romance or kisses or the future. I just wanted to help this ghost I cared about.

"Carol...?" I said, my voice gentle like she was a skittish deer.

"Barry," she said, her tone listless. "You..."

I nodded and did my best to smile. "I learned how to pop," I said. "I am, officially, the world's worst popper and never want to do that again."

She nodded, but, again, it was listless, barely there.

I walked to her and put my hand up, my palm facing her, but she didn't react and kept floating along with the squeaking swing.

I lowered my hand and said, "Can you hear me, Carol? I want to tell you about my life. About what you would have experienced if we had kissed on New Year's Eve."

She nodded, her eyes focusing on me and her form becoming just a little bit less wispy.

I had practiced this, but now that it was time I was finding it difficult to find the words. I had been looking hard at my life since New Year's and thinking about what my unfinished business might be. I didn't want to speak the truth, but I knew Carol needed it.

"My life was nothing," I said. "I distracted myself through most of it, letting my precious days leak away delivering packages for my job and then distracting myself with video games and TV shows in the evening."

Carol was still rocking gently back and forth with the swing, so I rearranged myself into a sitting position about three feet from her and matched her motion so she wasn't moving relative to me.

"I fell in love with my high school sweetheart," I said, forcing the words out. "She wanted to become a teacher, I wanted to be an electrical engineer and get into robotics, help bring the future to life. I asked her to marry me at our high school graduation and she said yes.

"We were too young. Everyone told us, but we were too young to listen. We went to different colleges but managed to keep the relationship going until our junior year when I went to surprise her and found her in bed with someone else. With my best friend.

"I know this happens. I know it's lame. But suddenly my life wasn't what I thought it was going to be and I lost all momentum. I was already working for UPS and picked up more shifts to distract myself. I started failing classes and dropped out of school.

"That one stupid thing, that one human thing happened and I was stalled, dead in the water, and I couldn't get out of that funk no matter what I tried.

"Five years later I finally was getting back to myself, taking night classes and trying to finish my degree, but then my brother got cancer. I was with him when he died. And I was lost again and fell back into the same pattern.

"I died delivering packages, a big pileup on the highway. I vividly remember lying on the blacktop, cardboard packages all around me, barely conscious, and some kids running up and stealing the packages, not even looking at me. It was summer, the sun was bright, but I was so cold. It felt appropriate that the kids weren't helping me, that they stole stuff and left me to die, because my life had no meaning, no reason, no purpose."

The breeze had calmed, the swing had stopped squeaking, and we had stopped moving. It seemed entirely too quiet. I felt wounded, like the words describing my empty life had cut me on their way out. But when I looked at Carol she was much more there, not very transparent and only a little wispy along the edges.

"I'm so sorry, Barry," she said.

"That's what you would have seen if we had kissed," I said. "But I want you to see me and I want to see you. Exactly as you are. I don't care that you lied. I don't care if we ever kiss. I just want to be with you."

I felt ghostly tears running down my face and saw them running down hers.

"I think I figured out why we bumped into each other at Thanksgiving," I said.

"Really?" she asked, wiping at the insubstantial tears on her face. "Why?"

"We're ghosts because we have unfinished business, right?" She nodded.

"I never thought about mine, continuing my distracting ways after I died, but I see it now," I said. "I never made anything of my life and what I need to do is make something of my afterlife."

She nodded. "That... that must be my unfinished business, too."

"And that's why our frequencies match," I said, holding my palm up again.

This time she placed her palm against mine and we touched with ease. "We have the same unfinished business," she said.

"And we can help each other," I said.

"How?" she asked.

"You have a passion and a mission," I said. "We can pop to Kenya, you can see exactly what is going on. Nothing can stop us, you'll have access to everyone in their most private moments. And the—"

"But so what," she said, cutting me off. "I can't actually do anything."

"But I can," I said, and I told her all about the SECI chamber, how I had learned to use it, how I could type out her articles, how firsthand reports from a ghost would be sure to get a lot of attention.

"You... you would do that for me?" she asked.

I shook my head. "No," I said. "I will do this with you. You can pop, you can take us anywhere. I can communicate with the outside world. Together we can make our afterlives count, make them mean something."

"Together," she said.

Just then the moon rose above the horizon, bathing us in its silvery glow and this yard didn't seem so dark and foreboding anymore.

Carol leaned over, our lips getting closer, but there was no hesitation this time, our lips finally meeting, and we kissed.

And... well, I'll keep most of it to myself, but it was way more than even the rumors had made it out to be. I saw her, really saw her, her highs and her lows, her good heart and the flawed human execution of her dreams, and she saw me the same way.

It was the most intimate moment of my existence and more than I could have ever hoped for.

When it was over, when I had filled myself up with her and only wanted more, she asked, "Can we go to Kenya? Now?"

"Yes," I said with a laugh.

I can't say it was that one kiss on Valentine's Day that changed everything, but I can say that bumping into Carol at the

Fraklin Family Thanksgiving Extravaganza changed both of us for the better and that means everything.

I'm no longer ghosted, but a ghost with an afterlife worth living. We have purpose and we have each other. What more could someone, living or dead, ask for?

She popped us to Kenya, and we got right to work.

BACKSTORY—GHOSTED

Holidays: Thanksgiving to Valentine's Day

The idea for this story is, of course, a simple one. Take the modern parlance for a relationship that ends silently, "ghosted," and apply it to the world of ghosts.

Just like "A Grave Kind of Love," "Emily Loves Christmas, Emily Loves Murder," and "A More Adventurous Afterlife," this story takes place in my ghost world. There are, to date, six novel-length books and many short stories written in that world. You can find out more at *ShuffledOff.com*.

These stories have some common themes: grief and making your life (even if it is an afterlife) worth living. This particular story adds to it finding a good partner, one that can understand you and where you are coming from, one that can accept you just the way you are. This is, in my opinion, one of the things that makes a life most worth living—in other words, I'm a big ole romantic and it shows in stories like this.

PART 10
LINE DANCING WITH VAMPIRES

LINE DANCING WITH VAMPIRES

I DON'T KNOW WHY BUT GETTING PUNCHED IN THE FACE always makes me want to drink, and not just a little, my faulting attempts at sobriety be damned.

One of my rules is to not drink when I'm working, and I was working when I took the punch, two jobs at the same time, in fact.

It was Saturday night at the Step Right Up, a country and western bar on the edge of Chandler, Arizona. The alcohol had flowed like a river and the Great Santa Line Dance had begun, a Vince Gill Christmas song throbbing over the speakers as people stepped gracefully across the dance floor doing the "tush push."

The place wasn't much more than a small warehouse decked out with a faux Western finish. The rough wooden planks on the wall contrasting with the modern high ceilings and exposed ductwork, but that was balanced out by vintage road signs and large reproductions of classic Western movie posters framed in neon.

Lining one side of the space was a huge bar made of rough-hewn pine logs with a long, lariat-edged mirror behind, and shelf upon shelf of liquid temptation. There were stools all along the bar with high, round tables lining the back wall.

On the other side of the building were bathrooms, a tiny office, and a storeroom. The rest of the space was the dance floor which was crowded with "tush pushing" Santas.

The mechanical bull pit had been put away to make room for dancing and the ceiling was strung with colorful Christmas lights.

It was sheer madness, beautiful, beautiful madness. Not long ago, I had been out on the dance floor with the guy that hit me. He, unlike almost everyone else, was dressed in high-end goth, not dime-store Santa.

My apparent job was as a bouncer, but the guy that punched me was drunk enough that he might not have known that. It's not like I wore a badge that said, "Hi, my name is Conner Bright. I'm from Scatterwood, Australia, and I'll be your bouncer tonight."

It was past midnight, officially Christmas Eve, and the air was thick with the smell of beer and what beer turns into, a group of patrons forming around us eager for a show.

The guy that punched me was about six-foot, two hundred fifty pounds, with a blocky face and slicked-back, shoulder-length, black hair. He had a good seventy pounds on me and was about fifteen years younger, but I had six inches on him and was regrettably sober. My sometimes nickname of "Scarecrow" was apt.

"That one was for free, mate," I said in my best B-movie quality Australian accent, tasting blood and rubbing at my throbbing jaw. The accent matched my outfit. I had left the 11-inch bowie knife in the car, but I still had on the wide-brimmed bush hat, cowboy boots, and a crocodile claw hanging from a leather strap around my neck.

"You stay away from my girl," he said, just managing to not slur his words and sounding as intelligent as he looked.

His "girl" stood next to the bar dressed in a short red skirt, a tight red sweater with a plunging neckline, and a Santa hat atop her wavy blond hair. She was my second job which I had been about when this goth-guy had punched me.

I caught the girl's eyes and gave her a smile that I am told can be quite charming. She smiled back sweetly, and my opponent charged like some enraged bull.

What this guy didn't know is I used to face enraged bulls professionally, and despite the way that job had damaged my body, I could still move when I needed to.

I ducked his ham-fisted swing, caught his leg with my boot, and he went sprawling on the sawdust-covered floor.

I caught the bartender's eye, a redheaded woman named Lori, and she gave me an approving nod. She was the manager tonight and I wasn't supposed to actually hit anyone.

"Stay down, mate," I said. "Just let me finish my chat with this delightful young lady, who, by the way, ain't yours. Women are no longer chattel for cavemen like you to do with as they wish."

That one got some cheers and made the bull madder, as it was supposed to. The line dancing had stopped, since watching a fight is even more fun than pushing your tush, and we were now surrounded by a sea of Santas making this one of the more bizarre fights I had ever been in.

The blockhead goth-guy hadn't come alone. There were two more of them in blatantly expensive black. They weren't as big as this one, but they looked smarter even though they had the same bad taste in clothing and haircuts. One was clearly the alpha, his clothes just a bit nicer and his face quite a bit prettier.

They were both flanking the woman, but another one of the

betas stepped into the open area. This was getting serious, so I caught Lori's eye again and tossed her my bush hat. She deftly snatched the hat out of the air and grabbed her phone to call the cops.

I still had reach on the second one, but not as much. He was tall with a pointy chin, pale, with a fair amount of eyeliner on.

"I'd hate to muss that makeup of yours," I said, dancing back as the first one got up, throwing in a few steps of the "tush push" for the hell of it. "Are you supposed to be a one of them mimes or what?"

"You're going to regret that," he said.

I shrugged. "Right-o, mate. What's one tiny regret piled onto the heap of 'em?"

As they both came for me, I was sure as hell regretting taking this second job tonight.

———

THAT MORNING, I WOKE TO THE SOUND OF SOMEONE pounding on the door of my dingy single-wide on the outskirts of Phoenix, Arizona. It was early, 10 a.m., and I had only been asleep for a couple of hours.

"Go to hell, mate," I called. My fake Australian accent was so ingrained after this many years that I did it by default. Even drunk. Even barely awake. That morning, though, I was regrettably sober.

The pounding continued, so I sat up and squinted against the light. My small bedroom—it is a single-wide after all—was barely big enough for the queen bed and the chair that dominated the space. All of it was covered with rumpled clothes, some food wrappers, and harsh, painful light was sneaking in around the drape.

Sleep, for me, is hell. If I want to have anything resembling real sleep, I have to be drunk, and if I want to be anything approaching a real human being, I have to be sober. I had been doing my best to choose being human lately.

"All right, all right!" I shouted. The pounding was particularly insistent. "I'm comin', mate."

I padded through the living room, decorated festively with more food wrappers, and touched the old cookie tin that contained my father's ashes and said, "Hi, Dad." It's the only time I don't put on the accent. Right next to the tin was a DVD of *Crocodile Dundee*, my father's favorite movie.

I didn't own a bathrobe, so I only had my boxers covering all six-foot-five and 170 pounds of me. That's what they get to waking me up so damn early. I was about to yell, when I saw it was two sheriff's deputies, serious looks on their too-young, well-scrubbed faces.

"Good morning, Mr. Bright," the taller one said with a faux cheerfulness that made my head hurt. He shoved one of those little portable breathalyzers in my face. "Detective Sanchez would like to see you, but only if you are sober."

DETECTIVE TRISHA SANCHEZ WAS ALL OF FIVE-FIVE AND 115 pounds soaking wet, but I would lay odds on her in a fight against just about anyone. There is this coiled energy to her movements like she's a dangerous animal that you have to watch every single moment.

But maybe that was just me. Sanchez, once a work colleague if not an actual friend, currently hated me. I had shown up to a job drunk and things had gone to hell.

The deputies had let me get dressed, in my usual Crocodile Dundee regalia, gave me 10 seconds to have some mouthwash for breakfast, drove me in, and abandoned me in Sanchez's small, plain office, leaving with such expediency that I was left to believe that I was not the only one she hated.

I stood across from the scarred metal desk that dominated her office, which actually made my single-wide seem roomy. There were some family photos on the too-white walls—she had a big family—but that was all that made it personal.

She was sitting, her long black hair pulled back into a severe ponytail, dressed in a crisp navy-blue pantsuit. I caught a whiff of soap—she wasn't much for perfume—and worried about how I must have smelled.

I was staring at her and she was staring at me, neither of us speaking. I hadn't seen her for a while, not since that stakeout I screwed up. She had sworn she would never hire me again.

"Rule number 1," she said, sounding bored. "No lies. Ever." I didn't say anything, so she continued. "Rule number 2, no booze. Ever. Not within twenty-four hours of working for me."

I still didn't say anything. She needed me, that much was clear, but I didn't trust myself not to say something stupid and screw this up.

"God, Bright," she said, leaning back, her ancient office chair protesting with a loud squeak. "You look like hell." She poked at phone that had way too many buttons and said, "Bring in two coffees. Black." She looked back up at me. "Can you at least sit? You are making me dizzy."

Was that a crack about my height? Had Trisha Sanchez almost made a joke? To me?

I nodded and folded myself into the hard chair across from her desk. I had made my apologies for the stakeout and was in no mood to do it again.

My little single-wide happens to sit on ten acres of land on the far outskirts of the Valley of the Sun. It is rare horse property, that the always-hungry metropolis hasn't gobbled up yet. I no longer have a horse because of that mistake. When the cops dropped me, many of my other PI clients did too, and my income cratered.

"What's the job?" I asked, leaving off the "mate." Sanchez didn't deserve it.

She nodded, almost like she approved. She didn't want to rehash the past either.

She opened a folder and slid three 8x10s over to me. They were security footage but each one showed a man with black hair dressed all in black, and we're not talking jeans and T-shirts here, but ties and jackets and tailoring. None of them were looking at the camera so you couldn't see their faces, but they all had identical John Wick haircuts.

"Vampires," she said, and I swear there was amusement in her voice as it got huskier. "I need your help with vampires."

I'M NOT WHAT YOU WOULD CALL A CONFIDENT BRAWLER— the only thing I'm confident about is that there will be pain—but it's fair to say that I am calm and assured.

A fair number of years ago, I worked as a rodeo clown. That's a job where you have to remain calm and you can be confident that there will be pain, and adrenaline, lots and lots of adrenaline.

The adrenaline made me forget what I was hiding from, forget why I had become "Conner Bright." The pain was something I thought I deserved. I did it until it was clear that I would ruin my body if I kept it up.

And here I am, considerably older, facing off against two wannabe vampires at the Step Right Up surrounded by drunk Santas on Christmas Eve.

Can't say I make things easy on myself. Can't say that I should.

My opponents were taking their time now, assessing their prey. Which meant they were thinking, and I didn't want them thinking.

So I got weird. Humans, by and large, aren't good with the strange and unusual.

"Ever heard of Scatterwood, mates?" I asked. "Deep in the outback where you are taught to wrestle with crocodiles young."

I moved my body in ways that probably didn't make sense to them as I mimed wrestling a croc. "You've got to get control of its mouth, right. Them teeth are lethal. They have tremendous strength closing their mouths, but are weak in openin' it."

The short, stocky one, the one that hit me, stepped close, his mate flanking me as I mined hugging a crocodile's mouth closed. He jabbed, but it was just a feint and I easily dodged it. The taller one swung hard, but I turned my pantomime into a roll and he swung through empty air.

"That's part one," I said cheerfully. "Then it's the tail you gotta worry about." I made some bizarre motions, dance moves you might call them, as if I was the dangerous flapping tail of a crocodile.

The tall one charged me, but this was calculated, not like the shorter one. He was trying to get me to step aside into the range of his companion.

I stepped to the other side, and he came face to face with a rather large Santa who shoved him back into the circle and growled, "Fight!"

I kept on giving a lesson in wrestling crocodiles, telling them the next move was to cover their eyes which will retract into their heads, but I knew something wasn't right.

I mean, I was stalling for time. Sanchez and her crew should be here soon with enough to arrest these two guys, but why had the blockheaded one started the fight in the first place? These guys haven't left much for the cops to go on, why in the world would they get into a bar fight?

Something was very wrong.

I stopped the lesson on crocs and sank down into my knees in a more formal boxing stance. The time for fun and games was over. The time for worrying about breaking the rules was past.

They slowly closed in on me from opposite ends of the circle. Their demeanor had changed too, gotten distinctly predatorial, and I realized that I wasn't the one that had been playing with them.

It's usually better to pick a fight with a bull than with two men. The bull is much more predictable.

"THERE'S NO SUCH THINGS AS VAMPIRES," I SAID THAT morning in Sanchez's cramped office. "Not the kind you wanna interview and not the kind that sparkles."

She nodded. "I know. But these boys are..." She hesitated, her brown eyes searching mine, like she was trying to figure out if I was up to this or not. She sighed and pulled out another photo, this one bright and glossy showing the darkest of things. A corpse. A young, blond, way-too-pale woman with two precise punctures in her neck.

"No way," I said, picking up the photo.

She shook her head. "ME confirmed. The punctures happened postmortem."

"Why?" I asked.

"Rumors get spread. People are gullible," she said.

I snorted my agreement. "So, cover?"

"Or bait," she said. "God knows why, but vampires are... sexy."

I sipped my coffee and didn't say anything else. I wasn't

awake yet, and the coffee was the dregs of an old pot, but the smell promised me that I would be at least awake soon.

Sanchez needed me, that was clear, but I didn't understand why and I was afraid to ask.

Sanchez nodded as if she understood my unasked question. "We haven't ID'd these guys, they have a knack for facing away from security cameras. Haven't caught them doing anything untoward. They go to bars, talk to young women, don't leave with them, but then the women soon disappear. Two have shown up dead, four others haven't been found."

My furrowed brow was my part answer to that.

"They've done this once before at the Step Right Up," she said naming the place I am a bouncer and suddenly things became clearer. "We got a tip that they'll be there tonight. They seem to have a good sense of when cops are in the room, but you, Bright, God knows you don't seem anything like a cop."

I ignored the backhanded compliment and asked, "What, exactly, is it ya want me to do?"

"Get between them and their next victim," she said. "We'll be close, call us in if something goes down. Anything. We need to be able to arrest them. Get prints. Doesn't matter if it'll stick."

There was more, I could feel it, so I just stared at her.

"Look, Bright," she said with a sigh and a stretch of her shoulders. "The media hasn't gotten a hold of this one, but they will soon. The pressure is on. I need you sober. I need you on your best game."

The constant reminders of sobriety were getting annoying, despite having earned them.

"In fact," she said getting up. "I've got some things to do. You can have the couch for the day. Sleep. Rest. Get ready."

"Stay sober, ya mean," I said. "That's why those boys wouldn't let me drive myself. You wanted to strand me here."

She gave me a sharp, "you're not as dumb as you look" smile and left me alone with the picture of the corpse.

Bulls are dangerous, very, but they are not predators. They are herbivores, their horns and their power dedicated to getting a mate and protecting them from predators.

These goth-boys, while they may not have really been vampires, were predators and I was their prey.

At the Step Right Up, the tall one with all the eye makeup pulled out one of those black expandable batons and my stomach tightened up. They may not have been aiming to kill me, but they meant to hurt me. Badly.

Adrenaline dumped into my system, things slowed down, and I was finally all the way awake.

The pretty, wannabe vampire was still standing next to the blond, holding on to her arm, as her blue eyes grew wide with fear.

My two opponents shared a look, like they had rehearsed this, and they started towards me about 120 degrees apart. I could see them both, see what was coming, but there was no way I could counter them both effectively.

I wasn't Bruce Lee. I was a bouncer that used to be a rodeo clown. I knew how to take a hit, but this was getting ridiculous.

And that look? This had all been planned, which could only mean—

"Shit!" I said. This was some kind of setup. Sanchez had a mole and I had to assume that reinforcements would be delayed.

This was all fun until they got serious, so I got serious. Besides, I didn't think these boys would be suing the bar if they got hurt.

I tripped myself—on purpose—looking like a clumsy oaf,

turned it into a role, and from my back, kicked the blockhead square in the groin.

The Santas cheered as he went down with a sharp cry and crawled away.

But it wasn't enough. The pretty boy left the blond and entered the circle, pulling a knife from his back pocket.

"Goddamnit, Frank," I growled as I got back up. Frank was the other bouncer on duty tonight and not only had he let these guys in armed, but he was nowhere to be seen and no one in the crowed looked like they wanted to join the fun.

I caught Lori's eye again and mouthed 911. Her first call had been directly to Sanchez, but I didn't think I could count on that.

THE STEP RIGHT UP IS A HOLLOW MONSTROSITY WHEN IT'S not filled with bodies and music. The sawdust covering the floor seems garish and the smell of stale beer and staler humanity is a bit revolting, but I arrived at work that evening dead sober and fairly well rested.

Sure, Sanchez had maneuvered me into it, but I needed this job. If I could only get back into her good graces, then—

I cut off the thought. It was a hopeful one and hope can be a harsh mistress, taking as easily as she gives. I didn't have room for hope. I needed realities.

"G'day," I said to Lori Reynolds who was behind the bar getting ready. The Great Santa Line Dance wasn't for the faint of heart, but Lori did, among other things, play roller derby and knew how to handle herself.

"Bright," she said with a small smile, pushing a strand of her auburn hair behind her ear. She was about thirty years old with an athletic build dressed in blue jeans and a red sweater with a Santa hat sitting on the bar for later.

"I need a favor, love," I said, ambling up to the bar which always felt like a dangerous proposition, even though I made it a point to never drink at bars anymore. I just drank alone in my trailer in the early hours and let the alcohol numb me enough so I could sleep.

Sad? Hell, yes. Was there a reason? Oh, yeah. Don't get me wrong, I'm not looking for pity here, but when I close my eyes, I often see and hear that hellish ten seconds that turned me into Conner Bright.

When I was sixteen, I drove over my best friend.

Sounds terrible when I say it like that, but I guess I should say it like that. It is terrible.

This was in Globe, Arizona, where I grew up. We were epically drunk, out at a party in the desert, and fighting over a girl. I was in my truck trying to leave and he was banging on the hood of my old pickup blocking my way. I had the clutch in, revving the engine, as we both screamed at each other.

My foot slipped and...

Well, you get the picture. It was the kind of story that was all over the news which is why I changed my name when I turned eighteen, even though it broke my father's heart.

"What's up?" Lori asked, a smile raising the plentiful freckles decorating her cheeks.

I shook my head to clear it. Thinking of that night just made me want to drink. "There's gonna be some men comin' tonight," I began. "Dressed in black, expensive, and heaps of trouble."

She pulled a can of pepper spray from her pocket and put it on the bar. "You finally ready to take one of these?"

I shook my head. "Nah. Not my way, love, but I appreciate it. Here's what I need ya to do..."

There is no easy way out in a bar fight with two wannabe vampires, one with a baton and the other with a knife. I don't wear a knife when I'm in the bar, so I can't whip out my eleven-inch bowie knife and quote a classic *Crocodile Dundee* line. "That's not a knife. That's a knife!"

That's the kind of thing that makes me think of my father and my past in the best possible way.

I thought about running. There's no way Sanchez was paying me enough to risk my life, but then I saw the wide-eyed blond, their next victim. She looked shell-shocked and was just sitting there when she should have been running. What would happen to her if I ran?

Back when I did this kind of thing at the rodeo, I was there to protect the cowboys from the dangerous animals if they got bucked off, and this wasn't really that different.

"Let's go then," I said, stepping over to the bar and grabbing a stool and flipping it around so I held it by the legs.

It wasn't great, but I had reach on both of them again.

Baton-boy took a couple of steps forward and took a swing at me. I blocked the baton with the stool and said, "Back, you beast! Back!" I banged him in the chest with it, and he stumbled. These stools weren't comfortable or padded, just hard wood so it elicited a groan out of him and a few cheers from the Santas. It was just a feint, though, and knife-guy took a swipe at me. I ducked under the knife and swung the stool around, clipping him in the leg.

We kept at this for another minute or so. One would come in, I would block them, and then the other would try to flank me and I would use the stool as a cudgel. A stool really isn't an agile weapon, but it was proving to be just enough.

There was regular cheering from the assembled Santas, and I'm pretty sure some were placing bets, and others figured this was part of the show. Humans, I swear. It's a wonder we've survived this long as a race.

I had worked up a sweat and was starting to breathe heavy as my arms began to tire.

One and then the other. Block, swing, dodge as we circled each other in the ring of cheering and yelling Santas. This was no longer the "Great Santa Line Dance" but the "Great Santa Fight Club."

I was listening for the sounds of sirens, but there wasn't any. At one point, Lori caught my eye and tossed me the can of pepper spray I had refused early. It was a brilliant idea, but they both rushed me at the same time, so I ignored the pepper spray, swung the stool around so I was holding it lengthwise, and rushed towards them.

The legs of the stool hit them both in the chest, but I didn't have reach on them anymore. The baton caught my shoulder, fiery pain erupting, as I jerked my head back just in time and avoided a knife to the face.

Behind me I heard a voice through the din, a female voice. "Oh, hell. You two can't even...? Useless." The voice was sensual but filled with distain and dripping with privilege.

I don't know how, but as I was holding off the two wannabe vampires with the stool, I felt it coming. Maybe the air moved, maybe I heard it, but I jerked to the side and a beer bottle came crashing down on the right side of my head.

It didn't hit me straight on, but that didn't matter. The glass broke, my legs turned to rubber, and I went down.

* * *

EARLIER THAT NIGHT, I CLOCKED THE BOYS DRESSED IN black as soon as they entered the bar. It was past ten and it was already a sea of Santas, the music loud and the alcohol flowing freely.

Lori caught my eye, and with a tablet in hand as she headed out the door. This is what I had asked her to do. She could review the security footage and ID the vehicle these boys came in.

I joined the line dancing some, roamed the bar, kept an eye on them from a distance, and saw that they soon attached themselves to a young blond woman who had set herself up at the bar.

Her Santa outfit was high-end and highly sexy, the plunging neckline of her fur-edged top displaying ample cleavage. To go with it she had blond hair that fell in waves past her shoulder and glittering blue eyes.

I waited until I had my chance. Two of the boys-in-black had gone to the toilet and the short, stocky one was distracted by a brunette and was a few feet away.

"Evenin'," I said with a tip of my hat as I ambled over. The bar was far enough away from the dance floor that you only had to talk very loudly to be heard, not actually yell. "Them boys botherin' ya, ma'am?"

This was, believe it or not, part of my job. Part of both my jobs tonight. The owner of the bar wanted women to feel safe and this was part of my job for Sanchez. If this young lady was their next victim, the more I could find out, the better.

"They're..." she began, her full lips quirking into a smile that I couldn't help feeling despite being much too old for her. "They are a little much, but I can handle them." She leaned forward and pursed her very red lips. "Why don't I just whistle if I need you."

There was something about her, something entirely too intriguing. Something very primal in me stirred and I searched my brain, which wasn't working very well, for a reason to stay there, for an excuse to find out what her name was.

Yes, this was what I needed to do for both of my jobs, but I wasn't thinking about that. I just wanted to—

The stocky wannabe vampire's fist connected with my face, and I stumbled back, wanting a drink so very badly. I had been so enchanted by her that I didn't see him come back. I was so enchanted by her, that I didn't see a lot of things.

THAT ENCOUNTER CAME BACK TO ME AS I FELL TO THE floor, broken glass from the beer bottle falling with me, and time seemed to slow way down. The bar fight with the wannabe vampires was over. This was it. This was the end.

Sanchez hadn't come in time. Frank, my fellow bouncer, had abandoned me. Start to finish, the whole damn thing had been a setup.

As I fell, I wound back what I had heard before the bottle came crashing down on my head. I knew who it was. It was the blond, the ones that the boys-in-black had been circling, the one that I had found so enchanting.

She wasn't their next victim, she was their leader.

And then I was on the sawdust-covered floor, the right side of my head on fire and I could feel warm blood oozing out.

I could see the two boys standing over me and then I could see Blondie's beautiful, cherubic face. She leaned down and said, "You and your little cop friend stay out of our business, or next time we won't be so kind."

I hadn't noticed her shoes before but they were red, those expensive shoes that look kind of like moon boots. Her boots stood out because that's that last thing I saw before she kicked me in the head and it all faded to black.

T**HEY DIDN'T KILL ME.**

That was the first thought as I rode a wave of pain back to consciousness. They didn't kill me.

Actually, it makes sense. A murder would have to be investigated, but just another bar fight where the bouncer was the only one hurt and a good show was put on for a couple of hundred people dressed up like Santa? Not so much.

"Come on, Bright," a voice said, a female voice, and for a moment I thought it was *her*. But this voice was a tad husky and way more world-weary than overprivileged. "Wake up."

"Setup," I said, finding it painful to move my jaw and hard to think with the stabbing throb thrumming through my head with each heartbeat. "It was a setup."

Sanchez let out a long sigh and said, "Yeah." A couple of heartbeats passed and she added, "Sorry about that."

I slitted my eyes open, finding the light painful but catching a glimpse of a vintage black and white Johnny Cash concert poster, which meant we were in the bar office which was right next to the bathrooms and smelled like it. That explained the lumpy kind of softness underneath me—the couch in here was old and was never comfortable.

I took a deep breath and managed to get a look at Sanchez. She looked rumpled and tired, her long black hair not rigorously contained in its ponytail, dark smudges under her eyes.

Lori was leaning against the desk watching. She brought over a bag of ice which I gratefully pressed to my aching head.

"God, Sanchez," I said. "Ya look like hell."

She gave me a wan smile and nodded but didn't say anything.

"Where were you?" I asked.

She sighed again like she was leaking air or something. "Getting chewed out. By my captain. For hiring you."

"He's in on it," I said.

"Yeah," she said. "He called me in and reassigned the deputies I had with me. I think he called the Chandler PD and had them drag their heels getting here."

"Frank, too," I said, nodding to Lori.

She took her turn sighing and said, "Yeah. Haven't seen him. Bet they bought him off. He's fired if he ever comes back."

I didn't deserve the beating I had just gotten, but it's not like I didn't have some payback coming to me for my other sins. This setup, though, made me mad.

I slowly sat up, treating my body like it might snap at any moment. I took a breath and told Sanchez everything. The predatorial wannabe vampires. The seductress running the show. My vow to accept pepper spray the next time someone offers me some.

That last part elicited a grin from Lori who had leaned against the desk, her arms crossed in stony silence the whole time.

"Your car's in the lot," Sanchez said. I knew she had sent some of those too-fresh-faced deputies to retrieve it. "But I don't think you should drive. I'll take you to the hospital or home, at least."

"Oh, hell no," I said. I looked at Lori and asked, "Did ya get it done?"

She nodded. "Dumbasses. All in black like that on a night like this. Wasn't hard to locate their car in the lot with the security video. It was a goddamn black Cadillac SUV. They are way too caught up in their image."

"What?" Sanchez asked, her head swiveling to look at Lori and then back me.

I pulled my phone out from my back pocket, glad to see it still intact, brought up one of those "find my phone" apps, and showed it to Sanchez.

"Good ol' Lori there," I said with a nod that brought on a

wave of dizziness. "She duct-taped a burner phone to their car. The bastards are in Scottsdale."

Sanchez's brown eyes brightened, and she gave me one of her patent-pending predatorial smiles that showed off her very white teeth. God love her, we only had a location and no plan, but she was in.

It was a stupid plan. It was a desperate plan. But I used to go up against literal raging bulls, so "stupid" and "desperate" are not foreign to me.

It took a bunch of middle-of-the-night driving to get the plan rolling and I was once again reminded that the Phoenix metro area is urban sprawl, pure and simple. The city expanded, first gobbling up the orange groves followed by agricultural fields and then spreading out into the desert like some kind of fast-growing fungus. Sure, there's a few obligatory high rises downtown that are mostly old and seem a little embarrassed that there are so few of them, but most of the area doesn't get higher than a few stories.

Cheap land. Lots of roads. Millions of cars. Filled with the hum of those cars all year and air conditioners most of the year. And don't forget the Circle-K on almost every corner of every major street.

Okay, so not a literal "Circle-K," which is not as dominant as it used to be, but one of those gas station/minimarts. You gotta feed those hungry cars and those hungry humans.

Still, I love it. You can see the craggy desert hills rising up out of the sea of humanity and, weirdly, imported palm trees line streets in certain parts of the city, tall sentinels in the desert sky.

I guess it's the desert I love, the raw honesty of it. The desert doesn't hide what it is, hide its danger.

Scottsdale is one of the swankier parts of town. It lies on the east side of the valley, a long, narrow corridor that hugs Scottsdale Road and all the high-end retail establishments perched there.

The house the burner phone led us to was a sprawling adobe the color of the desert, sitting on a small rise on the edge of town, and the wannabe vampires are awake. We could tell because they had left the blinds of the windows open. Not smart, but I can't say I blamed them. The city glitters at night with millions of lights, better than just about any Christmas tree.

I really enjoyed the time on the road with Sanchez, especially as we passed bits of Christmas cheer. A blowup Santa here, a palm tree with Christmas lights someone strung all the way to the top, the way the city seemed more at peace than usual.

We didn't talk much. We didn't have a warrant. We didn't have support. But Sanchez was sure that what these wannabe vampires were up to was human trafficking. She thought that they found their victims, mostly college girls, at the bars, charmed them into giving them their numbers, and then scooped them up later.

The dead ones were the ones that effectively resisted. The missing ones were likely out of the country.

This is how I found myself at the wannabe vampires' front door just before dawn with what looked like two pizza boxes in my arms. Well, the top box had pizza in it, you gotta have that smell, but the bottom didn't.

Gone was the Crocodile Dundee outfit and I had a cheap windbreaker on, covering a bulletproof vest underneath, with—God forbid—a red Santa hat on my head.

I had taken as many painkillers as I dared, munched a microwave burrito from a Circle-K, and was feeling almost halfway human despite my aching head.

I was hunched down to hide my height as I rang the doorbell for the second time and turned away so the door camera couldn't get a good look at my face.

"Go away," baton-boy said as he jerked the door open. He was still dressed all in black, but his clothing was looser and more comfortable. Soft pants and a black T-shirt that showed off his toned arms. "We didn't order any pizza."

"Ummm... well..." I began, discarding my B-movie quality Australian accent and making my voice nasally. "This is the right address... I swear."

He shook his head and was about to slam the door when I fired the taser hidden under the pizza boxes and he went down, convulsing quite satisfyingly like a fish out of water. I swear it made where he had hit me on my shoulder hurt just a little less.

Sanchez, dressed in tactical black complete with a bullet-proof vest, slipped in ready to knock baton-boy out, but as he convulsed on the marble entryway, he smashed his head on the stone and did that for us.

We pulled his body outside, zip-tied his hands and feet, and duct-taped his mouth. We reset and I rang the doorbell again.

It was risky, someone might have seen the doorcam footage, but we thought it worth it. This crew had a dangerous level of arrogance. They had the cops in their pocket and had just gotten way from my beatdown scot-free.

The next wannabe vamp that opened the door was shorter, stockier, and in obvious pain as he made the half step back when he opened the door. He looked exhausted as he pointed a gun at my chest and said, "Get the hell the out of here."

I straightened up, smiled, and said, "G'day, mate."

This was my arrogance. It hadn't even entered his blocky head that I might come after them. I was just some weirdo bouncer from a bar meant to carry a message back to Sanchez. As his eyes widened in sluggish recognition and his gun drifted away from me, I pulled the trigger on the reloaded taser I had hidden under the pizza boxes.

He didn't do us the courtesy of knocking himself out on the marble, so Sanchez did it for him and we dragged him out and trussed him up right next to his mate.

We had spent time surveilling the place. We were pretty sure it was just the four of them, although there were lots of rooms in this rambling house we couldn't see in. We moved in— she had a gun and I had the taser.

The living area was dominated by a tall Christmas tree decked out in white lights and huge blue and red ornaments. It was too perfect for my taste and seemed out of place with this crew. As we stepped in, I carefully put the pizza boxes down on a low bench.

"Don't move," a sensuous female voice said as we looked over the living room. Besides the Christmas tree, it was all leather couches, gleaming chrome, a huge flatscreen, and colorful but somehow generic artwork. This was clearly a vacation rental, albeit a pricey one.

"Hands up," a male voice said. "Nice and easy."

Oh, God. They're dialog was as stilted as their overly goth wardrobe. The queen and her pretty boy had snuck around, callously offering up Mr. Blockhead as a sacrifice.

I caught Sanchez's eye, and she gave me a pursed-lip nod. This wasn't our best outcome but one we had planned for.

A minute later we were disarmed, relieved of our bulletproof vests, kneeling on some gaudy throw rug over the garishly marbled living room floor, our hands zip-tied behind us and our ankles zip-tied together.

The queen blond was out of her red Santa outfit and wearing boring black, pacing in front of us. I couldn't see the pretty boy, but I could hear him breathing behind us.

"How long, love?" I asked with a nod. "How long ya been stealin' girlies and sellin' 'em to the highest bidder?"

She looked at me, her blue eyes fierce, a sneer turning her decidedly symmetrical features into something rather ugly. But, really, knowing what she was made her ugly regardless of the appearance her genes and lots of money had afforded her.

She squatted down in front of me, and my nose filled up with her overdone, expensive, cloying perfume.

"Long enough," she said. She ignored Sanchez, her eyes drifting up and down in a look of reassessment. "Didn't think you had it in you."

"And lookin' at you, love," I said. "I wouldn't think that human trafficking was in ya."

She shrugged and puckered her lips and tilted her head looking like she was posing for some crazy, cutesy photoshoot or something.

"How many?" Sanchez asked, her voice extra husky and sounding like a growl.

"Excuse me?" Blondie asked.

"How many girls you got in the back room?" Sanchez asked. "How many more are you going to ship off soon?"

She rolled her eyes like it was the most superfluous question in the world. "Just one," she said. "We've been a bit distracted. But after tonight—"

"That sounds like evidence to me," I said to Sanchez, cutting her off.

"That it does," Sanchez said. She caught my eye and yelled, "Execute!"

A bunch of things happened at once.

Queen Blondie blinked and looked confused. She was still right in front of me, so I reared back and headbutted her. Hard. I saw stars, quite literally. With a loud cry, she went down, her nose gushing blood, and I almost did too.

The sound of gunfire erupted from towards the front door. It was coming from the bottom pizza box, what we had spent much of the night sorting out. It was a cell phone, a good mic, a disassembled Bluetooth speaker, and some hacked software a friend of mine had put together.

Sanchez had triggered it by yelling "execute." It played the gunfire audio, called 911, and uploaded the recording it had made of all this into the cloud.

Pretty boy fell for it and started shooting, but above us.

When they disarmed us, they had missed the little knife in my right boot. It was hidden under the inside pull. Despite the world spinning around me, I slipped it out, cut my hands free, and then tossed it to Sanchez.

By that time, pretty boy was wising up, his gun coming down toward Sanchez, so I surged up and tackled him. My ankles were still zip-tied, so it sure wasn't pretty, but I managed it. We were wrestling for his gun when Sanchez delivered a swift kick to his head and lights out for him.

By the time I turned and saw Blondie running for the door, Sanchez had pretty boy's gun and fired, the bullet whizzing by her head and slamming into the doorjamb.

Blondie froze and Sanchez said, "I will shoot you. Happily and repeatedly. Please, run. I'd consider it my Christmas present."

Tip for all of you out there. Don't go doing any headbutting when your noggin has just had a beer bottle broken over it right before being solidly kicked.

The paramedics had me strapped into a gurney and were about to load me when Sanchez stopped them. The place was crawling with Scottsdale PD and the FBI. I knew there was

going to be long statements and grilling from several law enforcement agencies, but for now I was happy to be lying down and
not fighting for my life.

"There was a young woman in back," Sanchez said.
"Gagged. Tied up. Dehydrated. She's not hurt otherwise, but..."
The rest didn't need to be said, the girl would have plenty of
trauma to recover from.

"You're welcome, mate," I said with my best smile despite
the pain and dizziness. Sanchez wasn't going to thank me, it
wasn't her way, this was as close as I was going to get. "Ya see
another case I can help out with, ya got my number."

She smiled, and it wasn't fully sharklike. "You got it, Bright.
Next time I run across vampires or... aliens or bigfoot, I'll give
you a call."

"Aces!" I said as they loaded me into the ambulance.

"Merry Christmas, Conner," she said, a rare use of my fist
name.

"You too!" I said as they closed the ambulance doors.

I hurt bad, but I felt good, if you know what I mean. I had a
suspicion that maybe, for once, I'd be able to really sleep without
a belly full of beer.

Sanchez was true to her word. The next case she called me
on involved a purple unicorn. Seriously. But that's another story,
mate.

BACKSTORY— LINE DANCING WITH VAMPIRES

Holiday: Christmas

Conner Bright stories are a ton of fun to write (and hopefully to read), this one being no exception.

As of this writing, this is the first Conner Bright story, chronologically speaking. To tell this story, I needed to go back in time before all the other Conner Bright Mysteries to a place where Conner was a bit younger and in rougher shape.

The other Conner Bright stories have recently been released in a novel-length omnibus edition called *I Am Conner Bright: Four Essential Conner Bright Mysteries.* You can find out more at: *RobertJMcCarter.com/ConnerBright.*

PART 11
A MORE ADVENTUROUS AFTERLIFE

A MORE ADVENTUROUS AFTERLIFE

The graveyard feels empty tonight, only a few other spirits besides me roaming amongst the gravestones and the manicured lawn, their spectral forms looking to be made of moonlight under the blanket of stars on this moonless night.

A winter storm blew through Arizona yesterday, cleansing the air and making it one of those rare crystalline clear Tucson nights when you can really see the stars.

I knew Tucson when it was young, when "wild" was an apt adjective for this western town, when the roads were more dusty dirt than hard pavement, and when the stars were clearly visible most every night. My name is Fredrick Penny and I died in 1929 of Parrot Fever. I was a mortician and my life's work was caring for the dead, and, it seems, my death's work is the same.

I was one of the first ghosts at this graveyard and, as of this writing, I have been here the longest and must admit that I view this as "my" graveyard. The times have changed, to be sure, but the rules of a happy afterlife have not and I do my best to help those in need when I can.

It's Christmas Eve and that can be a particularly lonely time for ghosts. Well... it can be many things for a ghost. Dangerous as well as lonely, sometimes happy, occasionally joyful. It can bring back old griefs and reignite old angers. If a ghost is courageous enough—or stupid enough—it can lead to them trying to participate, in some way, with their living family members, and that can lead to madness.

These days when the veil between the living and the dead has become shockingly porous because of this SECI chamber, this typewriter for ghosts that I am writing to you on, the holiday season has become particularly dangerous. It has normalized the living communicating with the dead.

At first glance, it would seem that this would bring nothing but joy, given that some of the dead are not quite as dead as everyone once thought. But that is only at a glance. It often goes poorly when the dead and the living interact, and, unlike in the movies, the consequences are usually worse for the "dearly departed."

This season is, above all, a time that reminds the dead that they are dead and that is, indeed, a lonely thing.

"You okay, Fred?" Taylor asked.

She was a young ghost with long golden locks and a flowing blue dress encasing her lithe form, one that matched the color of her eyes.

I simply detest the name Fred, my name is Fredrick or Mr. Penny, if you please, but Taylor was young both in terms of being dead—only a few months—and the age she was at death—twenty-something, I am a poor judge of youth at this point—so I let it go.

And letting it go was the only thing to do here, I had corrected Taylor many times and it never did a bit of good.

"I'm fine, Taylor," I said. "Just fine."

"You don't look fine," she said.

I looked down at my ghostly form and it was crisp and only

slightly transparent. I was dressed, as always, in a three-piece suit that appeared to be made of fine dark grey wool with a lovely herringbone pattern.

But then I realized what the young lady was getting at, she was doing what the young often do and was asking me the question she wanted to be asked. "Is everything okay with you, Taylor?" I asked.

She shrugged and looked down at her feet which were encased in improbable looking high heels that would not have worked on this grass had she been alive. There are some benefits to being dead, after all.

Another benefit in that moment was that I couldn't smell. Taylor with the bangles on her wrists and large gold hoop earrings looks like the kind of young woman that would have doused herself in cheap perfume which I liked quite a bit less than the pungent smell of embalming fluid.

These little benefits of being dead are a wise thing to keep reminding yourself of.

"Taylor," I said, my voice as gentle as I could make it on this day with this ghost. "You know I am here to help if you have a problem."

She nodded, didn't look all the way up, and was now staring at my shoes, some fine wing-tipped Oxfords, of course. "It's..." she began, her voice sounding more like a girl's. "This is my first... you know... and my family... you know..."

Don't they teach the young how to speak anymore? In any case, her meaning was clear. She had heeded the warnings of what can happen when the dead interact with the living, especially a young ghost like Talyor, but it was Christmas Eve and she felt the pull to be with her family.

I sighed, which was a lapse on my part. Not having lungs, a sigh is an even more conscious gesture for the dead than it is for the living.

"It seems at least half the graveyard has lost their minds this year," I said, putting a little punch into it, hoping to get through to the girl indirectly.

"Can... can you blame then?" she asked, shyly looking up at me. "It's... it's Christmas, after all. Things have changed, the living know we are here, they might..." She paused, her eyes lighting up. "They might remember us."

I must admit to being a man from another era, one in which the norms for men and women interacting were far more conservative than now. I must also admit to having "shuffled off my mortal coil" early in the previous century and have forgotten so much about the ways of the flesh. But I must also admit that Taylor was a lovely young lady and in that moment her attention was flattering to this old ghost.

It is to this I must attribute my response and the unusually silly grin that was on my face when I said it.

"Well then," I said. "Perhaps we should go see what the hubbub is all about."

I SHOULD PIN THIS INTERACTION IN TIME A BIT TO properly frame it. For me, having been conscious for so many decades, time can get a little mixed up in my mind, but in this case it is important.

Taylor died and this interaction happened less than a year after the SECI chamber first opened and ghosts started writing their own stories. This was before all the strife that came later, when both the living and dead took sides in regard to this technology, some for and some against. And before a certain vocal minority of the living decided that the dead, and the SECI chamber by extension, were evil.

This happened when we are all a lot more innocent about

what might be coming, my greatest fear being the costs to the ghosts that went to see their families and saw things they couldn't unsee.

It was my own loneliness that drove me down this path. My children and grandchildren were all long gone and most of my fellow ghosts were off indulging in this new era, so why shouldn't I?

Taylor, being a young ghost and not skilled in our ways, did not know how to "pop," which is the aptly named process when a ghost goes instantly from one place to another. The name being a succinct description of the sound that occurs when this happens.

So Taylor took a hold of my arm and described her family's home, in great detail, and even though I had growing misgivings as she described it, I visualized her home my in mind, and willed us there.

And, with a sharp "pop" we were there.

I was, of course, not surprised by the house itself, having visualized it to get us here, but almost everything else was a surprise, but I shall start with the house and we will work out from there.

It was a large, sprawling affair perched on the top of a small hill in the faux-adobe style that upscale houses in the desert tend to have these days. That meant rounded edges, a nearly flat roof that hid behind the top of the walls, and textured stucco the color of the desert sand. This particular house strayed from the adobe aesthetics. having large windows in the front so those inside could clearly see the fine view of the city.

The house was backed against the cactus-filled Catalina Mountains and was, frankly, so large I couldn't comprehend a single family needing so much space.

That was the house, what I had visualized, and it was on a lot of approximately an acre inside a gated community. But what

I hadn't visualized was the flashing lights of a fire engine, two police cars, the smoke billowing out of the center of the house, and the screams coming from within.

I stood there blinking, trying to take it all in, my mind trying to take me back to the past, back to a dangerous place. Talyor was not frozen like I, she flew towards the house, her voice loud as she cried, "Mom! Dad! Oh no, oh no, oh no!"

This, my gentle reader, is why the dead should, as a rule, stay away from their living loved ones.

It is often more than a ghost can bear.

As I write this missive, I find that I must not assume that you, dear reader, have read the stories of other ghosts and assume you know how our world works, so let me give you a very quick overview.

We ghosts can see and hear, but we have no sense of smell, so, for example, I couldn't smell the acrid smoke flowing out of Talyor's house, but I could hear the crackle of the fire and the frightened cries of the living and see everything in crystal clear detail.

The other thing to mention is the "bardo." That gape-jawed, moaning ghost of legend is a ghost that has collapsed into their own regrets and are lost to them, inhabiting a land where they experience their regrets over and over.

The bardo is the chief danger to the dead. It is, quite literally, an individual hell custom made for a ghost.

This is what was so foolish about all those ghosts ignoring this danger in this new world where the veil between the living and the dead seemed to be thinner than ever.

I use the word "seemed" intentionally. As an undertaker, I never thought the veil was thick and knew it to be razor thin. I had seen it too many times, with one breath you are alive and then there are no other breaths and you are dead.

One more piece of background about ghosts. It is only those of us that have unfinished business that are ghosts and do not "move on" after death.

From the introduction of this story, you might just assume that this story is about Taylor's unfinished business, and indeed it is and we shall get to that. But it is also about my own unfinished business, otherwise I would not be telling the tale. It would be presumptuous of me to try to tell that kind of story for another ghost.

As young Taylor shouted and flew towards the burning house, flames now leaping out of the middle of the roof while firemen in masks and full protective regalia headed for the front door, I flew after Taylor and shouted, "Wait! Please, wait!"

My voice sounded desperate, because I was, indeed, desperate. I am not fond of fires, they are hungry, rapacious beast that will destroy everything in their path. Of this I speak from experience.

My instincts told me not to enter the building, that no good could come of it, but I had brought Taylor here and I bore some responsibility for what would happen to her in there, and I knew it could not be good.

My shouts did not one bit of good, of course. Not that they should have. These were her people, and even though the rare ghost or two has shown they can interact with the material world in a very limited way, there was not a thing she, being such a new ghost, could do to help anyone, and only harm could come to her.

I lingered but a few moments, my fear of the fire warring with my sense of responsibility. I had been weak in agreeing to bring her here. No, I take that back. She would have come anyway, flown across Tucson until she got here, but it was on me that she was there at this moment. A moment that could very likely find her falling into the bardo to be lost forever.

GHOSTS CAN SEE AND HEAR MUCH BETTER THAN THE living, which is probably poetic in some strange way since we have left both our eyes and ears behind in death. This meant that when I flew after Taylor, into her former home, I could see and hear everything, in startling clarity.

Too much clarity.

The front door opened up into an expansive living room with a tiled floor, comfortable overstuffed couches, and hardwood furniture. The high ceiling was accented with rough-hewn logs running the length of the room, and in the middle of it was a large and perfectly symmetrical Christmas tree that reached all the way to that high ceiling and was brightly burning like a torch.

It was this pitchy fir tree that had burned a hole in the roof. The fire was spreading out from the tree and soon the whole room and the whole house would be ablaze. It was clear to my eyes that the tree was the source of the fire.

A faulty wire, perhaps. A light that shorted out and sparked. It never seemed wise to me to put a fuel source in the middle of your home.

I have to imagine that the heat radiating off of it was intense, but I could not feel it, although the walls past the tree seemed to undulate as heat radiated out from that fire.

The two firemen in their masks with the oxygen tanks showed me just how hot it was for it was like they hit a wall when they entered the room, their hands held in front of them as if they could stop the blow of the heat that way.

I saw all of this in a moment as Taylor plunged forward,

straight through the burning tree, not something I would have recommended. While our ghostly forms are quite malleable, something in me tells me that they are not indestructible.

Nevertheless, I had made my decision and got over my fears and followed the young woman. I flew around the tree, hugging the wall which was hung with a fine Navajo blanket and a large, glossy photograph of the Catlina Mountains, flying deeper into the house.

"Mom! Dad!" Taylor shouted, trying to raise her voice over the roaring crackle of the fire, not that her parents could hear her. Not that anyone but the dead could hear her.

And that was my fear. While her parents probably couldn't hear her now, with the strength of this fire, they might just hear her soon.

As I rounded the tree and flew deeper into the house, I caught a flash of movement from within the conflagration. Or at least I think I did. The burning tree was, by its very nature, alive with motion, but this seemed different, felt different, and I felt like I was being watched.

But it was only a moment, only a fleeting thought, as I flew on. I discarded it, concluding it was my own fear of fire and past trauma, my mind playing tricks on me.

I found Talyor just inside what must have been, judging from its size, the master bedroom. It was huge, nearly as large as a house for a small family in my day, and in it was another Christmas tree, this one only eight feet tall and it too was burning brightly.

Two Christmas trees in the same house, both burning? Well, this defied all odds and had to be a malicious act.

Also in the room were a man and a woman dressed in silky pajamas, each about fifty years of age, both bearing some resemblance to Taylor. The woman had blond hair similar to Taylor's and the man was short and stocky, his sandy-brown hair sliding towards grey. These were Taylor's parents, of course.

The tree in the corner of the room was blazing hot enough that it was keeping Taylor's parents from the windows. As I wondered why they didn't just exit by the door, I wound my memory back—we ghosts have excellent memories, far too excellent if you ask me—and remembered seeing that the fire had reached the door making an exit that way unwise if not impossible.

As I took it in, as I fought my deeply instinctive desire to be anywhere but here, as I struggled to think of a way to help Taylor and her parents, to prevent this from being a tragedy for all of them, I realized that I was the exact wrong ghost for this incident.

For a moment, put aside that I very much hate fires and consider the fact that we have ghosts in the graveyard that eagerly meet challenges like the one I was now facing.

JJ Lynch, the first ghost to use the SECI chamber, entered into the bardo on purpose to rescue someone he didn't know—and, somehow, managed to defeat the bardo and return to us. Walter Anchor and Emily went around studying murders and Walter typed up the cases giving the police all the information they needed to arrest the guilty parties.

There were adventurous ghosts, and then there was me. I was ready to help, ready to give a word of advice or encouragement. I was the ghost that could tell you how to conduct yourself so that you stayed out of the bardo.

Entering burning buildings where it seemed you would witness your parents' horrific death was not something I would ever suggest.

Entering a burning building for any reason was not something I would advise a ghost to do, but here we were.

Talyor's father, who had the same blue eyes as Taylor, was guiding Taylor's mother into the large adjoining bathroom. They were stooped low and coughing as the smoke accumulated.

I saw him draw her into a large tub, one of those that shoots jets of water, and turn the water on.

"We have to save them," Taylor said.

She said "we" and the word echoed in my mind so much so that I could hardly think.

There is a ritual around the graveyard that we follow when we meet a new ghost for the first time. For me it goes like this, "Hello, my name is Fredrick Penny and I died of Parrot Fever in 1929."

The year is not, strictly speaking, part of the ritual, but I like to insert it, let the new ghosts know that I am well experienced and establish my place here as an elder.

But what that sentence hides is that six months before that I barely survived a fire in my own home and had the scars to prove it.

I am a ghost, my appearance malleable, and I am not stuck with my original, "default" appearance, so the scars that once marred my right hand, arm, and part of my face aren't visible and there are no longer any ghosts around that know that bit of history.

While it was Parrot Fever that officially killed me, it was the fire that weakened me and made me vulnerable to the dreaded parasite that causes that malady.

"There... there is nothing we can do," I said. "Your father is wise and taking the best course of action. We should leave."

The crackle of the fire was so loud, it was bringing me back to the past, back to the fire that nearly killed me and my entire family. I wanted to fly away... no, I *needed* to fly away.

"No!" Taylor shouted, her voice briefly louder than the blaze. "We must help them." Her blue eyes roamed around the room. The two windows looking out at the rugged cactus-covered hills of the Catalinas where too close to the fire, the window in the bathroom was too small, and the door was wedged shut from the outside.

The fire was spreading, licking up the walls of the bedroom, the large bed starting to smolder. There was no escape for Taylor's parents. This was up to the fates and the fire crew. Perhaps the water and the tub would save them from the fire, but if the firemen did not get to them soon, they would die of smoke inhalation.

"The door," Taylor shouted. "We must open the door. Help me!"

I HAVE BEEN DEAD FOR A VERY LONG TIME, BUT I AM QUITE aware that I do not know everything about being a ghost, and I am sure there are some capabilities I have not heard of and skills yet undiscovered, but moving physical objects... No. We don't do that. We are ghosts, ephemeral, gossamer spirits.

It is not within our abilities to move physical objects.

"Is there anyone else living here?" I asked Taylor, my voice also a shout as I competed with the crackling of the rapacious fire.

"No," she said, a strange emotion passing over her face. Grief, perhaps, maybe a touch of fear. "It's just them now."

This house wasn't built for two and there was clearly a story there, but we did not have the time.

"Taylor," I said. "Listen to me. We can't open that door, but there may be something else we can do."

"What!?" she shouted, her eyes roaming to the door, but

even if we could open it, the living room was further gone than this room.

"We can tell the firemen where your parents are," I shouted. "So they know where to go, so they know where to fight the fire."

I wasn't lying to Taylor, it wasn't just my desperate need to leave, to be away from the hungry flames and the caustic smoke. It wasn't just my past driving my words, but I didn't think I could stand being there much longer.

"How?" she asked.

"You have to trust me," I said. "And we have to go, right now."

I grabbed her arm, feeling the barely there sense of touch we ghosts are afforded, brought to mind a ghost that was much more suited to an adventure like this, and popped us out of the growing inferno.

JJ LYNCH IS FAMOUS AMONGST US GHOSTS. BEFORE HE DIED he was involved in the construction of the SECI chamber, and after he died he was the first to use it, confirming the theory of the afterlife to the builders of the device.

Famous though he may be, his presence is unpresuming. He has short brown hair, kind but intense blue-grey eyes, and looks like the thirty he was when he died, dressed simply in jeans and a long-sleeve black T-shirt.

Ghost can, if they know how, pop to a location, or pop to a person or ghost, which is, if you think about it, something of a movable location.

JJ was the only choice in this emergency because he knew how to use the SECI chamber, he also had one of the devices dedicated to him in a secret location that wasn't mobbed with huge lines of ghosts, each wanting to try to see if they could master the strange device, this typewriter for ghosts that allowed them to type with no hands and reach past the veil that separates the living from the dead.

Popping to a location can often be full of surprises, like when we just popped to Taylor's house, but popping to a person is often much more surprise filled. You know who you are going to see, but not where, and you will have no idea what they are doing.

Taylor and I popped into a dark space that felt fairly large, but with what appeared to be a dinosaur running towards us amidst a cacophony of sound and—oddly—music.

Sometimes it is just fine not having a heart, or mine would have been trying to beat itself out of my chest. It took me a moment to realize that this was a movie theater and the image I was seeing was not real.

"Fredrick," JJ said with a nod. "Taylor. I didn't think you were coming today."

With time on their hands, the dead see pretty much any and every movie that comes out. JJ was with a group of six other ghosts hovering over the living.

Amidst the madness of this adventure, I had forgotten that this was planned, a saner alternative to risking your wellbeing visiting the living.

"Please," I said. "This is an emergency and we need you."

JJ was, as I indicated before, an adventurous ghost. Perhaps it was being involved in the creation of the SECI chamber, perhaps it was his sudden death, being hit by a car full of inebriated college students. Whatever it was, he was a ghost not content with being like all the other ghosts before him, dutifully trying to stay out of the bardo and determine their unfinished business so they might move on.

I needed no more words, the small nod and the tightening of

his jaw spoke louder than any words could. We flew straight up and left the rampaging dinosaurs behind.

"My parents..." Talyor began breathlessly on the flat roof of the movie theater, the city around us relatively quiet as Christmas approached. "Fire... they are going to die... Please help."

The poor girl could hardly speak.

"We need you to go to the SECI chamber," I said, trying to let my firm tone and calm words help steady the girl. "Her home is burning with her parents trapped in it. They are in the north-eastern corner of the house, wisely sheltering in the bathtub, but they don't have much time."

JJ nodded, "Address?"

I looked at Taylor who, with a somewhat surprised look on her face, rattled it off.

"Okay," he said, looking at Taylor. "I'll do what I can." He turned to me. "But I can't pop. You'll need to take us there, Fredrick."

I am not, as you would say these days, a "fanboy" of JJ Lynch. I was there when he was a brand-new ghost, not aware of what was going on, frightened as the mass of us ghosts at the graveyard came to greet him—which can be, admittedly, quite overwhelming. But still it felt like I was about to be admitted to a secret society since I thought we would be popping to his hidden SECI chamber.

"Taylor, just stay here," I said. "After JJ is set, I'll come right back for you."

She nodded nervously and looked around, her hand at her mouth like she wanted to chew on the fingernails that were no longer there.

With that, JJ whispered the location of the secret SECI chamber. I grabbed his arm, and with a "pop" we were off.

I WILL NOT DISCLOSE WHERE JJ'S SECRET SECI CHAMBER was. Times have changed, the SECI chamber has evolved and isn't so much of a chamber anymore, but his was an act of trust, one I will live up to.

Nor will I describe the process with which a ghost "types," beyond saying it involves technology that can detect our very high-frequency electromagnetic emanations and converts those into letters.

To tell the truth, that first-generation SECI chamber was very hard to use, and I had not been able to master it. It was less like typing and more like sign language, and this fact just might explain why it has taken me so long to tell this story.

All that said, I popped JJ to his secret SECI chamber, he got to work, and I popped back to the movie theater roof, but Taylor was gone.

As I HAVE DESCRIBED EARLIER, POPPING IS ALWAYS something of a risk. You don't know what you will find, and this is why I didn't pop to Taylor. I was not ready to confront the heart of the hungry fire and I had absolutely no desire to watch Taylor's parents die from smoke inhalation... or worse.

If one or more of them became a ghost, then I could be of service, but for me it was something I could not bear to witness.

Earlier when I talked about the fire that I barely survived, I did not disclose that my youngest son, ten years old at the time, did not survive.

I carried his limp form away from the hungry flames before they had done more than lick at him, but I was still too late.

As I kneeled before him, trying to blow life back into his lungs when I wasn't coughing too much to do it, the crackle of the fire and the smell of the smoke taunted me. As the timbers of my home's roof failed with a series of sharp snaps and a wave of heat that took what breath I had away, I knew that I had lost my son. I knew it was the rapacious fire that took him. I knew from the screaming agony of my own wounds adding to the wailing of my heart and the cries of my wife as she saw her inert son that I would never be the same.

Therefore, I did not pop to Taylor. I simply could not. But I popped back to her house, the flames having nearly fully engulfed the faux adobe structure in the few minutes we had been gone.

I had done what could be done, enlisted the help of the adventurous JJ Lynch, but when I heard Taylor's scream rising above the hungry voice of the fire, I knew that it had not been enough. I knew that I should do something.

But I just floated there watching the house burn.

What could I possibly do?

***

THEY SAY THAT OUR FEARS ARE OFTEN IRRATIONAL. Witness my fear of entering Taylor's house again as the flames leaped higher, lighting the foothills of the Catalina Mountains with an eerie, flickering yellow, black smoke swirling up into the dark sky.

I was a ghost. I could not feel the heat nor could the flames harm me, but yet I feared.

This might, indeed, look irrational on the face of it, but that is only if you consider the "physical" aspect of it—as much as that can apply to one such as I. If you consider the emotional toll it would take on me and the potential of sinking into the bardo where I would spend the rest of eternity trying to resuscitate my son while my own burns screamed in agony, then you can consider my fear quite and very rational.

But I had spent my afterlife playing a particular role. I was the elder at the graveyard that I myself created when I was alive. I was the calm, steady presence to those new ghosts, showing them the proper temperament of a well-lived afterlife. I was advisor and witness to the more adventurous ghosts such as JJ Lynch.

I was not a ghost that stood idly by while others suffered.

And it was that schism that more than haunted me in the moments of my delay. There was danger, real danger to myself if I entered that burning building again. But there was also real danger if I did not.

Would I even be able to live with myself if I did nothing?

Without thinking about it or intending to do so, I had drifted higher and towards the burning building. There was, indeed, a slight breeze that night, but such things do not affect those that have passed through the veil. It was a part of me, the bolder part of me that had caused me to move.

So I accelerated that movement and soon I was flying over the house looking into fire, through the hole that had burned in the roof. I looked into the heart the blaze itself and I saw... I know not how to describe it, but I shall try.

I saw flames that seemed to be different than the rest. At first I could not discern the difference, it was more of a sense, a know-ing, but there were flames where the tree used to be that danced, somehow, differently than the rest of the flames. Its movements were less chaotic and more intentful, its dance seeming almost joyful, and I have never thought of fire as joyful. Hungry, yes, angry, to be sure, but never joyful.

And then I saw it. The flames were ever so slightly transparent.

The flames were a ghost.

This explained the thing I thought I saw when I passed by the burning tree earlier.

And this likely explained the fire. Besides being the first to master the SECI chamber, JJ Lynch learned how to, among other things, manipulate his ghostly form so that he could turn lights on and off, which he did to communicate with his living relatives.

But if you took that ability and turned it to nefarious purpose, like causing lights strung around a drying tree to short or spark, you could start a fire.

And I knew, as ghosts sometimes know the truth without proof, that this was what had happened.

As I saw the reality of this night, this fire, the ghost that was flames looked up at me, and while it had no face to speak of, I swear to all that I hold holy that it smiled at me, a wicked and terrible smile.

***

EVEN THOUGH MOST GHOSTS APPEAR AS THEY WERE WHEN they passed away, a ghost can appear to be anything they want... at a cost.

The more you look like you were when you are alive, the more you feel like you did when you were alive. So that cost to a ghost, such as the fire ghost I saw in Taylor's burning house, is you feel less like you did when you were alive.

And that leads, as all ghostly foibles do, to the bardo.

To put it another way, a stable, lifelike appearance lends to your emotional stability as a ghost.

Now there are exceptions, to be sure. All ghosts do not have the same abilities, and some are quite good at appearing as inanimate objects. We have ghosts like this that form the settings for the plays we put on at the graveyard at midnight.

My fear was not forgotten, but it was overridden by my horror at what this ghost had done. Before I could think on it, I shouted, "Who are you?" as I flew down to the fire ghost.

The large living room was fully engulfed except for the center area where the Christmas tree had been. In its place were the ashen remains of the fallen fir tree, darkened and skeletal.

The fire ghost did not run away from me but kept doing its joyful dance around the burning space, the crackle of the actual fire feeling like stabbing blows to my ghostly form.

"Why did you do this?" I shouted as the fire ghost danced around, joining and separating from the hungry flames as they devoured this house.

My mission, protecting Taylor, had not been forgotten, but it had been overridden by my strong emotions. There was something at play here that needed to be understood. Was this personal, was this ghost trying to kill Taylor's parents, or did we have a pyromaniac of a ghost and would we expect many more such fires, and many more lives at risk?

The fire ghost did not answer, it kept dancing around the room and I thought I heard laughter coming from within the roaring crackle of the flames. Manic laughter. Terrible laughter.

"Who are you?" I asked again, my words sounding weak and hollow now that I was in the house where the fire ruled.

My house, when it burned so long ago, was not big like this house, not roomy by today's standards, but it too was built of wood and was the ideal food for the rapacious fire.

As the fire consumed Taylor's house, as the fire ghost continued its dance, as its manic laughter rang out, I felt myself begin to fall.

There is no gravity for a ghost, there is only one place to fall, and that is the bardo.

"Father!" a boy cried out. I looked around, the fire ghost briefly forgotten. Was there someone else in here?

"Help me, Father. Please!" the boy cried, his voice desperate and small, much of the detail of it getting swallowed by the crackling flames.

"Johnathan?" I shouted, suddenly sure it was my son that was calling, the one that did not survive the fire that I barely did. "Where are you, son? I am here."

"The fire, Father!" he cried, his words being broken up by a wracking cough that tore at my heart. "I cannot escape it."

"Get low!" I shouted. "I am coming for you."

This is the way of the bardo, it lies. It called to me telling me that my son was alive, that there was a chance that I could save him, that I might see him again.

The bardo always lies.

And there was part of me that wanted to relax into the lie, to try to save my son again, even if I knew it was destined for failure, and that it would happen over and over and over again.

At least there would be that sweet moment of hope before defeat. I know, as all parents who have lost a child knows, that loss such as this leaves a hole that can never be filled, that can never truly heal.

Taylor's house didn't look the same anymore. I was in my old house. I had helped my wife and our daughter out through our bedroom window and had stumbled out of our bedroom in search of Johnathan as I stooped low and coughed deeply from the choking smoke which I could actually smell.

I was on my way and I think I would have fallen into the bardo if not for the other voice I heard. It was distant, but I knew it was Taylor.

"No!" she shouted. "Stay away. Who are you? What are you?"

And in answer to the external world impinging on my nightmare, the bardo lied to me some more.

"Father!" Johnathan cried. "Help me! Please. I can't open my window and the fire is coming close."

It was my son's voice, but this part had never happened. It was the bardo calling for me, my regrets ready to smother me for the rest of my afterlife.

"No," I said as I stood up and took a deep ghostly breath. I do not have lungs, so I could not cough, I also could not breathe, but the gesture is calming in us just as it is in the living.

"I am sorry, my son," I said to the bardo's representation of my long dead son. "I am so sorry," I said to my son dead these many, many decades.

I did not reach my son in time but I still had a chance to help Taylor. I left the lies of the bardo behind even though it was one of the hardest things I have ever done.

In all my decades as a ghost I had never come so close to falling into the bardo. I had heard the bardo lying to me before in the form of my son's cries, but I had never answered. I had also, mind you, stayed away from fire in all its forms, going so far as to a avoid lit fireplaces and looking askance at candles.

Something shifted in me in that burning house after turning my back on the bardo. I still heard my son's desperate calls, and although they had grown distant, they still tugged on my heart, but now I knew them to be lies. And that knowledge was power. I was a ghost, the fire could not harm me. I had turned my back on the bardo—it too could not harm me. I suddenly understood those adventurous ghosts such as JJ Lynch.

We ghosts feel insubstantial, as is appropriate in keeping with our nature. But there in the middle of Taylor's burning house I felt more solid, more real than I had since I had died.

There was work to be done here, and while I wasn't the most adventurous of ghosts, I was the ghost that was here.

I walked, very deliberately, towards where Taylor's parents were trapped.

Yes, I could have flown, it would have been faster, but I knew that by acting like I was when I was alive, I would feel more like I was when I was alive. How many young ghosts had I given that exact advice?

That simple act brought a greater feeling of solidity, and when I walked through the still blocked door into Taylor's parents' bedroom and saw the bizarre scene laid out before me, I did not hesitate. Not one little bit. I knew what to do and I acted with alacrity.

The expansive bedroom was fully engulfed, the hungry flames flowing over the ceiling like some strange, gravity-defying liquid, the large bed burning, black smoke billowing out, the hardwood dressers burning strongly. The fire had not reached the bathroom yet, but at this point there was no escape from it for Taylor's parents.

This was not what was strange. This was a fire, and while I still hated it, while being in the midst of it did not feel safe, it was not the distraction it once was.

What was strange was the fire ghost. It was in the bathroom poking at Taylor's parents while Taylor yelled at it.

The water had filled the large bathtub and was overflowing, Taylor's parents both had wet towels on their heads and wet washcloths over their mouths. I am no physician and I do not know how effective such methods are, but they were what they could do. Still, both of them were coughing.

The strange part of this whole scene was the first ghost. It was poking at Taylor's parents with a stabbing appendage of ghostly flame. First it stabbed at Taylor's father then at her mother, and each time they yelped in pain.

I saw all of this in just a moment, marched up to the fire ghost and grabbed it, and flew the two of us up through the roof into the Tucson night.

Now, such a feat was not a simple one. Each ghost is different, operating at, what I am told, is a different frequency of electromagnetic energy. If you don't match frequencies with another ghost you can't do things such as grab them, for your hand will just pass through them as it will the living.

But I had been a ghost long before we had such fancy explanations and I instinctively knew how to touch another ghost, even one that looked like fire.

And I did.

The ghost let out a scream that was itself the roaring of a mighty blaze, one that might level a whole town. This cry chilled me to my core and I almost let the beast go, but I persevered as the fire ghost twisted around me, changed its frequency trying to escape, and when that failed, wrapped me in what appeared to be crackling fire.

But I did not let go.

LIFE AT THE TURN OF THE CENTURY, THE TURN OF THE twentieth century to be specific, was hard, death awaiting around many a corner.

Tucson was a town of less than eight thousand people. The desert was a harsh mistress and there were no creature comforts such as air-conditioning to blunt the effects of the desert summers.

All of this is to say, I knew many a hardship when I was

young, and that night as I wrestled with the fire ghost above Taylor's burning home, I found the mettle I had long thought I had lost.

I had relegated myself to being the steady presence at the graveyard, the elder ghost, the mentor to the newly dead, but why?

Because I did not like adventure? But then why had I, as a young man, ventured out west before the turn of the century to find my fortune and make my way?

This view of myself as the elder stateman of the graveyard was a fine one, a useful one even, but was this all there was to my afterlife?

As ghosts we have what is termed in the parlance of the day, "unfinished business." Mine has never been in question. That fire took the life of my son and I was unable to save him. How could I ever "finish" that "business"? How could I ever do enough good in this world to balance the scales of a father losing his son to the beast that is fire?

Simply put, I cannot finish that business, which is why I have been a ghost so long. The past is out of my reach, but the present is here.

"Show yourself," I said as I grappled with the ghost.

The burning pseudo adobe house was a thousand feet below us, the fire looking small and congenial at this distance.

The fire ghost was all around me and we must have looked like some strange comet flying to and fro in the sky to any of the dead that were looking.

"I shall wrestle you all the way to hell," I said. "But I will not let you go until you reveal yourself and explain this madness."

I kept trying to fly us up, away from the living, and the fire ghost kept trying to fly us back to the house, giving the comet that we appeared to be an irregular bouncing path that didn't go anywhere.

I know how I appear to the other ghosts in the graveyard with my meticulously clean three-piece suit, starched collar, and pocket watch, with my greying hair and well-established crow's feet. They think I come from a kinder, gentler time and forget that my roots reach back to when the West was wild. It was my duty as undertaker to deal with some of the wilder effects of a young Tucson.

The fire ghost continued to fight, but I was a much older ghost and I had the advantage. We slowly gained elevation.

As many ghosts have said, without our flesh we are more intuitive than the living. Many would use the word "psychic" but I do not hold much respect for that word and for the charlatans that used it in my time among the living. But be that as it may, as we wrestled, I remembered asking Taylor if there was anyone else living in the house when we first arrived and she had said, "No, it's just them now."

This was not a house for two with its many rooms.

And then I could see it clearly. The parts of the large house I had seen were cold and barely looked lived in. There wasn't much life left in this house. Taylor's parents had lost her, but it was clear they had lost someone else too.

As I wound my memory back, I remembered a family photo I had glimpsed depicting a younger version Taylor and her parents with a boy with unruly sandy hair a few years younger than Taylor.

"You are Taylor's brother," I said to the fire ghost.

The fiery ghost I was wrestling with did not answer, but let out a shriek such as should only come from a beast straight out of hell, and in my surprise, the fire ghost slipped from my grasp and streaked back towards the house.

THE FIRE GHOST WAS TOO LATE. JJ LYNCH AND THE LIVING who managed the SECI chamber had done their part.

As the fire ghost flew as fast as it could, I saw three firemen carrying Taylor's parents out of the house with Taylor next to them.

It was an odd scene from my perspective. Taylor with her perfectly quaffed blond hair and flowing blue dress next to the ashen firemen carrying the limp forms of her parents.

The fire ghost, whom I suspected to be Taylor's brother, streaked towards them intent on doing harm, but this was a young ghost. I popped to Taylor and asked, "How did your brother die?"

The young lady was, understandably, a bit tongue-tied at my sudden appearance, at me knowing what I shouldn't know, at the state of her parents. At a glance, I could see that they were both unconscious but there was still life in them. They had a fighting chance.

"Was it a fire?" I asked as Taylor's eyes widened. "Did he die in a fire?"

Taylor mutely nodded, and although it was barely a nod, I took it as her assent to my assertion, and that was all I needed. I flew up and intercepted the fire ghost before it could do more damage.

I VIEW MYSELF AS NOT THAT ADVENTUROUS OF A GHOST, AND as such I don't see a need to regale you with a blow-by-blow of my battle with the fire ghost, Taylor's brother. Suffice it to say that it was a long conflict and I prevailed.

Ghosts cannot really hurt each other physically, since we are not physical, making a battle like this about endurance and experience, both of which I had much more of.

When the sun came up and Taylor's house was reduced to smoldering ashes below us, the fire ghost finally looked like a person, like a young man with unruly sandy-blond hair and eyes as blue as Taylor's.

"Let me go," he said, rather sullenly.

He was pitiful looking as a normal ghost, his ghostly form rather transparent and the edges diffuse. He appeared to be dressed in long khaki shorts, a baggy blue T-shirt, with those awful flip-flop things on his feet.

It is worth noting that I had never met this ghost before. There are, of course, legion upon legion of ghosts that I have not met, but few in this area that have not been by the graveyard.

This, in and of itself, was telling.

"Are you going to behave yourself now?" I asked.

He nodded.

"Then greet me properly," I said as I let him go and held out my hand.

He looked at me and then at my hand and I could practically see his thoughts, so transparent was his expression of emotion. He did not want to do this ritual, so basic amongst the dead. Or, at least, he did not want to do it with me. I had bested him and it was clear he would hold it against me.

"You can do it," I said. "But let me go first. My name is Fredrick Penny and I died of Parrot Fever in 1929 a few months after my house burned down and I tragically lost my son to the blaze."

I had never told anyone that last part, but I needed to reach this boy. I let my appearance change to be more like it was when I died with the right side of my face and my right hand badly scarred from burns.

The young man's jaw dropped open and he looked me up and down like he felt the need to reappraise me, for I wasn't what he thought I was. I, also, was feeling like I wasn't quite what I thought I was.

The young man took my hand, modulating his form correctly so we could actually touch, although it was that barely perceptible sensation of touch that we ghosts are relegated to.

"My... my name is," he began, his words halting and slow. "My name is Jared Youst and I died..."

He blinked, his eyes tearing up, a marvel that we can still express in biological ways even though we lack biology.

"It's okay, son," I said, a little surprised that I had used the word "son." While this was a common if somewhat old-fashioned way for an older male to refer to a younger male, and although I was plenty enough old fashioned for it, it was not a form of expression I used, for obvious reasons.

His jaw moved and his bright blue eyes looked anywhere but at me.

"You can tell me," I said. "I promise to keep it a secret, if that helps."

"You will?" he said, his eyes briefly meeting mine before flicking down to the smoldering mess that was once the Youst home. "After I...?"

"I'm sure you are done with such behaviors," I said. "So I will keep your secret if you like as long as you no longer engage in such activities or try to harm any living."

"Yes... yes, sir," he said with a deferential nod.

I slowly shook his hand and restated my name and cause of death and looked at him pointedly.

"My... my name is Jared Youst and I died..." He took a deep breath as if he needed to brace himself for the truth.

It is at moments like this that I still miss my long-gone biology, for this was a moment that would have paired nicely with some warming brandy.

The young man squared his shoulders, really looked me in

the eye, and said, "My name is Jared Youst and I died of electrocution in that house."

———

There was more to Jared Youst's story, and perhaps he should tell it himself, but for the sake of my own story, I will give you the briefest of summaries.

Jared was twenty-two when he died and still living with his parents. He was one of those young people, of whom there seem to be so many these days, that just couldn't find their way. Perhaps it was the relative wealth of his parents, perhaps it was something in his personality, or perhaps it was merely a sign of the times. Whatever it was is not for me to say.

To "pay his way"—his father's term—he did work around the house. Some of that work that was, in my humble opinion, good for him, character building, like tending to the pool and the lawn, doing dishes. Some of it, like the task that killed him, was too much to ask, again, in my humble opinion.

Jared Youst died when, at his father's insistence, he tried to replace some circuit breakers. His father was impatient, the jacuzzi kept blowing the fuse and he did not want to wait for, or pay for, an electrician.

After dutifully watching some videos on the topic, Jared proceeded to attempt the repair and electrocuted himself, managing to start a small fire in a nearby yucca.

As Jared told me the story, his form changed, fresh burns showing on his hands and arms, making me understand why I had called him "son." He was not the child of my loins, but we bore similar scars making us kindred spirits.

"Were you trying to kill your parents?" I asked as we hovered above the smoldering remains of the Youst home, the Christmas morning sun just peaking over the horizon and illuminating the charred scene below.

He pursed his lips and would not meet my eye, which seemed like answer enough, but then he said, "No... not at first. I... I think because of how I died, I can mess with electricity, like that other ghost."

"JJ Lynch," I offered.

"Yeah. Him," he said. "I stayed away, for a couple of years, just wandering around, but when I came back and saw that big Christmas tree decorated so cheerfully, I..."

He ended in a weak shrug. He had snapped.

"And when the tree caught on fire?" I asked.

"At first, I... I just wanted to mess with the lights. Get their attention. I was planning to do it in the morning when they got up. You know, let my folks know I was alive."

I nodded at him to continue, although it seemed he was looking to me for approval.

"When you do it," he continued. "You know, change so electricity can flow through you. It... it's wild. Energizing. And also..." He shrugged weakly again, seeming to lack the words, but I had heard JJ's story and it seemed to me like this was the closest equivalent to a strong drug a ghost had.

"So you weren't trying to start a fire," I said.

He shook his head. "No. Of course not. But then I did. I guess what I was doing, making the lights flicker, heated the wires up enough—not that I could tell—and caught the tree on fire."

"What did you do when the fire started?" I asked.

Jared looked away, his eyes straying down to the mess below us, the fire having escaped the house and crawled up the craggy hill behind the house a distance. His gaze didn't linger, and I realized that the bardo would soon be calling on Jared Youst if it wasn't calling right now.

"I... I tried to," he began, looking at me again. "I figured, you know, if I can change my form to mess with electricity then I could change my form to mess with fire." He ended in yet another weak shrug.

"And you lost yourself," I said. I didn't think it was wise to keep him here much longer, but I needed to know what had happened.

"It... I... I felt it," he said, his eyes wide and looking haunted. "I felt the fire. Like it was alive, like it was talking to me, asking me to do... things. Terrible things."

I had never heard of this, of a ghost taking on the spirit of fire, but I believed it. Having been inside a burning building as I struggled to save my family, I can easily believe that fire is alive, is a force, is evil.

"You were angry at your father," I said, attempting to prompt him to continue.

He nodded. "And my mother. She... she didn't try to stop me, just let my father yell at me until I did it."

"And for that, both of your parents have paid a heavy price," I said. "They have lost both of their children."

Jared blinked and stared at me. "Wait. What happened to Taylor?"

The boy had been so gone, so possessed by the fire and his own anger, that he didn't notice his own sister.

"That is not for me to tell," I said. "But I can take you to her."

He nodded, enthusiastically, his face lighting up and making him look more like a boy than a man.

It was touch and go for Talyor and Jared's parents, but I taught them how to tend to them, how to do what a ghost can most benevolently do for the living.

We call it the "warmth" because it is pretty much the only time we can sense heat. It is like a meditation. You open yourself up to the energy of the universe and let it flow through you into your loved one.

I know it sounds strange, like I am a charlatan trying to sell you something, but there is nothing to sell here, only energy to give. Another gift of being dead, it seems.

This was good. It gave them both purpose, something to do, a reason to ignore the beckoning calls of the bardo.

This, again, is more their tale than mine, but suffice it to say that Mr. and Mrs. Youst survived. A week later, Tayler and Jared found me in the graveyard on News Year's Eve.

It was another lonely night as ghosts tempted the bardo to be with their loved ones for this holiday. I was wandering the grounds, walking slowly and carefully between the gravestones, wondering at the stories at many of the stones that are yet to be known, what adventures these sprits had both while living and while dead.

Such a state, for a ghost, is restful and reflective, even meditative. This is why I did not notice Jared and Taylor Youst until they stood in front of me.

"We..." Jared began, his cheeks flushing just a touch red.

"We wanted to thank you," Taylor said with a rather dazzling smile, a smile I couldn't help but answer with a smile of my own. It made me understand why I agreed to take such a risk on Christmas Eve.

"Our parents are okay," Jared said, briefly meeting my gaze and then staring down at his flip-flopped feet.

"And that is all because of you," Taylor said, her smile becoming even more dazzling.

"It was JJ," I said. "He let the firemen know where to look. You should thank him. And it was the two of you staying with them so long and delivering the warmth."

If truth be told, my wanderings this night were not as restful as they usually were. I had been reviewing my sedate afterlife and had found it wanting. Was there no more that I could do? Especially now that I had faced the bardo and it had given me its worst in the form of the son I could not save.

Shouldn't my afterlife have more meaning?

"We will thank him," Taylor said. "But it was you, Fredrick, that knew what to do. It was you that went with me or there's no doubt my parents would have died and Jared and I would be... lost."

"And we were wondering," Jared said, taking a deep breath and squaring his shoulders, finally looking me in the eyes. "Can we... you know... come to you with questions? Can you, maybe, teach us some things?"

This was my chosen role here at the graveyard, but it had been a while since a ghost had asked me for help like this directly. There were younger, more adventurous ghosts that had been garnering this kind of attention. And perhaps that was because I had been coasting in my afterlife for quite a long time, becoming more and more adverse to risk.

In that moment, it occurred to me that these two young ghosts viewed me, Fredrick Penny, founder of this graveyard, long ago mortician, survivor of a house fire, as an adventurous ghost.

"It would be my most distinct pleasure," I said, and I'll wager my smile in that moment was more dazzling than Taylor's.

They both piped up and asked for three different things right away and it was clear that my afterlife was going to be a bit more adventurous from now on.

BACKSTORY—A MORE
ADVENTUROUS AFTERLIFE

Holiday: Christmas

This story wasn't written for an anthology but was a spillover from writing for the *Holiday Spectacular*. I was thinking about how lonely the holidays could be, especially for earthbound spirits in my ghost world and the start to this popped out.

In my ghost world, it's dangerous to communicate with your living relatives and I guess that extends to many of the living as well. Families can be amazing, they can hold you up and make you more than you ever thought you could be, but they can also tear you down like nothing else can. I guess some of those thoughts leaked into this and my own experiences of lonely Christmases (long ago, fortunately).

This was also an opportunity to explore one of the supporting characters in my ghost world. Fredrick has been around since the first novel, *Shuffled Off*, and it seemed high time to delve into who he is and how he died.

There are, to date, six novel-length books and many short

stories written in this world of ghosts. You can find out more at *ShuffledOff.com*.

PART 12
THE GREAT TURKEY HEIST

THE GREAT TURKEY HEIST

In the annals of the township of Oakmont, Ohio, the Great Turkey Heist of 1971 should stand out in the sleepy little community's history. It should stand tall as a shining example of youthful energy and ingenuity, of daring do and untold bravery in the noble cause of saving a Thanksgiving that was very, very much needed.

Except for a couple of important factors.

The eldest member of the team that pulled off this magnificent heist was ten, and the execution was so flawless that the only thing that could go in the histories would be this clipping from the *Oakmont Gazette*:

On Nov. 25, 1971, Doctor Elias Young, resident of Oak Street, reported that a roasting turkey was stolen from his oven. The Carroll County Sheriff's Office visited Doctor Young the next day in an attempt to calm the nearly hysterical gentleman. No suspects were found and the only witness, four-year-old Amelia Young, claimed, "Yucky turkey. Store man took it away." When asked to describe the "store man," Amelia Young said, "Thick mustache. Big belly. Very nice." Deputies found no indi-

viduals matching that description at the A&P whose where-abouts could not be accounted for. It is suspected that the evidence has been consumed and the perpetrators will not be found.

But that telling is entirely inadequate and I should know. I was there. I wasn't the brains of the operation, or the brawn, but it would be accurate to say that I was the reason for it all.

It's been over fifty years now and enough time has passed to tell this tale. Besides, not all of us are here anymore, and in this way I can honor my brave compatriots.

It all started on a sparkling Thanksgiving morning in 1971.

"BILLY RUDOLPH GRANGER," MY MOM SHOUTED UP THE stairs of our two-story split-level home. "Get out of bed and get down here. It's Thanksgiving. You know I need you. And something has come up. So get down here now!"

My mother wasn't a thespian, but good lord could she project her voice when she wanted to. It was almost like she was in the bedroom I shared with my little brother Anthony, who I called Ant.

"You heard her, Ant," I said groggily from the top bunk bed. "Mom needs help."

I peered at my little brother, he was on the floor in his pajamas playing with Legos. He had a tousle of brown hair and bright brown eyes, just like I did.

"My name is not 'Rudolph,'" he shot back.

I hated my middle name. It was way too "red-nosed reindeer" for me and a source of constant teasing. But this was important. We both knew Mom only used our middle names when she was serious.

I was eight and a half, Ant was six, and as such I was

required to be a proper "big brother," which mostly meant doing all the crap that no one else wanted to do.

To be fair, 1971 had been a hard year for our family and I understood why I was often called to duty, but sometimes I just wanted to sleep in.

I grumbled my way out of bed, into some jeans and my coveted "The Amazing Spider-Man" sweatshirt, avoided the landmine of Legos and other toys on our bedroom floor, and made my way to do my duty for the Granger Family Thanksgiving.

My mother had a habit of hitting me with a verbal list of things to do. Especially when she was in a hurry. It was rapid-fire, like a machine gun, and I was somehow expected to remember it all, execute it perfectly, and do so with a big smile on my freckled face.

As a kid, I just hated it. I didn't want to be that organized or that efficient. I wanted to go back to bed, go back to the Amazing Spider-Man comic that had kept me up too late, to dreaming of crawling up buildings and trading witty quips with nasty villains.

I most certainly did not want to peel potatoes, baste a turkey in an oven that felt as hot as a blast furnace when you opened it, and really did not want to prepare the mountain of green beans knowing I would be in trouble if one little rusty spot was found in the final product.

"It's all laid out," Mom said. She was fashionably dressed for the time in a paisley print dress, her shoulder-length chestnut hair curled to perfection. "You know this is a hard time for us," she continued. "Your Uncle Larry, you know he hasn't been right since he got back from that terrible war. He's having one of his... well you know... I'm counting on you, Billy. It's been a terrible year, we all really need a nice Thanksgiving. I'll be back as soon as I can."

And then she was gone, with only one more shouted directive, "And keep an eye on that darned oven."

"One of his... well you know..." meant that Uncle Larry was having an "episode," thinking he was back in Vietnam, and was probably terrorizing the neighborhood, or at the very least Aunt Jill.

With an appropriate amount of grumbling for an eight-and-a-half-year-old, I got to work.

"How is it going in the kitchen?" Mom asked.

I was using the rotary dial phone with the long cord in the kitchen. It was a shade of yellow like most everything in here.

I was born in this house, but as the story goes, it already had this vaguely yellow range top/stove combo and Formica counters when we bought it. My father hated it, but my mother leaned into it, declaring that she would have her kitchen "sunny side up."

She painted the walls yellow and the décor was all egg, chicken, and rooster based.

It was a lot.

"Great, great," I said, trying to make my voice match the cheeriness of the kitchen as I looked around at the chaos of chopped potatoes, pumpkin pie fixings, and the dreaded green beans. "How's Uncle Larry?"

She sighed. "It's going to take a while, but we'll get him there for dinner, but plan for six instead of four."

"Okay," I said. I had no idea what else to say.

"I appreciate you stepping up, Billy," she said. "I know it's a lot."

"Of course," I said, feeling a swelling sense of pride in my chest. My mom didn't often say things like that.

"And watch that oven," she said. "You know how it is."

"I am, I am," I said, not even looking at the oven.

I really, really should have been. Disaster was about to strike and I was oblivious.

———

I WAS THE OVEN BEING ON THE FRITZ AGAIN, ANT scrapping his knee pretty badly, and our next door neighbor Mrs. Thompson coming over for a cup of sugar, yet again, that led to the disaster.

That and boiling over potatoes, the liquid hissing on the range, and our cat Bartholomew helping himself to some condensed milk in a bowl I was going to use for the pumpkin pie.

By the time I dealt with all the little things, finding a cup of sugar, bandaging Ant up, and shooing away Bartholomew and deciding to forget he had ever sampled the condensed milk, our oven had decided to turn into the spawn of Satan we all knew it was and burn the hell out of our turkey quicker than you would think possible.

And it was a nice turkey. Mom had splurged. This was Dad's first Thanksgiving back from the war, and even though it had been a lot easier on him than on Uncle Larry, it hadn't been easy. At all.

"What did you do?" Ant asked, waving away the lingering smoke and staring at the blackened fowl sitting on the fancy Formica counter that seemed to be razzing me with its cheery yellow. There was nothing to be cheerful about.

"It was the oven," I said through gritted teeth. I was sitting on the linoleum floor—fortunately more beige than yellow—my arms around my knees. "And you and Bartholomew and Mrs. Thompson."

Dad had left for the war when I was six and I had grown up pretty quick in the intervening two and a half years. I cooked pretty often and, honestly, didn't hate it most of the time.

"This is bad," Ant offered, doing a good job of stating the exceedingly obvious. "Mom's been talking about this Thanksgiving since spring."

The door was open, letting the smoke out and the cool air in, and I heard a voice say, "What's 'ole Red-Nose crying about now?"

It was Chet Michaels. He was big and burly and ten with buzzed blond hair and he happened to be my best friend, which means he teased me mercilessly about whatever he could, mostly my middle name.

I didn't think about how Chet was over a year older than me and about thirty pounds heavier. I surged up off the floor, flew out the door, and tackled him.

We rolled around in the grass, crunched across the downed oak leaves, neither of us getting the upper hand. Which was surprising. Clearly the incident had affected me.

I finally got the upper hand and ended up on top of him. "Don't call me that," I said, my hand balled into a fist and my arm cocked back.

"I'll give you that one for free, but get off me, Billy," Chet said, not a trace of fear in his voice. "And tell me what's going on."

* * *

SITTING IN THE DRIED LEAVES FROM OUR BIG OAK TREE, THE leaves I hadn't gotten around to raking up yet, I told Chet what was going on. Halfway through, my neighbor, Alice McGee wandered over curious about the "hubbub."

Her word, not mine, as in, "What's all this hubbub about, boys?"

Alice was nine and a half, a little taller than Chet, and skinny. She had green eyes, reddish-blond hair braided into pigtails, and glasses with thick black frame. She was wearing overalls and a blue sweater which did nothing to blunt her bookworm appearance.

"Go away, Alice," Chet growled. "It's time for the men to talk."

Chet didn't like Alice, but I did. Not quite in the way I would like her in a few years, but we were friends. She was smart and fun and actually liked comic books.

"It's the turkey," I said. "The oven..."

"Satan-spawned contraption that it is," Alice said. She was my neighbor, we talked a little bit a lot. Her face squished up, her blue eyes getting that look, that Alice-has-an-idea look. "This will not stand, gentlemen. It is up to us, we must give the Grangers the kind of Thanksgiving they need, give these brave soldiers the day they deserve."

Alice was prone to speeches, and at our ages the controversies of the Vietnam War hadn't really filtered down. We knew that some adults hated it, and figured that was just them hating war, which seemed entirely justified and rational. If we even noticed that in many cases it was the soldier that the hate was heaped upon, it didn't really sink in.

Our young lives so far have been steeped in the news of war, and in our families a solider was to be respected.

"Are you offering your turkey?" Chet asked, a defiant sneer in his voice.

"No," she said, a twinkle in her eyes. "I am offering up the best turkey in town, the turkey of one Doctor Elias Young, who we all know is a turkey."

She grinned, seeming pleased with her dual use of the word "turkey."

"How?" I asked, confused. Doctor Young went on and on about his turkey, about how he "brined" it, whatever that was, and slowly roasted it for exactly six hours, basting it precisely every twenty minutes to "ensure a guaranteed perfect result."

Alice did a half snort, half laugh and said, "We are going to steal it, of course."

DOCTOR ELIAS YOUNG WAS NOT A DOCTOR, AT LEAST NOT IN the way that any of us would acknowledge at that age. He had a doctorate in business from Harvard University which he told people often, annoyingly so, in a way that made him sound silly to us.

He lived in a big house on Oak Street and owned half the buildings that bordered the park at the center of our town.

When you think of Oakmont, just visualize that Warner Brothers' backlot that has been used in hundreds of movies and TV shows like *The Gilmore Girls* and *Back to the Future*. There's a park at the center of town with large, mature trees, oaks in this case, with a big gazebo in the middle and mostly red brick buildings surrounding the square.

Oakmont has that wholesome Anytown, USA vibe to it.

And this Anytown, USA mostly belonged to "Doctor" Young.

"You just want to get back at him," Chet said on hearing Alice's plan. "Because of what he did to your father."

There was no love lost between the Youngs and the McGees and that goes back a least a century.

For the current generation, it was Alice's father that started an ice cream shop on the town square and it did very well. Then Doctor Young raised the rent, forced him out, and installed his own ice cream shop and there wasn't a thing Mr. McGee could do about it.

"It was real crummy what he did," I said. "And everyone knows it. He's such a Scrooge and never helps anyone with all his money."

Chet couldn't deny that and nodded.

"I'll admit, this a multipurpose thing," Alice said with a shrug. "So what? You boys in?"

"I don't know..." Chet began.

"Or are you chicken?" Alice asked, cocking her hip and putting her fists on her waist in a gesture that reminded me of my mother.

"I'm no chicken," Chet said, imitating her gesture in a way that was comical and not at all intimidating.

"Then we better get busy," Alice said. "We don't have much time."

It must be clear at this point that Alice was the brains, Chet was the brawn, and I was... well, I was the terrified kid that had to actually pull the very hot bird out of Young's oven and somehow get out unnoticed.

The stakes were high. Either this worked, or one way or another it was not going to be good for me.

Well, the burned turkey would mean ruining Thanksgiving for my father and uncle who desperately needed a taste of normal life, but getting caught in this endeavor would mean being grounded until I was old enough to shave.

And most days it would have been an easy choice.

I'm really not the courageous type.

But Uncle Larry and my dad needed this.

So as we sat under our big maple in our backyard, Alice gave orders and Chet and I did what she told us to do.

It was uncanny, almost like she had this plan in her back pocket all the time.

"We need fireworks," she said, looking at Chet.

"I don't have any—" Chet began.

"Don't bother," Alice said. "Everyone knows about your famous horde of fireworks. Get us some. We'll need a distraction."

She looked at me. "Billy, you are in charge of finding something to transport the turkey in. It needs to be able to handle heat and hold the liquid."

I shook my head. "I got a pan," I said. "But we can't be running around town with a turkey in a pan."

"No," she said. "I'm in charge of the disguise. We'll use Clara's stroller, dress it up like a baby, so you need to find something to put it in that is small, but waterproof and can handle heat."

My mind spun. How was that going to work?

"And Ant will need to keep your preparations going," she said nodding at the back door where Ant's head was visible in the window of the door watching us.

"What else?" Chet asked.

"You need to find us a volunteer," Alice said and then tapped on her chin with a finger and added, "Actually... you need to find us someone that will find someone else that will provide the distraction."

"Huh?" Chet asked, clearly not following. To be fair, I didn't either.

"Look, Chet," she said, pushing her glasses up and folding her arms over her overalls. "If you recruit someone directly, they might rat us out. But let's say you get your friend, we'll call him Tim, to get his friend, we'll call him Fred, to do what we need, then it will be harder for this to be traced back to you. Our 'Tim' will have to owe you or be terrified of you."

Chet got this silly grin on his face, made a fist, and punched his other open hand. "It's clobberin' time," he said. The Thing was way more Chet's speed than Spider-Man. He got up off the ground, now eager for this.

Alice held up her hand, a smile of pure joy spreading across her young face, her green eyes sparkling. "Not quite," she said. "We have to discuss my price first."

IN MY MIND ALICE MCGEE WAS ON THE CUSP OF EITHER becoming a hero like Spider-Man or a villain like Doc Ock. It could easily go either way. I had suspected as much, but that Thanksgiving day in 1971, I knew it to be true.

She was brilliant and relentless, the only question was whether she would use her powers for good or for ill.

Her price for her help saving the Granger Family Thanksgiving was twofold:

First, Chet needed to agree to be her protecter at school, to be her "knight," as she put it. It made sense, they were in the same grade and no one messed with Chet Michaels.

Second, I was to be her ears at school. If people said bad things about her, she wanted me to "infiltrate and report."

Seriously, she was on the cusp, sure to be a hero or a villain.

"You have to do it," I said to Chet. I had dragged him into our very yellow kitchen which still smelled smokey but at least I could breathe. He had flat refused Alice's "price."

"No," he said, folding her arms. "I will not let that little... that *girl* boss me around for the rest of my life."

"For me," I said. "Please. For Uncle Larry. For my dad. Please, Chet. I am begging you."

Most boys my age were afraid of Chet so he didn't really have a lot of friends, but my plea to our friendship failed. He just shook his head.

"Imagine how many enemies she will make," I said.

"I am," he said, loudly. Ant was staring at us as he pretended to sort through the green beans without really doing anything.

"Imagine how often it will be clobberin' time," I said, my voice low. "Alice is going to rule the school, you know that. Won't it be better if you are on her side? If we are on her side?"

He stood there blinking. Chet wasn't dumb, not at all, he just heavily favored his physical side and it took him a bit to think things through.

"You owe me," he said with a sigh.

"Big time!" I agreed.

Alice's plan was simple. Distraction at the front of Doctor Young's house giving me the opportunity to slip in the back, nab the bird, and slip back out.

Everyone knew that the kitchen was off limits during his preparing of the feast for his family, facilitating the ease of the op —"op" was Chet's word, he though it made it sound cooler and I had to agree. Doctor Young was so fussy about tending to the turkey that he didn't allow anyone to interfere lest they spoil it.

Doctor Young was married to a real doctor, a nice lady named Elizabeth who seemed to have very poor taste in husbands. They had three kids, the oldest Ant's age.

I felt a little bad for them. I did. I was hoping to deprive them of their Thanksgiving turkey, but this was too important to let such concerns get in the way.

The Youngs lived in a fancy Victorian house, two stories tall, built of brick with a covered porch, and a third story jutting up in a fancy little tower that had windows from which you could see most of Oakmont.

The house was on Oak Street. It had been built in the late 1800s by one of the city's founding fathers and was just a block back from the town square.

There were lots of bushes, some on the side of the house thick enough to hide behind even with the leaves shed for the season.

We were watching the kitchen window, waiting for the basting to happen, figuring he'd leave the kitchen afterward and that would be our window of opportunity.

I was shaking in my tennis shoes, pretty much literally, about what I was about to do, but I was also worried about Ant. He was younger than me, hadn't been heaped as much responsibility as I had, and there had only been ten minutes to tell him what to do with the Thanksgiving prep until we got back.

The primary thing was to answer the phone and cover for me if it was Mom. The nearly as important thing was to not burn anymore food.

We had walkie-talkies so he could talk to us in case there was an emergency which I was hoping, praying, and crossing my fingers and toes there wasn't.

"Is it bastin' time yet?" Chet whispered, a chuckle in his voice. He liked The Thing and The Fantastic Four, like I liked Spider-Man. At least he was having fun.

"Not so far," Alice said, completely ignoring the comic book reference.

I was worried about everything. Getting caught in the Young house. Getting the turkey back. And having it edible once we got there. I mean, how do you transport a baking turkey with all the bubbling juices safely? The oven will probably be over four hundred degrees and it's not like you can just dump it all in a plastic bag and call it good.

"Vulture, this is nest," the walkie-talkie squawked. It was Ant. "Vulture" referred to as in "turkey vulture."

It was turned down low, but I was worried that all of Oakmont could hear it.

"Go ahead, nest," I whispered into the walkie, hoping it was loud enough. "Over."

"Mayday, mayday," Ant said. "Mother hen called. She'll be home in an hour. And what do I need to do for the pumpkin pie? Over."

I froze. It was all too much for me. With my eyes wide and my mouth open, Alice grabbed the walkie. "Call your Aunt Kathy for help with the pie," she said. "We'll be home before then. Maintain radio silence. Over and out."

Yup, hero or villain, Alice was way too good under pressure, considering her age.

CHET REALLY CAME THROUGH FOR US, AND I HAVE NO IDEA how he did it. His role, assigned by the mastermind Alice, was to convince someone and have them convince someone else to provide us with our distraction.

He grumbled that it cost him *all* his fireworks, but when Chet used the walkie and said, "Vulture to Barbie, execute," it wasn't two minutes until a teenage girl came riding up to the Young house.

She was probably fourteen, much older than any of us, with long blonde hair and a pink bike with a wicker basket installed on the handlebars.

"You know her?" Alice whispered to Chet.

"Of course not," he whispered back as we peered through

the bushes. "I can follow instructions. I know of her, but we've never met."

Alice's eyes widened and she looked at Chet like she was seeing him for the first time.

Doctor Young had just basted and we had forty minutes to get this done, get back home, and get the Young's turkey in our oven.

My knees felt like they were made of Jell-O and I was quite convinced I would never eat again, my stomach was tied up in such a knot.

The teenage girl walked up to the door, knocked, and then Alice said, "Go!"

If Alice hadn't put some punch in her voice, I don't think I would have moved, but I did. I sinched up my backpack, ran to the back of the Young house, and peeked in the window of the back door.

The kitchen wasn't any bigger than ours, it was a very old house, after all, but the appliances were bigger, fancier, and nothing was any shade of yellow. The stove was gas, the metal on top gleaming. The counters were tiled and the cabinets looked to be made up of some fancy wood just like the floors.

I slowly turned the doorknob and almost passed out from relief when I discovered it wasn't locked.

I carefully opened it and sneaked in, figuring folks could probably hear my heart beating a block away in the town square it was so darned loud.

Once I got inside, the smell was so glorious, so enticing, that it confused my knotted up stomach. I couldn't tell if I was starving or if I was about to throw up.

I carefully closed the door and crawled over the hardwood floor to the oven. In the next room I could hear murmured voices.

Alice had said to Chet, "Your distraction must engage the Youngs for a least three minutes."

I had no idea what the teenage girl was talking to them about, but the impression I got was that they all knew each other.

I opened the oven and was hit in the face with a blast of scalding heat that made me want to move away and a blast of heavenly scent that made me want to move closer.

Whatever I thought about Doctor Elias Young, I no longer had any doubt that he was the Master of Turkey Roasting in the greater Oakmont area.

I shucked my backpack and prepared to transport the bird.

This had been my part to figure out, and at that point I was embarrassed to say that Ant came up with the key bit.

"It's a hot turkey, with bubbling fat," I had said to him in our "sunny side up" kitchen. I was packing my backpack and giving him instructions. "What am I going to do with all the basting liquid?"

Ant shook his head like he was the older brother and said, "Use the thermos, dummy."

And that was that, a simple way to transport the super-hot liquid.

The rest of the plan was pretty simple. I had a brownie pan in my backpack. The Young's turkey would go in that, I would wrap it with tin foil, wrap that with a towel, and put all of that in a garbage bag, and that would go in my backpack. I would then fervently pray it didn't melt the plastic.

I was laying out the tin foil when I heard a quiet voice ask, "Hello, who are you?"

I froze, my heart finding a brand-new high gear, bouncing around my chest like an out of control pinball. This was it. I had been caught. The best case scenario was that I would be grounded for the rest of my life.

I think there are many kids better suited to stealing a turkey than me. While I love to live the lives of daring characters vicariously via comic books, I had never really thought of myself like that.

I was the kid who did what they were told and kept the grumbling to a minimum, got good grades, helped around the house, and even occasionally made an attempt to clean up my room.

I wanted to be liked. I wanted to get along. Stealing Thanksgiving turkeys runs counter to that.

Kneeling on the hardwood floor of the Youngs' kitchen, sweating in the heat of the open over door, knowing I was caught, I ran the voice back through my mind and realized that all might not be lost. It had been a girl's voice that I heard, probably a little girl.

I slowly turned, plastered a smile on my face, which I'm sure was quite red from the heat washing out of the oven and from my embarrassment at getting caught.

The kitchen door was cracked open just enough for a tiny round face to peak through. It was one of the Young kids. I didn't know her name, but she was about three of four, dressed in a frilly blue dress with a matching bow restraining her curly blond hair.

I have no idea where this came from, but I quietly said, "Hello. I am the with the grocery store. I'm sorry to say that the turkey we sold your father is not any good, it will make you sick, so I am taking it back."

"Yucky!" she said, squishing her face up like she had just eaten some very bad turkey. The expression was so extreme it gave me an idea.

I nodded and said, "I like your bow. It's pretty."

"Thank you," she said, cheering up, her hand straying to the bow on her head.

"Do you like my thick mustache and my big belly," I said with wide eyes rubbing at my nonexistent mustache and cupping the air in front of me like I really did have a big belly.

Again, I'm not sure where this came from. Maybe from reading Oliver Twist. Maybe from Alice rubbing off on me. But I knew kids that age, and I knew how much they liked to pretend.

"I do," she said, her eyes getting wide and bright. "Do you like the faerie on my shoulder?"

I nodded. "She is very pretty and has nice hair just like you."

"Thank you," she said.

"You better go," I said, my heart still thundering in my chest. "You don't want your father to find you here." I ended by placing my index finger to my lips.

Her eyes got even wider and she mimicked my gesture and then was gone.

I liked the kid and once again hated that I was taking this from her, but I used the big forks I had in my backpack, pulled the turkey out of its pan put in into my brownie pan.

For a moment I thought this was all over. The turkey was huge, much bigger than ours, and didn't fit in the pan until I maneuvered it on its side.

With two oven mitts on, I silently thanked Ant as I drained the grease and the basting liquid into the thermos.

It was so hot, I had to be careful, and my heart started thumping even more. This was taking too long.

Out in the living room, I heard a voice say, "I need to go check on—" It was Doctor Young. He was about to walk in on me.

"Please, Doctor," another voice said, and I knew it had to be the teenage girl, our distraction. "I just have one or two more questions. You are really helping me out with this paper."

When the door didn't swing open, I realized that I really did owe Chet.

I double-timed it, capping the thermos and then wrapping up the bird.

***

IF I HAD BEEN WIRED DIFFERENTLY, I THINK THIS TURKEY heist could have turned my life in a completely different direction. I mean it was terrifying, yes, but it was awfully thrilling too.

That day, I discovered that I was no thrill-seeking adrenaline junkie and strongly preferred such daring do to be on the pages of books.

The turkey was in my backpack, the warmth of it on my back rather alarming, the oven was shut and I had crawled to the back door. I was silently cursing myself for closing it and had just started to turn the knob when I heard heavy footfalls heading for the swinging kitchen door.

I wanted to run, but I just froze, crouching there, my hand on the doorknob. My legs were Jell-O again and I was quite convinced that I was going to blow chunks at any moment and for some reason I just couldn't move.

This was it.

I was a dead man, or at least an extremely grounded boy that was about to visit more hardship on his family that didn't need one more little bit of it.

Then I heard a sharp crack and almost cried out because it sounded like a gunshot. Doctor Young wouldn't shoot a kid stealing a turkey from his kitchen, would he?

The resounding answer my brain gave me was, "Of course he would, dummy."

But the single sharp crack was joined but dozens more of them and I knew this was the distraction, part two. Chet's coveted fireworks were being set off.

And then I realized I owed Alice, big time. She hadn't shared all the details of her plan, just said, "Trust me," but I was quite sure she had been watching the back door, saw the knob turn, told Chet it was time, and Chet had radioed whoever was setting the fireworks off.

The brilliance was lost on me in the moment. I got out of there as quickly as I could and joined my fellow conspirators behind the bushes.

"Got it?" Chet whispered, his eyes wide.

"Got it!" I said, feeling a rush like I had never felt before. I shucked the backpack and put it in Alice's little sister's stroller.

Alice put a blanket on top of the backpack and put a life-sized doll's head with a hat on it and said, "Then let's run."

And we did, Alice pushing the stroller, the three of us only containing our giggles for a few seconds.

We were a block away before the popping of the fireworks ended. Chet really did blow his stash for this, proving beyond a shadow of a doubt that he was the best friend a kid could have.

THAT DAY I LEARNED A VERY IMPORTANT LESSON ABOUT heists, they are not over when you think they are. And in this case, the Great Turkey Heist was not over until the turkey was eaten.

We were riding high, walking the down Oak Street away from the Youngs' and towards my house chatting and laughing, feeling good about how clever we were, when suddenly Mrs. Cranshaw was heading toward us.

She was a blue-haired granny with a thick a woolen winter coat on even though it was barely cool.

"Is that Clara?" Mrs. Cranshaw asked. She loved babies. I mean LOVED them. She wanted to squish them into uncomfortable hugs, kiss them, pinch their cheeks.

I hadn't fallen prey to such treatment in a year to two, but she would visit the same thing on any of us if she got the chance.

"Shhh," Alice said, putting her finger to her lips, proving once again she was a villain or a hero in waiting. "She's asleep. Been very fussy today and these kind young gentleman agreed to accompany me on a walk around our fine town. We just got her to sleep."

Mrs. Cranshaw gave a knowing nod and smiled and we passed by without any squishing or pinching of cheeks.

I thought we were done, that the brilliant Alice had saved the day. Again. But we were not.

"What is that?" came Mrs. Cranshaw's quavery voice a few seconds after we passed each other.

"What's what?" Alice asked as we all stared at the stroller wondering if the doll head had fallen off the backpack or something.

"That trail of... of..." Mrs. Cranshaw said, her bony finger pointing at the sidewalk behind us. "It's coming from the stroller." We all looked and saw a thin greasy trail going back a good six feet. The turkey had started to leak.

We were doomed. I was sure of it.

Alice emitted a burst of nervous laughter and said, "Please, please don't tell anyone." I was then extra sure we were doomed. Alice had cracked. She was going to spill the beans.

But I, once again, underestimated Alice. "Clara is...," she began, her cheeks flushing red. It seemed Alice McGee, the future hero or villain, could blush on command, which made me think she had teetered to the villain side of things. "Well, the poor girl is having terrible problems today. I guess she needs to be changed and I didn't notice. Please, please don't tell anyone or I'll get in terrible trouble."

"Well, I..." Mrs. Cranshaw began. "Oh, poor little girl."

"Thank you, thank you," Alice said, her voice rising till it was almost a squeal. She ran to the older woman and voluntarily subjected herself to a thorough squishing and cheek pinching.

Once Mrs. Cranshaw was out of earshot, which didn't take long since her hearing wasn't very good, we laughed all the harder as Alice rearranged the blanked to catch the leaking turkey juice.

"Thanks, Alice," I said, standing in the grass between our two split-level houses. Chet had already gone home and it was time to get this turkey in the oven and prepare for Thanksgiving.

She smiled and nodded, her green eyes intense as she looked at me, almost as if seeing me for the first time.

"You and Chet did good," she said. "I wasn't sure you two had it in you."

"Ummm... thanks. I guess," I said.

She smiled, stood up straight, took a deep breath, and said, "Remember the lessons I have taught you today, Billy Granger. They will serve you well in your life."

"Oh, you can be sure that I will," I said, knowing full well that this was a day I would never forget.

"And don't forget your promise to me," she said.

"No way," I said. "One of the lessons I learned today is that you, Alice McGee, are legitimately scary. I'd much rather be on your team than off it."

Her face was stony for a moment and I was quite sure I had said the wrong thing, but then she cracked a smile and said, "I have taught you well."

I SAUNTERED INTO THE KITCHEN, MY SHOULDERS BACK, MY spine straight, thinking I was something special. I had the Youngs' turkey in my backpack and Thanksgiving was clearly saved.

"They're here," Ant hissed, his eyes wide. He had on a white apron, far too big for him, and the kitchen was a fright, not looking "sunny side up" at all. The pies were half-assembled and not baked, the green beans weren't on to boil, and he had, somehow, managed to get flour all over the place.

Mom would freak. And the turkey was still in the backpack I was holding.

"Get out there," I said, grabbing the knife he was holding. "Stall her."

"How?" he asked.

"Be sweet," I said, helping him take off the apron, remembering how well it had worked with Mrs. Cranshaw. "Wish her happy Thanksgiving. Give her a hug."

His face squished up and then he blinked and got this contemplative look on his face that reminded me of Alice. "Done," he said. "If you give me your Superman comic book collection."

I heard the front door open and voices spill into the house. It sounded like everyone was here. Mom, dad, Uncle Larry and Aunt Jill.

"Yes," I said. "Pushing him towards the door. I need five minutes."

Giving away my Superman comic book collection hurt, but

Ant was my little brother, and he was Ant. He'd mess up somewhere in the future, need me to cover for him, and I'd get them back.

It really did seem like I had learned something from Alice.

———

By the time Mom came in to check on me, I had the apron on, the ill-gotten turkey was in the oven, and the kitchen was just short of disaster.

"How's it going, honey?" she asked. She looked tired, more tired than I felt after all the madness of my day.

"Great," I said. "How's Uncle Larry?"

She took a deep breath and let out a noisy sigh. "He needs some help," she said. "And we are going to get it for him. But I'm hoping a nice home-cooked Thanksgiving dinner at least makes him feel like he's really back home."

She was still for a few breaths and then shook her head like she was trying to shake of her day. "Let me see how we're doing," she said and headed for the oven.

"I got this, Mom," I said with the sweetest smile I could manage. My heart was thumping along because I had figured out something in the last few minutes. The Youngs' turkey was considerably larger than ours and there is no way she wouldn't notice. In my panic, the only thing I could think of was to not let her see it until it was on the table where she wouldn't want to make a scene in front of Uncle Larry.

I was resolved to being grounded for the rest of my childhood, but I really wanted to see this meal through.

"Why don't you get Dad to make you one of those high ball things and relax," I said.

She blinked and nodded, looking around at the disarray. "You sure?"

"I am," I said. "You know, I figured out something today. I really do like to cook."

She blinked and a quizzical smile lit up her tired face. I had been helping in the kitchen but this was the first time I had admitted to liking it.

"You are growing up," she said, with a smile. "I like it."

THE GRANGER THANKSGIVING OF 1971 WAS A FEAST TO BE remembered. We had the biggest, best turkey in town, my father and my uncle were back from the war, and nothing was burned.

The dining room was a small alcove off the living room with a wooden table that could just sit all six of us comfortably.

When I brought the turkey out, my legs Jell-O again and my hands shaking a bit, Mom's eyes got wide, but she didn't say a thing.

After saying grace, Dad carved the glorious bird and everyone dug in.

Uncle Larry looked worn, more worn than the rest of the adults, be he really seemed to like the food. "You really outdid yourself this time, Maggy," he said to my mom.

Mom smiled and said, "Thank Billy. It was mostly him this year."

"Is that so?" Dad said. "Well, I don't know what you did, son, but I think this is the best turkey I've ever had. And this gravy...? It's fantastic."

"It's all in the brining," I said, nodding like I knew what I was talking about.

"Billy's become quite the creative cook," Mom said, giving me a look that made my heart leap into overdrive again. "I think in a year or two he'll be a better cook than I am."

There was agreement all around the table but it didn't last

very long because everyone got right back to that delicious turkey.

My mom knew. I know she did. When word spread the next day that Doctor Elias Young's Thanksgiving turkey had been stolen from his oven, she really knew.

But much to my surprise, she never said a thing.

"She can't," Alice told me one time when I asked her about it. Being the probable evil genius that she was, I was sure she could explain it. "If she acknowledges it, she has to tell your dad and punish you and that would tarnish the Thanksgiving you all needed."

And while Mom never said a word, she started putting me to work in the kitchen. All the time. Maybe she thought it was punishment, maybe she was pushing me towards what she saw was my vocation. It didn't really matter and I didn't grumble about it too much.

Chet, Alice, and I didn't know it yet, but during that crazy day, all of our fates were sealed to some extent.

Chet and I kept our promise to Alice and ended up having a pretty decent time at school and stayed close. In their senior year, Chet and Alice even started dating, but it didn't last past graduation.

A broken-hearted Chet ended up joining the army and served in the first Gulf War with distinction. He became a fire fighter in Chicago after that. He was kind of famous for yelling, "It's clobberin' time!" before entering a burning building. He died about ten years ago in a fire after saving six other people. He was the real hero.

Alice was valedictorian and went to college, Harvard, no less, and studied business. She was running one of those crazy companies in the first dot-com boom in the nineties. She, of course, got out right before the bust and after it was all over came back to Oakmont. One by one, she bought up space, bettered one of the businesses the Youngs owned, and slowly put them out of business.

She was relentless, making sure the McGees had the upper hand in everything. She now lives in that fancy Victorian house not far from the square.

I no longer think in black and white terms, heroes and villains, but I would have to say that in those terms, Alice was pretty much Doc Ock for a while and is a little more Spider-Man now. Unlike Doctor Elias Young, she has done a lot for this town, pretty much single-handedly keeping the food bank running, and of late has been on an affordable housing kick.

Me? I became a chef. I studied in Paris and New York, worked for a few years in Chicago, but came back to Oakmont and opened my own place. It's called The Sunny Side Up. It's on the town square in one of those lovely brick buildings with a very yellow interior and an eggy-chickeny decor. Every time I walk in, I remember my mom. She lived to see it and absolutely loved it.

Alice came in the other night and I sat down with her after she had eaten. Time had done to her what it had done to all of us, adding pounds and wrinkles, but I could still see that genius kid with pigtails and glasses.

"Tell me truth," I said. "On Thanksgiving 1971, were you the reason our oven went on the fritz and burned our turkey?"

Alice had testified to Congress after the dot-com bust. I had watched it on C-Span. She adjusted her glasses and gave me the same response she had given the senators a few times but with a dazzling smile they hadn't seen. "I don't seem to recall the details, Billy."

I smiled. It was all I was going to get from her, but her

answer was clear. Alice had been running the show the whole time and likely spent months planning it. It was the first step in her long game of the McGees taking the over town.

I laughed and we shared a bottle of wine I had been saving for a special occasion. We toasted our dear departed friend, Chet Michaels, and talked about The Great Turkey Heist of 1971 late into the night like only very good and very old friends can.

BACKSTORY—THE GREAT TURKEY HEIST

Holiday: Thanksgiving

This story combines three of my favorite things: Thanksgiving; clever thieves (just like "Dealing Seconds" but in a very different way); and adventurous kids stories (think of the movie *Stand by Me* or the TV show *Stranger Things*).

It's the last one, adventurous kids, that I had so much fun with here. When you are young, everything is new and exciting, and while you certainly don't have it all figured out, you are more willing to take chances, trying things, and make mistakes.

You world is also a lot smaller and simpler, and when something is important to you, it's *really* important. Like making sure your family has a turkey on the table for an important Thanksgiving no matter what it takes.

In the Afterword I talk about "Meet Cute: The Musical" and how there is usually one story that is the inspiration for putting together a book like this and that's true, but in this case it was actually two stories that I was just itching to get out, this one being the second.

I hope you enjoyed the untold tale of the Granger Family Thanksgiving of 1971.

AFTERWORD

"Meet Cute: The Musical" was the story that initially inspired me to put this collection together (there's usually one of these that inspire me to create a collection). That story did not make it into the *WMG Holiday Spectacular* the year I wrote it, which doesn't bother me a bit. I recently read an article about the TV show *Survivor*, which I love, where Jeff Probst, the long-time host, said of the game, "If you play to not lose, you will never win."

That's the way I feel about writing in general and this story in particular. It was what I think of as a "big swing" story. I was trying something, had a blast writing it, and the story still delights me.

Does this story, that is, basically, a prose musical, work? Well, that's for you to decide with that story and each of the stories in this collection. If they work for you, that's all that counts, and I certainly hope many of them did, and I hope you enjoyed your escape into these unusual holiday stories.

If you enjoyed these stories and want more like this from me, check out *Contemporary Musings: Sixteen Contemporary Stories from a Sci-Fi Writer*. It contains two stories that could have fit in this collection: "A Game of Kat and Mouse" which is tonally a lot like "Dealing Seconds" and "Haunted by the Past," a Conner Bright story similar to like "Line Dancing with Vampires."

In addition, my story "Sprits of Christmas" was part of the 2024 Holiday Spectacular and recently appeared in *Winter Wonderland*. (And, yes, that title is very similar to the title of this volume and that was not on purpose. I originally planned to publish this in 2024 before *Winter Wonderland* was released.) You can find out more about the *WMG Holiday Spectacular* at *TheWmgHolidaySpectacular.com*.

Sadly, *WMG Holiday Spectacular* ended in 2024, but I am grateful for five years of writing holiday stories for it. I have two more holiday stories coming out in two different anthologies in 2025 and I still have more in my catalog and I just might write a few more holiday stories, so who knows, there may be more *Winter Wonders* coming your way.

ACKNOWLEDGMENTS

First and foremost, I have to thank Kristine Katherine Rusch. None of these stories would have existed without her and, much to my delight, several of these stories have appeared in her *WMG Holiday Spectacular* and the following anthologies. If you love holiday stories, the anthologies that came out of this program are very much worth checking out.

Big thanks to my team that work so diligently to catch my mistakes and make these stories better. That would be my fabulous beta readers: Peter Klein, Roni Hornstein, and Eliot Schipper; my amazing proofreader Diana Cox; and my always encouraging, ever understanding about all the time this takes wife and first listener, Aleia.

And thanks for reading. I hope some of the warmth of the holiday came through these stories as you read these winter wonders.

ABOUT THE AUTHOR

Robert J. McCarter is the author of more than fifteen novels and over one hundred and fifty short stories. He is a regular contributor to *Pulphouse Fiction Magazine* and his short fiction has also appeared in *The Saturday Evening Post, Andromeda Spaceways Inflight Magazine, Everyday Fiction,* and numerous anthologies.

Robert writes in a variety of genres from contemporary fantasy to science fiction and just about everything in between. His diverse background–including a career in software engineering, growing up on a ranch riding horses, and acting–colors the stories he tells.

He lives in the mountains of Arizona with his amazing wife and his ridiculously adorable dogs.

Find out more at:
RobertJMcCarter.com

BOOKS BY ROBERT J. MCCARTER

Short Stores Collections

- Life After: Stories of Life, Death, and the Places in Between
- Anomalous Readings: Thirteen Curious and Confounding Tales
- Creatures Featured: Thirteen Stories of Monsters and Other Creatures
- Contemporary Musings: Sixteen Contemporary Stories from a Sci-Fi Writer
- Finding Time: 12 Meticulously Crafted Time Travel Stories

Books in the "Ghost's Memoir" world:

Find out more at ShuffledOff.com

The Carterville Mystery Series

Find out more at CartervilleAZ.com

The Wood and June versus the Apocalypse Series

Find out more at WoodyAndJune.com

The Neutrinoman and Lightningirl Series

Find out more at Neutrinoman.com

Other Novels:

- Seeing Forever
- Where the Past Belongs: An Angelica and Ash Time Travel Adventure

For a complete list, go to RobertJMcCarter.com